The
Earth Goddess

Also by Richard Herley

The Stone Arrow, 1978
The Flint Lord, 1981

THE
EARTH
GODDESS

RICHARD HERLEY

William Morrow and Company, Inc.
New York

Library of Congress Cataloging-in-Publication Data

Herley, Richard, 1950–
   The earth goddess.

   Sequel to: The stone arrow and The flint lord.
   I. Herley, Richard, 1950–   . Stone arrow.
II. Herley, Richard, 1950–   . Flint lord.
III. Title.
PR6058.E65E2   1986   823'.914   85-30992
ISBN 0-688-06213-X

Printed in the United States of America

First U.S. Edition

1 2 3 4 5 6 7 8 9 10

BOOK DESIGN BY JAYE ZIMET

The
Earth Goddess

PART ONE

1 In the grounds below his fortress Lord Heite, Gehan of the Gehans, had built a small pavilion by the lake. On spring mornings such as this he liked—when the burden of his duties allowed—to come here to meditate or perhaps to receive in privacy an especially favored guest. Constructed of fragrant timber, five-sided, and with a gently sloping roof, the pavilion stood at the very water's edge and allowed the occupants to hear each nuance of the quiet surge of ripples on the shore. The sun had just come out: the ripples were being repeated as a network of light on the cedar uprights and supports, on the lintel and across part of the ceiling. A chiffchaff began to sing from the leafless sallows. Lord Heite looked down again, at the water, and breathed deeply. He was at peace. He had made the right decision.

A dry branch snapped on the path behind the pavilion. His bodyguards were waiting at a distance, on duty in the grove. They had let his guest come through.

"Please join me, General Teshe," he said, and looked around.

The General mounted the steps and, bringing his bulky form to a halt, gave a correct but informal salute. His eyes were friendly; his broad, blond-bearded features were about to break into a smile. He had been traveling all night, but he looked, as ever, immaculate. The gray leather of his dress armor creaked softly as he accepted the unspoken invitation to seat himself beside his lord. In the regulation manner he drew about him his finely woven cloak, gray and darker gray, edged with black serpents along the hem. His kneeboots gleamed. Even when seated, he kept his shoulders perfectly square; yet he was also at ease. There was something permanent about the man, timeless, infallible. It had been the same twenty years ago, when he and Lord Heite had been boys together at the academy.

"Well, Kasha," said Lord Heite, free now from the ears of his entourage. "Tell me. How are you?"

"Growing older, liege." The smile broadened; his teeth were white. "The pagans in my care would age even Heite Gehan."

"How did you once describe them? 'Fractious'? Was that the word?"

"Let us say that their resentment of authority is second only to their idleness."

"On the contrary, Kasha. You have tamed them remarkably quickly. The returns from your province tell me so."

"You flatter me, my lord. Much remains to be done."

"But not by you." For a moment Lord Heite regarded the peaceful waters of the lake. Then he said, "Do you remember my kinsman, Brennis Gehan Fifth?"

"Only vaguely."

"His father tried to make the island country independent of the mainland. When he inherited Valdoe, Brennis Fifth pursued much the same idea. We tolerated the position until he, fortunately or otherwise, went out of his mind. It then became necessary to replace him."

"With General Hewzane," General Teshe recalled.

"Exactly. That was seven years ago. Did you ever meet Torin Hewzane?"

"Yes, my lord. He is of the Garland."

"Well, now of course he is Lord Brennis. Unlike you, Kasha, he lets such titles go to his head. I must say he has disappointed us. A mistake was made. We misjudged him."

General Teshe sat forward, incredulous.

"We are informed," Lord Heite went on, "that he has been stealing from us. He wishes, apparently, to finance the start of his own dynasty. In private he is already said to style himself 'Brennis Hewzane First.' We understand that next year he will be strong enough to approach the barbarian warlords in the east. There is no reason to imagine that his envoys will be received other than cordially. First to be attacked would be our eastern holdings; from there he would encroach upon the citadel itself, using Brennis as a base."

"Forgive me, liege, but is your information reliable?"

"Yes."

General Teshe was plainly stunned.

"Even had this matter not come to light, we should by now anyway have considered transferring him to some lesser post. He has failed to carry out his brief. Settlement and forest clearance have not progressed at the expected rate. Only three new forts have been finished. Fraudulent or not, the harvest returns have been consistently bad. He is unable to control the farmers without recourse to the most absurd and destructive measures: at least seven villages have been burned to the ground. As a result, a substantial number of people have returned to the mainland. More are expected to follow. The whole system of taxation in Brennis is in jeopardy. With Hewzane as their model, corruption has spread to the regional commanders, to the beilins, and even to certain officers and Trundlemen at Valdoe. Until we know how far it has gone we dare not risk a move. By the autumn, though, our information will be complete. At that time, Kasha, you will accompany Bohod Khelle and his annual commission of inspection. On arrival at Valdoe, you will publicly dispose of Hewzane and announce yourself Protector of Brennis Gehan Sixth."

"I . . . do not understand, my lord. I thought Brennis Fifth died childless."

"So it is generally believed." A note of distaste had appeared in Lord Heite's voice. "Lady Brennis, as you may have heard, was with child at the time of her husband's death. Unluckily she was lost during the siege of Valdoe, and although her body was not accounted for, the Prime is satisfied that she was killed." Lord Heite paused. "However, among the various aberrations leading to his downfall, Brennis Fifth contracted a liaison with his sister, the Lady Ika. The result is a boy, now six years of age. In the absence of a legitimate heir, the Prime has decreed that this child shall be designated 'Brennis Gehan Sixth.' Until he comes of age you are to be his guardian at Valdoe. In effect you will control the island of Brennis and be accountable only to me."

"Where is the boy now?"

"At Valdoe, with his mother. During the siege she escaped to a village close by. On my orders she was found and brought back to the Trundle, where she has remained ever since."

"Does Hewzane know all this?"

"Of course. But he would not dare harm the child. I had even hoped its presence might have reminded him of his true position and tempered his conduct. There are still many people in the Valdoe domain who remember Brennis Fifth, if not fondly, then at least with a certain nostalgia. At least he made things work. The farmers knew where they were. I suspect the appearance of another Gehan at Valdoe will be met with equanimity, or even approval. That is one of the main reasons the High Council has

decided to confer Brennis on this boy." Lord Heite stood up;
the General did the same, still trying to absorb the implications
of all he had been told. "Shall we view the herons, Kasha?"

More than two hundred and eighty years earlier, at the foundation of Hohe and the Gehan empire, herons had begun to nest
at the lake below the citadel. Overlooked by the temple, they
had established their colony in the southern end, among islands
wooded with alder and birch. The trees were bleached with drop-
pings; almost every fork and crutch among the outer branches
held its mattress of sticks, repaired and built upon year after year
or, for no obvious reason, abandoned and allowed to disintegrate.
To the priests in the temple, and then to the men of the garrison,
the birds had become sacred symbols of the Gehan ideal. The
grace of the heron's flight, its patience, persistence, and skill in
hunting, its noble and independent nature, its courage in the
defense of its young, its cooperation with others of its kind to
secure the continuance of its race: all these made it an exemplar
of the eternal truths. Gentleness through strength—this was the
path to the highest goal of the empire and of the Prime, and as
the empire grew and prospered, so did the heronry, until the
trees were full and ninety or more pairs came each year to breed.
On a morning such as this, viewed against the rise of the citadel,
the air above the heronry was a confusion of arrival and departure:
in many nests the hungry young birds, gray and fluffy, could
already be seen.

But Lord Heite, one hand on the rail of the viewing platform,
was more interested in observing his guest.

"You do not seem to be enjoying the spectacle, Kasha."

On the way here, following the plankwalk through the ornamental marsh, the General had been rather quiet, and for the last
few minutes he had spoken hardly at all.

"I am troubled, my lord," he said at last.

"Duty is always onerous," said Lord Heite. "That is how we
grow stronger."

"I know, my lord. But I remember Torin Hewzane as a brother
officer. An officer of the Garland. What I must do is not easy."
The General put both hands on the rail. "Is there no way he can
be saved?"

Lord Heite did not answer at once. Out of respect for his friend,
he briefly reconsidered the decision with which he had been
struggling for many weeks past.

They were separated from the trees by a hundred yards of water. Wildfowl of many sorts were lazing in the sunshine, safe in the lee of the island; bright reflections, sisters of those that had lit up the pavilion, were moving across the bare branches above their heads. It made a peaceful scene. Lord Heite allowed his gaze to travel upward, to the herons, and then to the sheer wooden walls of the temple and of the citadel.

"There is no choice," he said. "Hewzane must die."

2 "Listen, father," Paoul had said. "The beechmast sounds like rain."

Tagart had not noticed, but it had been true. Yesterday afternoon, all through the beechwoods, uncountable numbers of husks had been opening to let their contents fall. As each nut fell it had struck, perhaps, one or two yellowing leaves before hitting the ground, just as a raindrop might. Tagart, for all his years in the forest, had marveled that he had never heard the sound before.

He was thinking of it now, when his mind ought to have been on other things. With Paoul sitting here beside him, cross-legged on the gleaming boards of the Meeting House floor, the arguments of these village elders seemed infinitely less important and interesting than the sound of falling mast.

Bocher, the head man, glanced yet again at Paoul. Tagart could guess his thoughts. The sight of Paoul made Bocher dissatisfied with his own small son. It was the same in almost every village: the boy sitting cross-legged on the floor was extremely beautiful. There was no other way to think of him. Tagart tried to see him through Bocher's eyes, through the eyes of someone unprepared for his appearance.

He was seven. He might have been a year younger, or a year older, but his beauty was ageless. It came from within, from some deep source that defined and brought to life each detail of his outward form, blending him into an exact, ideal, and self-contained whole. In coloring he was dark, with brown eyes, as his mother had been; in general cast of feature he resembled his father, who, as even his victims had admitted, had been a handsome man. There the resemblance ended: Paoul's gaze was open, innocent, and sane. His limbs were smooth and clean, his skin utterly flawless. His hair had been cut very close, revealing the perfect shape of his head. The ears were neither small nor large, modestly molded, of such delicate make that light seemed almost to pass through them unhindered. His cheekbones and the structure of his jaw made a face that was at once striking and mild, softened still more by the gentleness of childhood. His nose was straight, his mouth exquisitely formed; but something in the set of his lips was uncompromisingly masculine. So too were the repose and the attentiveness with which he sat listening to the arguments of the adults.

Trouble had come to Sturt. Besides the crushing weight of ever-increasing taxation, besides the number of people who had left the village and gone to the mainland, besides last year's drought and this year's floods, besides the diseased animals and blighted crops, the village had been singled out for especially harsh treatment at the hands of the spirits. The head man's daughter had been struck down by a horrible ailment. He was being punished. Gauhm, Spirit of the Earth, was angry. Because of all their troubles, the villagers had been neglecting the observances. It was Bocher's fault, his responsibility, and now Gauhm could be appeased only by a huge sacrifice. This the village could not afford. Many pigs would have to be slaughtered, many bushels of wheat and barley burned. Bocher had begged neighboring villages for help; it had been refused. They too had suffered from the drought and the blight, and they too were subject to Valdoe's taxes. The taxes had always been heavy; since the arrival of the new Flint Lord they had grown intolerable—and Sturt had yet to be assessed for this year's harvest. Several villages in the region had been ruined. Others had been destroyed by the soldiers themselves, in retribution for real or imagined crimes against the Valdoe domain.

All this and more the elders were debating at length, just as if it had any bearing on the matter in hand. Tagart cared nothing for their gods. Excepting the daughter's illness, the troubles of the village, such as they were, had probably arisen from the villagers' own indolence and lack of foresight, or from the greed of the Gehans, over whom even the gods had no control. But Tagart well understood why the villagers felt the need of a supernatural explanation for everything bad, and by now, after a hundred such debates at a hundred such villages, he had learned to listen with patience and apparent humility.

He and his party had come seeking work. The crops had long been in, but one of the villagers, the councilman in charge of field drainage, had wanted to offer payment and a week's lodging in return for clearing a blocked ditch in the south meadow. The task was unpleasant and greatly overdue; despite the councilman's complaints, nothing had been done about it all summer. Now the winter and perhaps further flooding were on the way and, like it or not, the ditch would have to be cleaned. If the villagers were reluctant to do the job, the councilman had argued, why not give it to this band of vagrants? Others on the council, though, had objected to the cost, so Bocher had convened a meeting. While most of Tagart's party waited outside the village, he himself had been brought into the Meeting House to listen to the interminable talking and to answer the council's questions.

His head ached. His eyes hurt. The room was dazzling, filled with reverberating light. The long southern shutters had been laid open, letting sunshine pour in. The walls were limed, the floor and beams highly polished. Even the altar at the far end was of glaring, spotless white stone. But the doorway, overhung by a thatched porch, was in shadow, and beyond it, beyond the village houses and the palisade, there was a wide view of the wooded, gently rising slope. The trees there had started to turn: oaks mainly, one or two maples and cherries. Their foliage formed a continuous mass, invested by the warmth of the afternoon with a barely perceptible haze. The air was quite still: he faintly heard the cry of a soaring buzzard.

Even on such a luminous autumn day as this, three weeks after the equinox, the village of Sturt might at one time have seemed to Tagart a squalid and confining place. He would have been made uneasy by the closeness of the palisade; he would have despised the way of life of those who had built it. And, even in the years before he had known anything at first hand of the farmers or their fields, he would have taken an instinctive dislike to this shifty and indecisive head man.

But it was no longer in him to have such feelings. He was too tired, too old, too weary of wandering from place to place. He had seen his own and all the other nomad tribes destroyed: the old way of life was finished forever. Its freedom and plenty, its grinding hardships, its terrors and grandeur, everything he had lived for, everything was gone. Even had there been enough people to make a spirit group, there was nowhere left for them to go. The trees had gone from vista after vista, cut down or ringbarked and left to die. The ancient territories of his people had been laid waste, and still Valdoe's blades were at work. Once he had been angry; recently he had begun to fear that, one day, he would view it all with indifference.

By his reckoning he was thirty-three. The last eight years he had spent in pain, and now he could scarcely walk ten steps unaided. His hair was turning gray, years before its time. Often at night he longed for release. It would be better then for the others in his party, the people who still called him their chief. Including himself and Paoul, only eleven remained. They carried him everywhere on a wicker seat. He was aware that he made a strange and pathetic sight, at the gates and meeting houses of villages throughout the domain; the children still sometimes threw stones, even where he and his party had been before.

Were it not for Paoul, he knew he would have killed himself long ago.

"What do you say, then, Bocher?" asked one of the elders, when the debate came at last to an end.

Tagart stared at the floor. In his bones he knew he was going to be turned away. Once again he would have failed to find his people decent food and shelter. They all thought they depended on his ability to negotiate, but he knew they were wrong. He was useless. He was stupid, too. By letting the ever-curious Paoul accompany him like this he had succeeded only in antagonizing the head man: he had made him jealous because of Paoul.

But Bocher had yet to answer the question.

Tagart looked up and for the briefest and most extraordinary moment sensed Bocher's dilemma, glimpsed somehow the inmost workings of his heart. Bocher had recognized the source of his own hostility. His eyes were drawn to Paoul's. The room might have been empty of everyone else. The child was looking at him calmly, with complete confidence in the fairness of the outcome. He had said nothing, not a word, since the start of the meeting, but it now seemed as if he were not only a party to the negotiations, but benignly overseeing them. He was content to put his trust in Bocher. He had placed Bocher entirely at liberty: he was free to choose as his conscience and judgment directed best.

"Well?" said the elder.

"Let them stay."

"And the payment?"

"It is little enough. Give them what they ask."

The dawn of their last full day in Sturt brought cold air in from the north, and suddenly it seemed that winter was very near. The previous night the sky above the village had been threaded with the thin calls of migrating redwings. Tagart had lain listening to them for hour after hour, kept awake by the pain in his legs and lower back, while all around him, in the straw, the other members of the group had slept. He had heard the furtive movements of Munt and the girl Tanda; he had heard Fodich talking in his sleep; he had heard one man and then another getting up, at long intervals, to urinate. He had heard Paoul close by: the steady tenor of his breathing, the occasional rustle when he shifted or turned. And slowly, like the growing chill in his joints, Tagart had watched the gray morning light pushing back the darkness to reveal the interior of the ruined barn which was serving the group as a dormitory.

There would be one more night here. Tomorrow they would have to leave, to continue their wanderings. At this season work became hard to find. Most of the farmers themselves would be hungry by the spring: the harvest taxes saw to that. By midwinter, when the snows came, Tagart and the others would again be fending for themselves in the woods. Last year they had built a makeshift camp and subsisted on the few beasts that the able-bodied men had managed to kill. The weather then had been kind, but the preceding year two of their number, an old woman and a child, had succumbed to the cold. Perhaps this winter it would be Tagart's turn. Or perhaps the camp would be attacked by wolves again, as it had been two years ago, when three people had been lost.

The group was steadily getting smaller and weaker. Sometimes, when the sun shone and food was plentiful, it was almost like a real tribe, or a large family, but more often there were arguments, bitterness, endless jealousies and complaints. Munt, Einthe, and his woman Igmiss had once been slaves. Except for Paoul, all the others were of pure nomad stock. That was one source of friction; and then Tanda, free of the restrictions of tribal law, had made trouble between Munt and Worley which had lasted until Worley's death.

At the beginning, when Altheme had been alive, Tagart had hoped to find further remnants of the nomad tribes, but it had never happened. The survivors of the siege, of the fighting at Valdoe, had scattered in all directions. Most had gone north, back to the forest. His own group had spent three years there, searching, visiting all the old camps and hunting grounds. They had found nothing but desolation, the results of clearance and of the Gehans' campaign of extermination. By now, after seven years, there could be little hope. Tagart's party, as far as he knew, was the only one left.

Once it had numbered nineteen. Now it was reduced to eleven. Two of the slaves had managed to join villages, and a third had been recaptured and presumably taken to Valdoe. Soon there would be too few people left to support him and Tagart knew the group would break up. At that time his life would end. Fodich would want to stay, and Maert, Fodich's woman, but he would be too much of a burden and eventually they would have no choice but to leave him. No village would take him in. Alone and crippled, he might last about a week.

He did not care. He cared only about what would happen to Paoul.

Without thinking he reached for the pouch he wore on a cord around his neck, and as he clasped it saw Altheme, dying under the oaks, tormented by insects, disfigured by exhaustion and pain. Her features were blurred now. He had never so much as thought of her in that way, but her face and the faces of his women, the two women he had known in the old time, had become interchangeable and confused. The second woman had been false; the first had not, and she had borne him a son. They were dead too.

Paoul was his only son now. The boy believed him to be his father. Five years ago, on that long and terrible summer evening, Tagart had been charged with bringing him up in ignorance of the truth, in ignorance even of his mother's true name. Altheme had exacted this promise and in secret had given Tagart her pouch. It contained what was left of her valuables, the bits and pieces of jewelry she had snatched up before leaving the Trundle. They were for Paoul, she had said, whenever he should need them. Their worth, Tagart believed, was trifling; but, despite all the privation she and the others had endured, despite the almost continuous temptation to exchange mere trinkets for food and shelter, he had been unable to bring himself to sell the least part of Paoul's inheritance.

The time was drawing near when Tagart would have to do it. He did not know how. He knew only that the boy was too young, too defenseless, to be left to the mercy of circumstance. Alone, or with only Fodich to guard him, he would end in slavery or suffer some even more appalling fate. For months, years, Tagart had been worrying and wondering what to do. In vain he had examined each village with an eye to leaving Paoul as an adopted son of one of the kindlier families. Certainly there would be no trouble in finding him such a home; there had even been an unprompted offer, earlier this year. Refusing it had made Tagart realize much about himself. The family had been unsuitable, but his refusal had been immediate and instinctive, and he had seen for the first time how much he dreaded giving Paoul up. Since then he had tried to be unselfish, to look without bias at prospective homes, to be less critical and suspicious. Even here, in Sturt, he had made himself overcome a feeling of unease which formerly might have impelled him to take Paoul and leave. The head man, Bocher, seemed to be watching the boy. His own son and Paoul had become firm friends—everywhere he went Paoul made friends with all the village children and left a deep impression on their parents, but something about Bocher's interest had struck Tagart as undesirable. Perhaps not suspicious or threatening, but unwelcome just the same. Paoul's friendship with his son was unfortunate. Because of it Bocher and his wife had been able, at leisure, to evaluate the most obvious of Paoul's gifts, none of which he was old enough to know how to conceal.

Everyone in the group loved him, but only Tagart, who had spent so much time in his company, had glimpsed the full extent of his qualities. It had always been accepted that Paoul was special, but recently, in the past few months, Tagart had begun to realize that he was very much more than that.

He feared for him. Paoul made friends too easily. Tonight, as usually happened at the end of a stay like this, Tagart was due to go to the head man's house to collect the group's wages and, as proof of the council's satisfaction, a clay tablet impressed with the village seal. Because of Paoul's effect on the head man and his family, the occasion had been turned into a sort of farewell meal to which Paoul had also been invited. This had happened before, at one or two other villages. Tagart did not like eating with these people. He much preferred it when they treated him with incivility. It was safer to keep a distance. So far he had not found the heart to teach this to Paoul, but he would soon, gently, have to tell him that not everyone could be trusted.

As the daylight grew Tagart heard waking sounds and voices from the village compound. Presently, after a breakfast of oatmeal and milk, the others would leave him behind for the day. They would go out to the fields and by their labor provide his food and shelter while he, to make himself feel useful, would sit outside the barn and repair, for nothing, such broken weapons and implements as the villagers cared to bring. It was then that he chafed most harshly against his fate and wished that Brennis Gehan's spear had done its work properly and left him dead on Valdoe Hill instead of half alive. That he had been crippled was bad enough, but then to be given Paoul like this—to be unable to protect him—was unbearable. Like Paoul's father, the man who had wielded the spear, the irony of this circumstance was too cruel and complicated for Tagart to understand.

He watched Paoul sleeping for a moment longer. Fodich awoke with a yawn. Einthe sat up and stretched. Then there arrived, at the barn door, the two village girls with the pails containing breakfast, and everyone else began to stir.

3 At bedtime—especially when the evenings grew dark and the table lamps lit either side of his bed—Hothen's second self emerged. Gone were the tantrums of the day; forgotten were his cruel words and threats, his transparent, ugly little deceits. In the unsteady lamplight he looked almost like a normal child of his age, but more helpless, and sad, and Rian felt she might one day even bring herself to pity him.

She stroked the hair from his eyes and arranged his arms on the counterpane. "There," she said. "Now you're nice and clean, your mother will come to tell you a story."

"You tell me a story," he said. "Are you a slave, Rian?"

"Yes. I am a slave."

"Can I have some more blackberries tomorrow?"

Rian stood up without answering: the Lady Ika had appeared at the door. Rian moved back from the bed. "Good evening, my lady."

"I came in too late," Ika said. "Was Hothen asking for anything special?"

Even his own mother had trouble understanding his stammer. "Just some blackberries, my lady. For tomorrow."

"Of course you can have some blackberries, dearest." Ika felt for the bedpost and guided herself to the seat. "You can have anything you want."

As usual, Rian settled herself in the far corner, leaving her mistress to hold Hothen's hands and to recount in a soothing voice the tales he liked so well. Rian did not pick up her sewing; away from the bedside lamps it was too dark. Her corner, like the rest of the room and, it seemed, the rest of the world, had suddenly been banished, excluded, shut out from the illuminated scene of mother and child together. Its radiance did not even reach the ceiling; the shapes and identity of nearby furniture receded into the gloom. Ika's face was three quarters turned away, her thick blond hair plaited into a mass which caught the light only at its edges. But Hothen, his pillow, and the carved bedhead above him were fully lit. The bedhead was made of blackened oak. On it, within a stylized border of wreathing vines, each scale of the Gehan serpent threw its upward shadow. The original pigments of red and green had mostly flaked away, for the bed was old, a hundred years at least. It had been made for the first Flint Lord and used by his descendants and successors—five in all, the five Brennis Gehans, the last of whom had been Ika's brother. The bed had been kept in a larger, much grander chamber then, but under its covers Hothen had been conceived.

Rian looked on bleakly, reminded again of her former mistress. In this bed unhappy Altheme had also slept. Rian had worshiped her; she still mourned her loss, eight years ago this winter. Where was Lady Brennis now? What had become of her unborn baby, the Flint Lord's first and rightful child?

Dead, both were surely dead. After the siege of the Trundle, Altheme had fled into the forest with the savages—the remnants of those who had vainly tried to take the fort. In the following years the last of the savages' tribes had been systematically destroyed by Torin Hewzane, the new Flint Lord, the man installed by the Home Lord and the mainland Gehans; the man who had betrayed and murdered Altheme's husband. If she had survived, Lord Torin would have found her. She had not been found: Altheme and her child were surely dead.

Yes, they were dead. Brennis Gehan Fifth had left only a single monument to himself, perhaps a fitting one—defective, inbred, reared on a diet of lies and intrigue. How much more terrifying would be Hothen's rages if he knew the extent of his importance abroad, at the citadel? For Rian had heard that he was being kept here as a check on Lord Torin. The Home Lord, as did the whole fort, the whole of Valdoe, knew Hothen's parentage; if ever it became necessary or expedient, there might yet be a Brennis Gehan Sixth.

The stories Ika told him often concerned Brennis Gehan First, founder of the Valdoe domain, builder of the Trundle and, after her own father, chief inspiration of her brother's life. At least, the stories purported to detail the valor of the first Lord Brennis, but in many episodes Rian recognized a subtly fashioned portrait of Hothen's father, and sometimes, unconsciously, Ika gave her hero her brother's features, demeanor, and manner of dress—far removed from the ugliness and austerity that were said to have characterized his ancestor. Yet she never spoke of him directly, not to anyone, least of all to Hothen.

On her brother's death she and a servant, a certain Rald—who had also shared her bed—tried to escape from the new Lord Brennis. They did not get far. On the orders of the Home Lord, Ika was brought back and given medication for the blinding she had received in the siege. During this treatment it became apparent that she was pregnant. The priests, aware of the rumors that had been current just before the siege, questioned her closely. At first she maintained that Rald was the father. Rald, who had red hair and green eyes, was interrogated and the nature of their relationship was established. The last union that could have given rise to a child had taken place at least two months before the siege.

Hothen was born two hundred and eighty-four days after the start of the siege. He was fully formed; he had been carried for the full term. His hair, like his father's and mother's, was blond. His eyes were blue, and that was how they remained. There could be no doubt. Hothen was the son of Brennis Gehan Fifth.

To everyone but Ika, it was obvious from the start that the child was not normal. He was slow in learning to suck; in the cradle he lay inert, taking no interest in dangled toys or his nurse's finger. He did not recognize his mother, and was nearly three before he uttered her name. About that time the convulsions began. Mercifully they had now abated, but in their place had come fits of frightening and inexplicable rage. These always followed the same course. Some tiny incident, at the meal table, for example, would be enough to spark one off. Hothen's eating habits were disgusting. Rian might reach out to wipe his chin, to offer the mildest possible word of correction; and it would start. First, with miraculous fluency, his stammer forgotten, he would say the worst and most hateful things he knew. Rian was dung, vomit, spittle. Somewhere—no doubt from the soldiers in the enclosure below his window—he had learned a variety of profanities, all of which he knew how to use with telling effect. Rian tried not to listen, but often his words struck deep and she was hurt that such things could be said at all. He seemed to have a cruelty far beyond his years. And then, without warning, in the middle of this stream of vituperation, he would slur his speech, shouting and struggling uncontrollably, upsetting dishes and bowls and platters, become incoherent, demented, and, just as suddenly, quiet. He would drool, pull faces, perhaps begin to laugh. His head would twist to one side and then the other. His eyes, which always seemed slightly filmed, would become yet more opaque, unfathomable, and withdrawn. Very often he would bring up whatever he had eaten. Afterward, much subdued, he would allow himself to be cleaned and carried to his bed: these rages always left him much exhausted. Even in his sleep he made Rian more work, for he was still not properly trained. Sometimes she had to change his bedding twice or more in one night.

Looking after him, and she had always been his nurse, was grueling work for a woman of her age. By rights she should have had assistance, for she was also Ika's body slave, and by rights Hothen should have had his own body slave as well as a nurse. But Rian had to do it all. In just the same way were the quarters for Ika and Hothen dingy and cold. Their food was inferior, and their clothing had to last. They were Gehans, members of the Home Lord's clan, but the other slaves and servants, the workmen and soldiers, treated them with ill-concealed contempt. Their movements were closely regulated. Ika—because, they said, of her blindness—was not allowed to leave the Trundle on her own. Accompanied, she could go as far as the settlement fields, but no farther, and the road to Apuldram, where the ships docked, was strictly out of bounds. Ika and her son were prisoners, and that made Rian doubly a slave.

Perhaps she was lucky to have a position of any kind. At least it was keeping her alive. She might easily have followed all those whom Lord Torin had suspected of loyalty to Brennis Fifth. In the weeks after he had taken power, many, many people had been put to death—not only here at Valdoe and in the outer forts, but in the villages also. And though Rian knew she was too old and unimportant ever to be considered dangerous, still she was very guarded in what she said. She did not care so much about herself, but her own three children—who had long since grown up— were all in service here.

She leaned back, glad of this chance to rest before her duties of the evening. Tonight there was to be a banquet, and Ika had to go. Each autumn a commission was sent from the homelands to inspect the domain: it had arrived this afternoon. The custom was for a welcoming feast attended by everyone of rank. Lord Torin and his lady would of course be there, as would his two generals and their ladies, the commanders of the outer forts, and the most important priests and Trundlemen. There would be other freemen too, those who were rich and who benefited from

Valdoe and the Home Lord, and everyone else whom the commission expected to see. They would be expecting Ika. Tomorrow they would probably come to check on Hothen.

Rian's eyes wanted to close. The smell of burned incense, combining with Ika's voice, had made her sleepy. The incense was used each day to purify the air in Hothen's room; his mother's voice was like the smoke, soft and warm, drifting through a story told many times before.

"And that's the end, Hothen." Ika put a caressing hand to his cheek. "You must go to sleep now. You're very tired."

She kissed him and Rian forced herself to rise. "Good night, Hothen," Rian said, and touched his forehead with her lips. She put out the lamps and followed her mistress into the adjoining chamber.

Ika's finest white robe had been laid out across the bed. On the dressing board, on its inset rectangle of soft green leather, waited her best remaining jewels—those left to her by the exigencies of life under Torin, Lord Brennis: a jade and ivory necklace, matching bracelet, and large ivory brooch. She would wear them all, and new slippers lined with leverets' fur, but first she had to be bathed and dried, manicured, anointed with herbal oils, powdered; her lips had to be darkened, and her hair— highlighted earlier with a camomile rinse—brushed and carefully plaited with freshly picked flowers. Only then would she be fit to be dressed and brought into the presence of Lord Brennis and of Bohod Khelle, chief commissioner from the homelands.

"Send for hot water," she told Rian, discarding her day robe.

It was time to make ready for the feast.

Bocher's house was the biggest of all the thirty-eight dwellings in the village. Set in its own garden surrounded by a quickthorn hedge, it shared the larger precincts of the Meeting House and stood almost exactly in the center of the compound. It was made of stone and weathered oak, with a conical roof for the main chamber and flat roofs, covered with turf, for the others. The winter shutters had yet to be fixed; all the windows were open except one, in the rear, which was his eldest daughter's sickroom. Paoul had, earlier in the week, been allowed to peep inside. The sight of a girl of fifteen so wasted and pale had affected him deeply. One skeletal arm, contorted somehow and drawn up, had protruded from the bedcovers. Her brittle dark hair, her sunken eyes and speechless mouth had been those of a corpse. "What's wrong with her?" Paoul had whispered. "She's dying," her brother had said.

She had been bedridden since the spring. Now she was getting weaker. The priest had tried everything. At last he had been forced to tell her father that this was the work of the Earth Goddess. Only a great sacrifice might save her, if it was not already too late.

The girl's name was Utara. Her affliction seemed to fill the house. It had come to dominate the family; every aspect of the household had been subordinated to its needs. None the less her brother Berritt, a boy the same age as Paoul, had daily been allowed to invite his new friend to spend time quietly indoors or in the garden, and tonight, for the farewell evening, most of her family—father, mother, uncle, brother, and younger sister—had gathered and a special supper had been prepared.

Usually Paoul did not like village food, but he had never tasted anything quite like this before, succulent lamb roasted with hyssop and served on a steaming bed of tender vegetables. Sometimes in the past he had been given mutton, but it had always been stewed, gristly, and overcooked; and he had certainly never tasted such vegetables or the flavor of such a subtle and delicious herb. The hyssop was from a special bush which grew only in Bocher's garden. Paoul had seen it there, together with many other herbs, all of which were tended and propagated by Bocher's wife, Dagda. Berritt had named each kind for him and explained some of its properties and uses. The cultivated herbs were even more interesting than the ones Tagart had taught him, the wild plants of the wayside. Berritt said that sometimes the flint sellers would bring a new sort, and then the price would be high. Paoul knew that dried herbs, some very rare and expensive, were sold at the great Valdoe fairs. Dagda had told him that the priests at Valdoe grew or stored every herb ever known, including secret ones which it was forbidden for anybody else to have.

Almost every day this week Paoul had eaten a meal at Berritt's house. Here, in this room, he had begun to understand why people chose to live in villages. Life in the woods was hard; the forest only seemed beautiful if you were not hungry or frightened or cold. But if you had a solid house with a hearth, and a palisade to protect you from the wolves and bears, there was time for other things besides survival. Berritt's sister—the one who was not sick—had shown him the leather pictures she had made, and Dagda, whom Paoul did not really like, had taught him to eat properly, with a spoon. She had presented him with his own clay spoon, fired in the village kiln and fitted with a wooden handle, but at other meals, in the barn, Paoul had been too embarrassed to use it.

When he had learned that both he and Tagart had been invited here tonight, the spoon had given him hours of worry. If he used it, Tagart would think he had been less than open, concealing from his father the acquisition of manners which could so easily be taken as criticism of the way he had been raised. This deceit, which he had not intended, would make Tagart unhappy and disappointed. But in turn, if he left the spoon in his tunic and ate with his fingers, Dagda's feelings might be hurt, and besides, she would ask him where it was. So this evening, an hour before the meal had been due to start, Paoul had made a point of showing Tagart the spoon.

His reaction had been strangely subdued. Paoul was still puzzled about it. They had never been shown such hospitality before, and yet, as the meal drew toward its close, Tagart appeared to be growing more and more anxious. Even as they had crossed the compound from the barn—even as Fodich and Uden had helped him through Bocher's gate and along the path—Tagart had seemed uneasy. His eye had been drawn to the Meeting House, where four or five young men had been sitting on the steps, indolently watching, and then, on seeing Dagda's burly brother by the hearth, he had grown more uneasy still. Paoul could not understand why. He wondered whether Tagart's anxiety could be related in any way to himself, to the incident of the spoon—to his friendship with Berritt. He realized keenly now, too late, that throughout the week Tagart had mutely disapproved of his visits to the head man's house. Paoul regretted that he had ever set foot here; he was ashamed that he had craved, even for a moment, the advantages of a settled life. For Tagart was very wise and if he disapproved there was always a reason, and if he felt threatened there would be a reason for that too. Paoul began to wish that Fodich and Uden had not been so quick to return to the barn.

The meal ended with cheese for the grown-ups. He and Berritt, who were sitting together, next to Dagda's brother, had been given fruit junket in wooden bowls.

Utara, meanwhile, was being cared for by Bocher's mother. The old woman came out of the rear chamber once again, collected a bowl of junket, and crawled back through the low, narrow doorway, letting the leather curtain fall behind her.

When she had gone, Bocher glanced at his brother-in-law, reached back and took something from one of the shelves by the hearth. "This is our seal," he said, handing it to Tagart. "Your people have done a good job here. The council is pleased."

Tagart examined the seal, holding it closer to one of the rush lights, and slipped it into his tunic. "We're glad to have been of use."

Bocher wiped his mouth nervously and offered Tagart a platter of oatmeal biscuits. "Where are you making for next?"

"I'm not sure. We might go north."

"Up to the Weald?"

"We might go that way, yes."

Bocher shot an odd glance at his wife. Paoul did not understand what it meant, but he saw that Tagart had noticed it too and suddenly felt alarmed. Dagda was big and raw-boned, like her brother, with red hands which she was always wiping on her smock. Her voice intimidated him a little, and he had pitied Berritt, whom she was always scolding, for having such a mother. Whenever Paoul tried to picture his own mother he always imagined someone very different from this.

No one else would know, but Tagart had become extremely tense. Paoul could tell by his eyes, by the minute changes in his expression.

Bocher reached over his shoulder once more and gave Tagart a goatskin pouch. "This is what we owe you."

Even to Paoul's eyes the pouch appeared much too big and heavy for a week's wages, but Tagart quietly opened the flap and looked inside. He took out the first flint to hand, a blue pressure-flaked spearhead of the finest Valdoe quality, and tested the edge with his thumb.

"This isn't what we agreed," he said. "You're giving us too much."

Despite Dagda's brother, despite the young men on the Meeting House steps, Bocher was terrified. He had reached a cliff edge, goaded here, driven by his wife, by forces stronger than himself. A moment more and it would be too late, not just for him, but for Paoul too. Paoul sensed it but did not understand how. His instinct was to reach out for Tagart, to shelter behind him, but he knew that would only make things worse. He saw Bocher pleading silently with his wife: she had fixed him with an insistent, accusing stare which pushed him and pushed him until he toppled forward into the void.

"We want to give you more," he said.

"Why?"

"For the boy. We want the boy."

Falling, helpless, Bocher had finally hit the rocks below. Paoul felt the impact just as if, yard by yard, he had fallen with him.

"It's like this," Paoul heard Bocher say. "You've seen how well he and my lad get on. Dagda and me, we've talked it over. We reckon he deserves better. Better than he can get on the road with you. It's not your fault, I know, but look at his clothes. Look at the state of his feet. What's it going to be like for him when you're dead?"

Paoul hardly dared breathe. He could see how desperately Tagart was searching for a way out: but there was none. There could be no question of a fight. If it came to that, Bocher would win. He was the head man here. There were only nine people in the barn: nine friendless, rootless people, against more than two hundred villagers. Whatever Bocher chose to insist upon, whatever he wanted, that he would surely have—if Tagart allowed it to come to a fight. But by the same token there could be no question of subterfuge. Tagart could not pretend to accept the price and then later try to rescue Paoul. Judging by the young men at the Meeting House, such a rescue had already been anticipated; and anyway, even Bocher would never believe that Tagart cared so little for his son.

The only solution was to be patient. If Tagart pretended to yield, Paoul would somehow, later, make his escape. He did not understand why these people wanted him; he understood only that this was the answer. This was the only way to get back to Tagart. But Tagart had not seen it. His face, molded by years of pain, exhaustion, disillusionment, revealed that the final blow had been dealt to the very center of his suffering—to his pride. A hammer blow, wielded by a stupid man who had suddenly become the focus of a lifetime's rage. Paoul had never guessed the depth of his frustration. Tagart was finally losing control, in a long, slow slide that had begun in earnest earlier this week and that was now accelerating, speeding, racing toward its ends.

"He's not for sale," Tagart said.

"You don't seem to understand," Dagda said.

"Keep out of this," Tagart told her. He did not take his eyes from Bocher's face.

Paoul wanted to say, "It doesn't matter, I'll do anything they ask, just as long as you're not hurt," but when he tried to speak the words would not come. He was too frightened.

"Paoul," Tagart said. "Run to the barn. Tell Fodich we're leaving."

"Stay where you are!" Dagda cried.

Before he could even think of moving, Paoul felt a large hand grasp the scruff of his neck. He had been seized by Dagda's brother.

Turning his head, Paoul missed the beginning of what happened next. For weeks, months, afterward, he tried to reconstruct these few instants in their true sequence. Each time he tried it became harder, until the disparate fragments of vision and memory would not fit together at all and made sense only in his nightmares. With the flames of the rush lamps wildly agitated, casting insane shadows across the walls and ceiling, he had seen Tagart attacking Dagda's brother, heard her husband's shouts and the piercing screams of her daughter; he had witnessed the jerky, dreamlike, flickering movements of Dagda with arms raised high, clutching in both hands what Paoul later knew to be a hearthstone, heard the sound made by a jagged edge of the stone brought down with all its weight on the side of a man's head—not just any man, but Tagart, his father whom he loved, whose dark blood was suddenly spattered in spots and streaks on Berritt's face, and, looking down, on Paoul's tunic and the backs of his hands. And afterward, while he was being restrained, he had seen his father's body dragged heel-first through the doorway and out into the autumn coldness of the night, to lie alone in the compound till morning, till ignominiously taken away. And among the terror and screaming in Bocher's house he had heard the orders given by Dagda and then by Bocher to the young men, who had grown in number until they were a mob armed with picks and mattocks, the orders meant to forestall any further trouble from these vagrants, to prevent them from biding their time beyond the palisade, to stop them coming back for revenge. He had heard the orders sending the young men running to the barn, heard them, but remembered only one, the one that Bocher had shouted last, crazed, unhinged, like the mob, no longer human:

"Kill them all!"

4 It was one of Rian's duties to accompany Ika whenever needed, to be her eyes; and though she had attended many social functions with her mistress, she could never quite feel easy when other slaves, some much more elevated than herself, behaved as if she were a rightful member of the gathering. And even now she felt awed by the presence of Lord Torin, who tonight was wearing the black, white, and gray dress uniform consistent with his rank. Something about him—his dry, bloodless lips, perhaps, his thin, spare frame, his fastidiousness—always seemed to her to be peculiarly arrogant and repulsive. He was three years short of forty; his blond hair was cropped in the formal manner; he was clean shaven, and by any standards would not be judged ugly, but Rian could not image how his wife managed to submit to him—if, indeed, she ever did.

"What is Lord Torin doing now, Rian?"

"He is talking to the Commissioner, my lady."

"Tell me more about what Lady Torin is wearing."

Rian had done her best to describe the elegance and richness of Lady Torin's green and cream robes, just as she had tried to describe the appearance of the other guests. In this one room were assembled all the most important people in the Valdoe domain: the highest-ranking officers, the wealthiest and most exalted freemen, the most influential priests and Trundlemen. They had all gathered to honor the arrival of Bohod Khelle and his annual commission of inspection. He had been brought by a Gehan ship which, flying the Hohe standard and carrying his inspectors and a nominal guard of ten men, had docked today at Apuldram. The four inspectors were here tonight as well; and most of the ten guards had taken up position among the resident Trundle guards, by the doors and along the walls.

"Did you say Bohod Khelle was wearing maroon?"

"Yes, my lady. With a sable collar."

It was hard to believe that even Ika could not see by the light of so many lamps. There were hundreds, large and small, on poles and stands, sconces and brackets, glaring whitely or giving

off an oily yellow glow. The odor of scented lamp fat permeated
the length and breadth of the Receiving Room; the rafters, even
at this stage of the proceedings, had been lost to the smoke. From
here, toward the back of the hall, the faces of Lord and Lady
Torin and of Bohod Khelle were already becoming indistinct.

All the guests, except those on Lord Torin's dais, were seated
on the floor, on bleached rush matting. Rian and her mistress
had been placed near one of the side doors. Rian had thought
this odd: at previous autumn feasts, Ika had always sat in the
center of the hall, just behind the Trundlemen and their wives.

Although it was late in the evening, the banquet had yet to
start. Lord Torin and his retinue had only just arrived; the guests
were still settling in. In a moment Lord Torin would make his
speech of welcome, and then, probably at length, the Commissioner would reply.

Rian felt a touch on her shoulder and looked around. A young
usher, whom she knew slightly, had appeared from the shadows
of the doorway. He squatted and spoke close to her ear. "Please
inform my lady Ika that she is requested to spare you for a brief
errand."

Rian was instantly apprehensive.

"What is it, Rian?" Ika said.

"I do not know, my lady. I am needed for an errand."

"A request of Lord Torin, I believe," said the usher, and Rian's
apprehension grew.

"Request? What request?" Ika said.

"It will not take long."

Rian put her hand on Ika's forearm. "I ought to do as he says."

The corridor beyond the doorway was lit by several flaming
brands. The usher took one down. "We are to fetch Master
Hothen," he told Rian, and then, seeing her expression, he added,
"Please. Don't worry. No harm will befall him, I assure you."

"What do you want him for? He's only a child."

"I understand he is to be presented to the gathering and honored in some way. That's all I know." The usher's pleasant manner had begun to dispel Rian's doubts.

"Who sent you exactly?" she said. "Lord Torin himself?"

"The chamberlain gave me the order. But it came from Lord
Torin, or so I was told. Please," he insisted, taking her elbow.
"We're wasting time. Lord Torin will be angry."

Hothen's room was on the far side of the building. The usher led the way, along gloomy corridors and up dark flights of creaking stairs.

Rian woke Hothen as gently as she could. At the usher's insistence, she dressed him in the rather musty military-style clothes he had last worn some months ago, at an official audience with Lord Torin. Hothen was too sleepy to notice or object; his head drooped as she fastened the collar. Her fingers pushed against the defenseless softness under his chin. She looked up at the usher. "Are you certain he'll be safe?"

"Yes. Quite certain."

Yes, Rian told herself. Of course Hothen would be safe. Lord Torin would never harm him in public.

"Please hurry," said the usher. "We must be getting back."

They had almost reached the Receiving Room when it happened. Coming down the stairs and along the final corridor, approaching the brightly lit doorway, Rian heard Lord Torin addressing the assembly, his high, precisely modulated voice clearly enunciating each word. He was saying something about the homelands, praising the citadel, when there was a sudden loud noise: a thud or a smack, so loud and unexpected that it seemed in its wake to fill the room with a swaying, unreal, transparent silence. Rian saw guests in profile, horrified, appalled; only Ika's face remained, for the moment, calm. Then there came, out of sight, from the front of the hall, the sound of someone falling, crashing backward. A woman screamed. Reality rushed in and the whole hall was a turmoil of shouting, confusion, of people rising to their feet.

Before Rian could prevent it, Hothen had been snatched by the usher and propelled to the doorway. A soldier, one of the Commissioner's men, seized him and he was bundled through the throng, toward the dais.

Only then did Rian realize that Lord Torin had been shot. She could see nothing of him—the dais had been surrounded, and whether he had been killed or merely wounded she could not tell. His bodyguards were forcing their way to the back of the hall: the arrow must have come from there. But many of the other soldiers, and all the Commissioner's men, were making no attempt to help find the assassin. Instead they were forming an orderly line, pushing people back from the dais and opening up a passage from the main doors.

A prolonged and imperious roll of drums silenced the assembly and halted the bodyguards. Even Lady Torin looked on, stunned, incredulous, as the doors swung open and a broad-shouldered man of forty or fifty, his dark-gray cloak sweeping the air behind him, strode to the dais and mounted it. Rian had never seen him before. His uniform was that of a general, the highest rank below a lord's. On his breast was the green and scarlet emblem of the Garland, the elite of officers dedicated to the Home Lord, and Rian began to be aware that everything this evening had long ago been planned.

He glanced sideways and down before levelly contemplating the faces of Lord Torin's dinner guests.

He did not choose to speak at once. The leisure of his silence charged the hall with menace, power, inexorable right; he was all these things himself, but what he represented was even stronger, more certain and implacable. He represented the Home Lord: he represented the Gehans.

"My name," he said, "is General Kasachie Teshe. I am commanded by Lord Heite, Gehan of the Gehans, to make known a proclamation of the Prime. By order of the High Council, meeting in the third session of the second quarter of this, the Year of the Blue Hare, be it known that Hewzane, Lord Torin of Brennis, has been tried in his absence and found guilty of the following capital crimes against the empire. One: treachery. Two: murder. Three: theft. You are to know that sentence has been executed in accordance with the decree. The traitor's corpse will be dismembered and burned. You are to know also that Balom, General of Valdoe, Abisende, General of the Coast, Crill, Commander of the Weald, and Tourse, Commander of the East, have been tried in their absence and found guilty of capital crimes against the empire. They will be conveyed to the citadel for execution of sentence."

There were cries of astonishment and dismay. Rian looked and saw that these men, four of the highest officers in the land, had been pinioned and rudely stripped of their weapons and insignia.

"Finally," said General Teshe, "I am commanded by Lord Heite, Gehan of the Gehans, to make known a proclamation of the Prime concerning the lineage of Brennis Gehan Fifth and the rightful inheritor of the Valdoe domain." He turned to Bohod Khelle and Rian's blood ran cold. The General spoke and she heard what she prayed she would never hear. She heard the words that signaled catastrophe, for herself, for her children, for all that remained at Valdoe of human feeling. And for poor Hothen too.

For the General had said: "Bring forth the boy!"

The system of exploitation devised by Brennis Gehan Fourth was so reliable that it had survived unchanged to the present day. Although based on the methods used in the homelands, it was more flexible and better suited to the needs of an island domain.

Most of the Flint Lord's income was gathered, not through taxes, but less directly, through trade, for he controlled the extraction and price of the flint upon which forest clearance and the production of crops depended. Fishing, the breeding of livestock, and certain other trades were taxed at source, by means of tithes and imposts—to which the harvest surpluses of consistently successful villages were also liable.

The harvest inspectors, nominally soldiers with a military rank, were experts in everything to do with the land. Many were themselves the sons or grandsons of farming families, and well understood the problems caused by the weather, by disease, and by evil spirits. Often, and this was a measure of how well the system was accepted, their technical advice was sought and closely followed. During drought or pestilence it was in their discretion to waive or reduce liability to impost, and even, through their regional commanders, to seek direct relief from the Trundle.

That was the tradition. In practice, the reputation of the harvest inspectorate had declined since the days of the Brennis Gehans. Under Lord Torin the inspectors had become increasingly disliked, and then hated, by the villagers in their control. Their visits now gave rise, not to grudging resignation, but to dread.

Farming villages received three inspections a year, the first in spring, the next in the growing season, and the last in autumn when the crops were in. Few villages now escaped the impost. Even the meanest and most wretched settlement received its three visits each year. At the third the harvest was assessed and arrangements were made for the impost—in grain, meat, hides, or sometimes in crafted goods—to be carried to the nearest fort.

It was this autumn inspection that the farmers dreaded most. Once regarded as incorruptible, the harvest inspector and his men now saw nothing wrong in accepting whatever welcome each village had to offer. Depending on the warmth of that welcome,

the assessment might or might not be revised. Some of the
inspectors attached to the eastern forts had, so the rumors went,
taken this practice one stage further. With the complicity of Commander Tourse himself, they were now demanding outright bribes.

Beilin Crogh had heard these rumors, and it was a source of
regret to him that he had been posted to Matley fort, at the
westernmost edge of the domain. The villages in this region were
mostly quite new and undeveloped, offering little scope for the
imaginative methods adopted by his colleagues in the east. Beilin
Crogh hoped one day to be transferred there, or at least to a fort
with a less conventional commander than his. He needed more
than a soldier's pay; he dreamed of settling eventually at Valdoe
Village, in the shadow of the Trundle, where he would live with
his family and slaves and earn his bread by keeping bees.

But time was getting short. Already he was thirty-four and his
eldest son was almost grown. His dream was beginning to look
like nothing more than that. Younger men had been promoted
instead of him; Beilin Crogh had come to realize that he was not
well suited to this work, and now it was too late to change. He
was too generous, too unsuspecting. His men, he felt, laughed
at him behind his back. All his attempts to toughen up had come
to nothing: he forgot each resolution as soon as it was made. This
was not the way to achieve life's ambitions; this was not the way
to eminence in the harvest inspectorate.

"You," he said to the man walking beside him. "Walver. Fas-
ten that breastplate. Are we soldiers or what?"

Walver looked at him in surprise. After another two or three
steps he tightened the straps of his leather cuirass, glancing for
an explanation at Lorco, an equally insolent soldier who had only
recently been moved to Beilin Crogh's team. Lorco's front teeth
had been lost in a disgraceful brawl at the fort. He smiled at his
superior, showing newly red gums, raising his eyebrows, and
ostentatiously checked the straps of his own armor and leggings.
Beilin Crogh suppressed a stern rebuke. What could he do with
men like these, the dregs of the domain? There was not an ounce
of sense among the four of them.

"Lorco," he said. "What is the name of this village we're
coming to?"

"Sturt, sir."

"Very good. And what is their crop?"

"Can't remember, sir."

"Tell him, Fairmile."

In a resigned tone Fairmile recited the tedious inventory of the summer inspection. So many roods of emmer, so many of oats, barley, lentils, millet; so many swine, goats, milk beasts, heifers, a solitary bullock . . .

Beilin Crogh allowed his mind to wander. He liked the woods at this time of year. They exhaled a special smell: damp, rotting, melancholy, which meant the onset of another winter, the season when he had least work to do and could spend some time at home. This village today would be one of the last.

The road, leading downhill now through the oaks, became much wetter, strewn here and there with red and yellow cherry leaves. It had rained heavily every day for the past week: at the bottom, near the edge of the fields, Beilin Crogh saw to his annoyance that the mud was so deep as to be impassable. He would have to force a way around it, through the undergrowth, and, of more importance, carriage of the impost to Matley would be delayed.

This was the first matter he raised with Bocher, the head man, who received him, as usual, in the Meeting House. Upkeep of official roads within two miles of the village was Bocher's responsibility, not Valdoe's.

"I'm sorry," Bocher said. "We'll see to it. More ale, master?"

The customary form of address, coming from Bocher's lips, sounded unpleasantly servile. Some radical change in his manner had taken place since the last inspection. Beilin Crogh narrowed his eyes.

"No," he said. "No more ale. I would like to begin at once."

5 Between sleep and waking, Paoul heard unfamiliar sounds outside and adapted them to his dreams. He was dreaming again of the Meeting House on that first afternoon, when Tagart had answered the council's questions and Paoul had sat beside him listening. The sun was beating on the polished surface of the floor, pouring through the open shutters, bleaching the interior of all color and yet imbuing it with its own special, ethereal light. Through the doorway he could see, with a clarity remarkable even for his eyes, each detail of the rising slope of trees. The shape and pattern and color, the very texture of each leaf was quite distinct. His gaze lingered on the finely toothed edges of the cherry leaves, the cherry leaves beginning to change from green to yellow to red. They were real, and not real, for he could see through them and they were nothing. Coming down the path below them—the path that he and the others had walked just now—he could see nine soldiers like those he had seen at the Valdoe fairs. Four of the soldiers were carrying a tenth, their leader, on a wicker seat. This man had Tagart's face: he was Tagart, dressed, not in armor like his men, not in the clothes Paoul remembered, but in crude, grimy, and ill-fitting furs and skins. His arm was wounded and he was in pain. Paoul saw him raise his hand and the blood trickled across his palm and down the backs of his fingers.

But Tagart was also beside him here, in the Meeting House. Yet this Tagart did not have Tagart's face. He was well fleshed; his thick, curly brown hair had no trace of gray; his dark eyes twinkled. His beard had been shaved a few days since. For some reason Paoul liked this other Tagart. He knew him to be a friend.

The negotiations were over: Tagart stood up. So did Bocher, and Dagda, and the whole village council. They were afraid. They were afraid of the soldiers coming down the hill.

"It's there, isn't it?" Tagart said. "By the stone."

Despite Bocher's denials, and then his pleas, Tagart made him fold back the altar mat. A large trapdoor had been cut into the floorboards. On either side, let into the wood so that it lay flush, was a white rope handle.

An unpleasant smell which Paoul had noticed earlier now grew stronger.

"This will go badly with you if you're lying," Tagart said. "Open it."

"But, master—"

"Open it, I say!"

Bocher and his wife each grasped a handle and heaved. The trapdoor was heavy and very stiff. As they pulled, as it juddered and creaked, Paoul knew what they would find. Floating in the bilge under the Meeting House floor, under the altar stone, they would find, face up, the source of the sickly sweetness that Paoul alone had been aware of till now. They would find his father's corpse.

But the trapdoor would not open. Tagart spoke more harshly, threatening to bring his men. Bocher and Dagda pulled harder, forcing the door, scraping one edge against the cobbles. From the widening crack came daylight which spilled into the dank, greenish darkness of the tool house and hurt Paoul's eyes.

He sat up, flinching and holding up his hands, and discerned the shapes of two men—one of them Bocher—standing in the doorway.

"I told you, master," Bocher said.

The next voice, the voice of the other man, Paoul had heard before, but only in his dreams, and so he knew he must be dreaming still.

"What's that in there? Is it a child?"

"Nothing for you to concern yourself about, master."

"Who is he?"

"A slave. We found him in the woods. My woman's brother has gone to make a price."

"Bring him outside."

"The tool house contains no produce, master, and slaves do not count toward the impost."

"I wouldn't treat a dog like that. Bring him outside at once."

"May I remind you, master, that I am head man?"

"Do you seek to argue with me?"

Paoul remembered where he was, in the village tool house, among the racks and stands and bundles of communal implements. This was the only securable building in the compound, with solid walls and a close-fitting door, against which Bocher had wedged a prop so that Paoul could not escape. He had been here for many days, perhaps nine or ten, grieving, remembering, lying in the darkness and listening to the rain. Until this morning the rain had scarcely stopped, if at all. It had blurred one day with another and he had lost count. Each morning he had been allowed out, for an hour or so, to keep him healthy. He had seen nothing of Berritt or the other children: the whole atmosphere in the village had changed. Accompanied by one of half a dozen different villagers, he had been made to walk inside the palisade until it was time to go back. Although they had also fed him well, kept him warm and, in the past few days, given him infusions in milk or water of centaury, brooklime, and then willow-bark, he had become more and more feverish, so that now, even though he was beginning to think that he might after all be awake, this version of reality seemed very little different from the one in his dreams, or rather, in his nightmares, each of which had flowed into the next to make a continuous and inconclusive whole. His father was dead. Tagart had been murdered for his sake. Tagart's body, and the bodies of the others, of all the people he had loved best, had been dragged away and hidden in the woods. Only Paoul had survived. He had been the cause of all their deaths—how, he did not understand—and now he was utterly alone.

He allowed Bocher to pull him to his feet and lead him out into the unbearable brightness of a fresh and cloudy autumn day. Flinching and shielding his eyes, he could not believe at first what he saw. The other man, the one Bocher had called "master," was the second Tagart, the Tagart of the dream.

"How he stares at me," the man said. Gathering up the folds of his cloak, he dropped to his haunches so that his face was just below Paoul's. "What is your name, boy?"

Paoul was afraid to speak. The man's eyes were kindly, dark, precisely as he had seen them a moment ago, in the bleached, unearthly light of the Meeting House. This too was certainly a dream, the strangest dream of all: this too was taking place in sleep. If he spoke he would wake and lose even this imaginary friend.

"How long has he been in there?"

"A day or two," Bocher said. "He has not been well. We thought it best to keep him safe. If he tries to go back to the woods alone, he will surely die."

"How can he go back to the woods? The gates are barred; without a ladder he can't climb the palisade."

"He might try, master, and that too would be dangerous."

"Can he talk?"

"Yes. But he is not well."

"I forbid you to put him back in that filthy hole. Look after him properly. Let him have the run of the village, at least until your woman's brother gets back. He can't possibly escape."

"As you wish, master."

"Good. Now, I think we are more or less done. It is time to fix the impost." He took a last, not unsympathetic look at Paoul. "He won't fetch much, you know."

Bocher humbly agreed.

On the man's initiative, he and Bocher set off toward the Meeting House, leaving Paoul alone, still feeling dazed, standing in the thick gray mud by the tool-house door. The man was slightly taller than Bocher, but rather round-shouldered. His drab military cloak was stained with much travel; his boots looked well worn. Paoul had already guessed that he might be a beilin, a harvest inspector, for he had seen one before, in another village. Beilins were soldiers, and soldiers came from the forts. Everything to do with the forts, according to what Tagart had told him, was to be shunned and feared. But this beilin was just a man, an ordinary man. At no advantage to himself, he had made Bocher let Paoul out. Perhaps he might be trusted: he might even turn out to be a friend.

Bocher and the beilin were about fifty paces away when Paoul began to follow. He saw them disappear behind the low, gray walls of one of the stone dwellings, then reappear, walking along the duckboards that led past Bocher's garden hedge. They entered the Meeting House precinct, climbed the steps and, removing their boots at the threshold, pulled on sheepskin house shoes and went inside.

The rain began falling again as Paoul crossed the compound, keeping where he could to the raised walkways. He drew the surprised glances of two women at the bakery, but most of the villagers seemed to be indoors or in the fields, and he reached the Meeting House steps without attracting any great attention.

One by one, he mounted the wide, rain-soaked boards. Under the thatched overhang of the porch they became pale and dry, and here, by the ornately carved doorpost, stood three pairs of boots, two large and one small. Paoul timidly sat down and looked into the Meeting House chamber. Bocher and the beilin were seated near where Tagart had sat on that first afternoon. Between them, set out on a dining mat, were many small bowls and dishes, patterned and plain, heaped with dainties. A girl was filling Bocher's upheld beaker from a wooden jug.

The beilin, beaker in hand, noticed Paoul and turned. Paoul wanted to draw back. The unthinking courage that had brought him here had suddenly dissolved. But he remained where he was. The beilin spoke to Bocher and then beckoned. He smiled: for this was a whim, a diversion, a break from routine. And it confirmed his ascendancy over Bocher.

Paoul hesitated. He had made Bocher very angry. Later, Bocher would punish him for this.

"Are you hungry, boy?" the beilin said. "Take your boots off and come inside."

"Yes," Bocher said, with a marked lack of enthusiasm, when prompted by his honored guest. "Come inside. Help yourself."

Paoul found himself obeying. He felt dizzy. The floorboards were warm and smooth against his feet.

"Have some of this," the beilin said, giving him a basket of honeyed reed-bread. "I think you might like it. Then try the apple jelly. What would you like to drink? Strawberry juice, perhaps? Or milk?"

"Milk, please," Paoul managed to say.

"So he can talk, after all. My young friend would like some milk. Can that be arranged, head man?"

Bocher nodded: the girl fetched a mug of cool milk and served it to Paoul from a tray. He was thirsty. As he drank he sensed that Bocher wanted to get rid of him but did not know how. Refreshed, already feeling better and more confident, Paoul wiped his mouth and carefully set the mug in its proper place on the tray, just as Dagda had taught him.

The beilin noticed. "If you sit there quietly and don't interrupt," he said, "you might learn something interesting. We're fixing the impost. Do you understand what that means?"

"Yes, master."

"Really?"

"The impost is the proportion of harvest taken by Lord Brennis.

You are deciding what the proportion will be and in what form it will be delivered."

With an incredulous glance at Bocher, the beilin smiled and looked back at Paoul. "Who taught you that?"

"My father."

"This is serving no purpose—" Bocher began.

"Was your father a slave too?"

"No, master, he was not. And nor am I. Nor did Bocher find me in the woods."

Again Bocher tried, with greater determination, to intervene: the beilin ordered him to be silent.

"Tell me where Bocher did find you."

"I came here with my father and our friends looking for work. The villagers let us work for a week, then murdered everyone but me."

"Don't listen to him, master! He's lying."

"How many of you were there in all?"

"Eleven, master."

"So you say ten have been killed."

"Yes."

The beilin gave a mischievous smile. "What made you do it, Bocher?"

The dull and humorless Bocher did not understand. "He's making it up, master. That's obvious. He's making it up."

"I'm not," Paoul said, becoming heated, feeling his advantage slipping away. "I'm not. I'm telling the truth!"

"Then ask him where the bodies are," Bocher said. "We'll soon find out who's telling the truth!"

"In the woods! They're in the woods! Hidden in the woods! All except . . . all except my father, and he's under the altar, under the secret door—" Paoul clapped a hand to his mouth. How could he have said anything so foolish? He had ruined his case, his attempt to win the beilin's trust and sympathy. The trapdoor, like the bilge under the floor, like the memory of Tagart's corpse, existed only in his nightmares. In reality the Meeting House was quite different: tangible, solid, ordinary. There was no smell, no strange light, no assembly of councilmen.

But his words had produced an astonishing effect on Bocher which did not escape the beilin's notice. "Secret door?" he said. "What's all this?"

"Nothing, master. Can't you see he's just a little liar? He's been lying since the moment we found him."

The beilin put down his beaker and looked around, toward the altar at the far end of the room. His eye dwelled on the white stone itself, on the votive wreath of box-sprigs placed on its top, then moved to the expanse of rush matting laid before it.

Slowly and deliberately, the beilin rose to his feet.

Beilin Crogh chose another pouch at random and opened the drawstring. This one, like many of the others, was filled with seed rather than dry leaf. He took a pinch between his fingers and sniffed it. "And this?"

Bocher was almost beside himself with fear. His denials had turned to bluster, then to pleading, attempted bribery, and finally to abject terror. At first he had merely sweated. Now he was weeping too. "Coriander, master. I think coriander."

"Also a forbidden herb, if I'm not mistaken."

Intrigued, Crogh peered again into the space under the trap-door. It was about three feet square and four deep, lined with broad shelves. Here, in trays, boxes, and leather bags, he had found enough illicit produce to have Bocher burned alive, and the whole village with him. Besides no less than three types of sacred herbs whose possession was, outside the red priesthood, punishable by death, there were several pecks of the permitted kinds—the equivalent of many bushels of grain. But far more remarkable than the value and variety of this hoard was the manner in which he had come to unearth it, and more remarkable still were the reactions of this strange young boy. The discovery of the very thing to which he had wanted to draw Crogh's attention had left him speechless. It was unlikely that the boy could have known of the trapdoor by normal means. Probably in all the village no more than a dozen people knew of its existence. How, then, had the boy known? And why had he said that it would conceal, not illicit herbs, but the body of his father?

At first, before Crogh had had the presence of mind to send him away, the boy had stood there watching, incredulous, in a sort of reverie. From his expression Crogh had seen that he now felt pity for Bocher and could understand, if not forgive, his crimes. Crogh himself found Bocher pitiable. The excuses he had made were human enough. He was frantic to cure his sick daughter and could not afford the necessary sacrifice. During the summer, at a secret clearing in a remote part of the woods, he and his wife had grown these herbs. The illicit ones they had obtained as seed, in tiny quantities, from a Trundleman's slave at the spring Valdoe fair. They were planning to barter the hoard with neighboring villages once the autumn inspection was complete.

Crogh reached into the hole once more and drew out a somewhat larger and heavier bag. It contained a variety of crafted goods, evidently the spare treasure of the entire village, put here for safekeeping: stone buttons, pendants, combs, bone fishhooks and needles, unusual shells, a damaged ax head of ornamental limestone. Tipped out on the floor, this hopeless collection of rubbish came close to touching Crogh's heart.

Reconsidering, he looked up. The serving-girl was also no longer here; like the boy, she could no longer witness what was taking place. Bocher had sent her away even before the mat had been moved. Crogh and Bocher were alone.

"They're yours, master," Bocher said, resuming his clumsy attempt at bribery. "It's all yours, the herbs, everything."

Crogh looked out of the window and into the rainy compound. His men were nowhere to be seen, still sampling the beer provided by overfriendly villagers, no doubt. He looked back at Bocher, into the hole, at Bocher again. He had never in his life been tempted by such a blatant or valuable bribe. If his commander got wind of it, Crogh would be finished. But then he thought of his family, his future, his dream of a leisured life. What would his commander do for him when he was too old to be of use? Nothing.

On the other hand, the price of the herbs, great as it was, would not go far toward paying for his dream. It might be better to win favor with the commander by reporting the matter fully; it might secure the promotion which so far had been denied, a promotion perhaps to another fort—perhaps even to the east!

"Then there's the boy, master. He's yours too. He's worth a lot, much more than the herbs. My woman's brother has gone to the priests about him. They'll want him, I know they will. You've seen for yourself."

So that was it. Crogh suddenly understood and, understanding, suddenly became excited. This mooncalf Bocher was not so stupid, after all!

Crogh looked away. Earlier, he had rather liked the boy. He had felt unaccountably drawn to him. He liked him still, but now he was also a little uneasy. The boy was more than merely strange, an adult in miniature. He did not seem like a child at all.

Crogh felt a twinge of fear. It might yet be better to report this business in full.

"Here, master," Bocher went on, fumbling to open his tunic. He brought out a doeskin wrapper and hurriedly unfolded it. "Here, master. Look."

"Where did you get these?"

"They belong to the village, master."

"Impossible."

Bocher did not reply, and Crogh saw no profit in pursuing an explanation which would anyway be tendered in the form of further lies. He was already engrossed in the wrapper's contents: the most wonderful jewelry he had ever seen, a small tangled heap of jade, amber, ivory, and, most precious of all, copper. Gently he extended a forefinger and lifted clear an extraordinary necklace made from interlocking scales of nacre and blue lapis. This one piece alone, this string of scales dangling from his fingertip, would take him at least half a year to earn. No: a year. Two. No; he would never be able to pay for such a thing. Or this, a tiny serpent, half the width of his palm, in copper and amber, adorned with brightly colored stones whose name he did not know.

Obviously Bocher had no idea what he was offering, for he need only have revealed one piece and everything would have been settled.

Did the jewelry have any connection with the boy? It had to. In that case, he could not afford to leave the boy behind. He would have to question him at length about the jewelry before attempting, cautiously and unobtrusively, over the years, to sell it. Besides, the boy would indeed be worth a good deal in his own right. There would be no difficulty in getting him to Valdoe: the autumn inspection was nearly over, and soon Crogh would have time to spare.

He rapidly came to a decision. He would accept the jewelry and the boy, but not the herbs. The forbidden ones would have to be destroyed, likewise the secret field in the woods. The rest he would allow Bocher to keep. The sick daughter would get her sacrifice after all; the boy would be released from captivity and spared an uncertain fate, for, if the priests did not want him, Crogh would not sell him to Valdoe, but to a private home. He might even keep the boy himself. As to the question of the murders—and Crogh was inclined to believe the boy's version—that was a matter for Bocher, the village, and the Earth Mother.

After another moment's hesitation, Crogh reached out. He took the wrapper from Bocher's hands, poured in the jewels, and carefully began to enfold them.

6 All trace of Lord Torin had been expunged.

Lady Torin, her four children, and the principal members of her late husband's entourage had already sailed, in disgrace, for the mainland. His bodyguards had been dispersed and enslaved; his personal slaves had been put in the mines; even his hawks and his matched pair of deerhounds had been given away. His clothing had been burned with his corpse. His paintings, rugs, tapestries, and other valuables had been put in storage to await transmission to the homelands, where they would be sold or otherwise disposed of.

For the past three weeks, since the morning after the assassination, laborers and craftsmen had been at work in the private residence. On the orders of General Teshe, the main room upstairs—in which the prospective young Flint Lord was to eat, sleep, and conduct his affairs—had been completely stripped. The ceiling had been cleaned; the walls had been broken out and freshly rendered with Cornish clay, smoothed, limed, smoothed again, and decorated to the taste of General Teshe with murals of birds, bears, and dragons. The floorboards had been torn up and replaced with seasoned maple, abraded with sandstones, repeatedly waxed and polished, and brought to a sheen. The doors, shutters, and all internal fittings had been renewed throughout the whole of the private residence. Rooms had been prepared not only for the customary domestic entourage—the various body slaves, the cooks, the food taster—but also for Hothen's tutor and for his nurse.

Rian's chamber adjoined Hothen's and shared its southerly outlook, toward the marshes and the distant sea. The chamber had once been Altheme's sitting room. Leaning on the window ledge, Rian could see beyond the inner palisade to the roofs and chimney holes of the vansery, the priests' quarters. The vansery had not been there in Altheme's day; neither had the stone temple on the hill. Like his father, Gehan Fifth had abhorred the red priesthood and, except for a few apostate doctors and a single astronomer, had kept it resolutely out of Brennis. Soon after Lord Torin's accession, however, a delegation from the citadel had arrived to supervise work on the new vansery and temple. It had been finished within two years. The Prime himself had risked the crossing to consecrate the altar and make the first oblation, conferring on Valdoe the highest possible status. From then on, the priests had assumed more and more importance in the affairs of Valdoe and of the whole domain. Another vansery had recently been built, at Cissbury, and Rian had heard that yet another was being planned elsewhere.

She had no feelings, good or bad, about the priesthood. It existed: it was just part of the system that had placed her and was keeping her in the condition of slavery. The aims and learning of the priests were utterly beyond her grasp. As men, as individuals, she found them intimidating. Their self-mastery, the complete absence of any human weakness or failing, were as incomprehensible to her as their prayers, their rituals, or their special signs.

They wore special clothing, too: voluminous gray tunics of the finest cloth, gray leggings, kneeboots, sometimes a gray cloak and soft hat, sometimes gray robes. On entry to the hierarchy, each priest received a red tattoo on the left side of the body: three lines along the arm, flank, and leg, ending in a pentacle on the instep and one on the back of the hand. The lower priests of the villages were marked in a similar way, but in blue, and always on the right side. The blue priests were not required to be celibate. They were common people, farmers, chosen from the village elders. Sometimes the head man himself would serve. He would go to Valdoe or to one of the forts, where a senior blue priest would show him the necessary rites and observances. He would be taught how to pray, and how to divide the year so that his village would know when to plant and when to reap. Then he would take the blue tattoo and return to his home. Of the mysteries, of the red priests' world, he would have learned nothing.

About twenty red priests lived at Valdoe. Their studies here, it seemed, had much to do with the sky. In clear weather Rian had seen them leaving the Trundle and walking down to the temple, where they would remain till morning. Sometimes they lit fires on the beach or on surrounding hills; sometimes they erected great crosses, or poles marked in black and white, or stakes around which they would draw their sacred ropes. Once, at noon, she had seen them flying a kite and marking the position of its shadow with white pegs in the grass.

They studied other things also. At the settlement farm near Valdoe Village they bred animals and birds and maintained several plots where they tested different kinds of cereal crops. Nearby was a young orchard and an area for soft fruit, mostly blackberries and gooseberries. Rian did not know whether they ever ate the produce. Perhaps it was magic, like the plants in the physic garden. This was laid out between the vansery and the inner palisade, protected at either end by a high spiked fence. The garden was usually tended by an old priest named Kar Houle, a doctor who had once treated Ika's eyes; he had eliminated her pain, but had told her that her sight could never be restored. During the treatment Rian had got to know him quite well—as well as a slave could ever know a red priest—and, somewhat against convention, he now always acknowledged her and occasionally even exchanged a few words.

Yesterday he had told her that the choice of Hothen's tutor had been settled. The tutor was to be a young priest recently arrived from the citadel, a teller of the legends called Ilven Loes. On five mornings a week Ilven Loes was to take Hothen for exercise: for walks on the hill and, in warm weather, to Apuldram for boating and bathing. The afternoons would be spent in the residence, where Hothen would learn his numbers and speech. Later he would be taught drawing, writing, pottery, movement, and history. When he was yet older he would be prepared in earnest for his coming of age. Other priests in the vansery would teach him mensuration, strategy, agronomy; he would spend three years in the homelands, at the military academy, learning the workings of the empire. At fifteen he would enter the Valdoe barracks part time to be taught the control of men. On his twentieth birthday, provided the Vansard—the arch priest—agreed, Hothen would become Flint Lord in fact as well as title and General Teshe, or whoever then was his guardian, would step down.

That was the plan. Rian did not know how far Hothen would get with it. They must have known how backward he was, how incapable of assimilating such learning, but still this elaborate scheme for his future had solemnly been laid out. Perhaps it was all a charade. Perhaps the Home Lord did not intend him to finish his education or to assume control of Valdoe. The appearances, however, would have to be observed.

The first stage in this process was beginning today. At any

moment now the tutor would be coming over to be introduced
to his charge. The Vansard would accompany him; General Teshe
had arranged a small ceremony to mark both this event and the
refurbishing of the residence. Food and drink had been prepared;
three musicians had just arrived and were tuning their instru-
ments. Hothen had been ready for at least an hour. He was sitting
with his mother in the main room, while the slaves straightened
mats and hangings that were already straight and Rian looked
nervously out of the window toward the gate of the inner palisade.

She still could not believe that events had moved so quickly.
She still could not believe that Lord Torin was really dead or
that Hothen, poor little Hothen, had been propelled with such
speed and force into the highest and most dangerous reaches of
power. Three weeks ago he and Ika had been nothing, despised,
ignored. Now Ika was important. She had new clothes, new jewelry, her own suite of rooms, body slaves, everything she wanted.
By sled or litter she could travel anywhere she pleased. Hothen,
naturally, also had his own retinue: Rian's work had been reduced
to a tithe of its former amount. In three weeks her life had been
transformed. It was unbelievable, but true. And for proof, she
saw at last two gray-clad figures passing through the inner gate
and crossing the mist-soaked turf toward the residence.

"They're coming," she said, and hurried back into the main
chamber.

"You must leave us now," the older priest said.

Beilin Crogh stood up, turning his hat in his hands, and looked
anxiously at Paoul. The younger priest took his arm and drew
him to the door. "The first examination will last till sunset. Come
back then."

Paoul did not look around. He heard the door close behind
him and felt even more afraid—Beilin Crogh was at least familiar.
Paoul had begun, almost, to like him.

They had been staying in Valdoe Village, at the house of Beilin
Crogh's father.

The walk from the west had taken four days. From Sturt, Beilin
Crogh had moved Paoul to another village, nearer Matley fort.
He had remained there for five days until collected by Beilin Crogh
and two of the soldiers who had been at Sturt. In the interval, it
seemed, Beilin Crogh had heard some momentous news about
Valdoe, about the Flint Lord. Because of it he had been on the

point of abandoning Paoul to the village; then he had changed his mind. At a rapid pace they had traveled the roads and tracks Paoul had last walked with the group. Each familiar bend and prospect, each river crossed, had reminded him of Tagart, of the old life which now was over and would never come again. Paoul was bewildered as well as frightened and unhappy. Beilin Crogh had asked so many questions that he had made Paoul cry, but Paoul's own questions had been ignored or evaded. He knew that Beilin Crogh had bought him from Bocher and that he was going to Valdoe to be resold, as a slave. But he also knew that he was too small to work usefully in the mines or anywhere else, and he could not understand why he warranted this special treatment— why a harvest inspector and two soldiers were troubling to escort him sixty or seventy miles across country, or why Beilin Crogh was so anxious to know every last detail of his life. Beilin Crogh had interrogated him most closely on the subject of his parents. Paoul remembered nothing of his mother, but Tagart had told him that she had been kind and beautiful and had died after drinking bad water. Beilin Crogh had insisted on hearing about her, not just once, but over and over again. And her husband, Tagart, had he always been a vagrant, a nomad? How had he come to be crippled? Was Paoul sure that his father had never been connected in any way—especially by blood—with the important families of Valdoe or the mainland? And his mother? What had been her name? Had she ever owned precious objects? Necklaces, for example, or brooches? Was he sure? Had anyone in the group, anyone at all, ever owned or come by such things? And how had he known about the trapdoor? Was it truly a dream that had shown him, or did he have access to the spirits? How often did he have such dreams? Had he ever seen the future before? Never? What did he know about magic, or ritual words, or secret markings, or how the pentacle was made? What did he know about the heavens? What did he know about the sun, the moon, the seasons of the sky? Nothing? Was he sure?

On arrival at Valdoe the questioning had finally come to an end. Beilin Crogh had seemed satisfied, even pleased, with Paoul's answers. He had become more affable; he had promised Paoul that nothing bad was going to happen.

They had arrived in the village at noon, in drifting fog which had wreathed the base of Valdoe Hill and obscured the Trundle at its summit. After a meal, Beilin Crogh had taken leave of his father and had climbed the hill, returning very late at night. From his corner of the rear chamber, Paoul had strained to overhear the ensuing conversation between Beilin Crogh and his father. He had heard "the boy" mentioned once or twice, and "Dagda's brother," and he had been able to distinguish a few other words and phrases, but nothing to signify what was happening or what the future held.

Early this morning, for the first time in his life, he had been bathed in hot water. Beilin Crogh's mother had scrubbed him with a doeskin pad soaked in a sort of colorless jelly. Afterward she had rinsed and dried him, cleaned out his ears and nose, examined his hands and feet and teeth, and pronounced him ready to be dressed—in new clothes, clothes of a quality Paoul had never seen before: a supple jerkin with braided seams, a doeskin blouse, kidskin leggings and breeches, hide boots lined with marten fur and fastened with horn-toggled straps.

Paoul had sniffed at his hand, tasted his skin. Even a summer bathe in the cleanest pool had always left him smelling very slightly of mud, of natural things; even a swim in the most dazzling surf had made his skin smell of the sea, but today he smelled of nothing, not even of himself. He could smell only the sickly odor of leather dressing, coming from his new clothes.

"Where's that other boy you brought here, Crogh?" Beilin Crogh's mother had asked her son.

"I think you must have left him in the bathwater."

And another boy, it seemed, had been left on the long ascent of the hill, approaching the dark ramparts and palisades of the Trundle, another as Beilin Crogh had led him through the jaws of the southeast gateway and into the enclosure, another as they had gained admittance to what Paoul realized were the priests' quarters, and yet another as the door had shut on Beilin Crogh, leaving Paoul alone with his two examiners.

"Now, Paoul," the older and more important one said, rising from his seat. "There is no need to be frightened. Nobody is going to hurt you." He beckoned. "Come to the light. We want to see what you're made of."

Paoul had never been spoken to by red priests before. He had never seen them so close to. He knew they were red priests by their tattoos, and by their gray clothing. He had occasionally glimpsed such men at gatherings or festivals or, once or twice, when traveling on the road. Tagart had told him that they were to be feared, much more than the blue priests of the villages, much more than the soldiers or the Trundlemen, more even than the Flint Lord himself.

"Come along," said the younger one. "Don't keep Kar Houle waiting."

Paoul stood up. He made himself walk to the window. The older priest, a man of great age with a shock of white hair and very clear blue eyes, laid a hand on Paoul's head and gently felt his skull.

"Why are you trembling so much, boy? Keep still."

"I . . . I want to know why I have been brought here. Am I . . . am I to be sacrificed?"

The old priest looked highly amused. "What makes you think that?"

"I once heard someone say . . ."

"Say what?"

"That children were sacrificed to the Earth Mother. By the red priests. By you."

"I'm sorry to disappoint you. Here we cut no throats at all. Not even children's."

"Then . . . am I to be made a slave? Tell me what you want of me."

"Just be quiet. You talk too much."

The old man continued, with gentle yet insistent fingers, to explore the shape of Paoul's head. "That's interesting," he said. "Yes." From a bowl beside him he took a small, flattened stick, squatted and, opening Paoul's mouth, pressed the stick against his tongue. "Easy. Don't tense." Paoul watched his eyes making a swift, darting examination. Paoul started to gag: the stick was instantly taken away. Next the old man's fingers probed under his jaw, feeling his windpipe and neck. "Turn your head. Now the other way. Back again. Now come closer to the light." Paoul felt his left ear being pulled, the end of a short tube being inserted. "Yes. And the other. Yes."

The younger priest had meanwhile left the room. From somewhere just beyond the doorway came a very faint tinkling sound, as of fragments of shell being blown by the wind. "Do you hear anything?"

Paoul nodded.

"Hold up your hand when it stops."

The test was repeated with a variety of sounds and whispered words, and repeated again, first with the right ear blocked and then the left. At the end, the old man seemed satisfied. He next made an extended and meticulous examination of Paoul's eyes, folding back the lids, asking him to look from side to side and up and down and, with the lids closed, lightly pressing the eyeballs in a dozen different ways. After this he directed Paoul's attention outside, into the enclosure. A black board, marked with concentric patterns in red, green, and white, had been hung from a post some twenty paces from the window. Using either eye, and then both together, Paoul had to describe the markings in great detail.

As question followed question, Paoul began to feel less fearful. He was even beginning, in a curious way, to enjoy himself.

"And inside the inner one? Is there anything else?"

"No . . . there might be. I'm not sure. Is it a dot?"

Once more the old man squatted, to share Paoul's view of the board, and Paoul noticed how lithe, how controlled, how unlike those of other old men, his movements seemed to be. Paoul allowed himself to become aware of what he had not wanted to acknowledge before: an indefinable, tingling sensation of fascination, attraction, a desire to please, to win the approval of his questioner. "Don't strain," the old man said. "Blink normally. Breathe easily. Don't screw up your eyes. Just guess. It doesn't matter if you're right or wrong."

Suddenly Paoul knew the old man did not intend to hurt him. And if the old man did not intend to hurt him, then neither, perhaps, did the young one nor any of the other priests, and perhaps Beilin Crogh's promise, that nothing bad was going to happen, had after all been true.

"So. What do you think it is, Paoul?"

"A cross. A white cross. Is it a cross?"

"You tell me."

"Yes. It's a white cross."

The old man rose to his feet. "Please remove your jerkin and blouse."

Over Paoul's head the young priest said, "He might even do, Kar Houle."

"There's a long way to go yet. But I agree, he might. If, that is, we decide to meet the beilin's price."

The beilin's price? Paoul did not understand; but he dared
not ask.

"Quickly, boy," the young priest said. "We've better things
to do than wait for you." And, firmly but not at all roughly, he
helped Paoul pull the new leather blouse over his head, deftly
folded it, and laid it on the shelf.

7 Paoul was examined daily for almost a week, usually by Kar Houle, who was always present, but often by other priests too. On the first day they completed the examination of every part of his body—his frame, his muscles, tendons, the shape and feel of his internal organs—and, with a graduated rod and large and small pairs of pivoting, sharp-pointed tongs, they measured his height, girth, the length and thickness of his limbs, the size of his head, and the proportions of his face. They immersed him in a vat brimming with water and balanced him on a counterpoised beam. They made him run against an older boy, made him step up and down on a log, jump, lift stones, throw spears, and bend bows. They felt his neck and counted his breaths, listened to his chest through a small tube, made him perform a number of contortions to test his suppleness.

The next day another priest, younger than Kar Houle but still very old, gave Paoul a selection of strange objects—both man-made and natural—and asked him to guess their origin and function. He then set Paoul some puzzles. At first they were simple and Paoul could answer without hesitation. Later they became harder, much harder, until, however much time he took, he remained baffled. After this the priest showed him a tray of small objects: a feather, a crab's claw, an acorn, a toadstool, a dead mouse. Almost at once he covered the tray and asked Paoul to remember what he had seen. That was easy. Paoul could name all the objects, even when more were added or some were taken away; but, by the time there were twenty or twenty-five to remember, and the time was reduced to just a few moments, his memory began to falter.

On the third day the same priest sat with him in the examining room. Much of the morning and the whole of the afternoon were taken up with a difficult series of tests, using pebbles at first, then wooden shapes, and then multicolored cubes laid out on a large checkered board. The markers formed confusing patterns which Paoul had to study and, if necessary, complete, by moving, adding, or taking away one or more of the markers. When the tests became too complicated they began again, but this time the priests engaged in distracting conversation which made it even harder to think.

By dusk, when Beilin Crogh again came to collect him and take him down to the village, Paoul felt exhausted. He was beginning to feel angry and resentful, too: for not once had Kar Houle or any of the others told him when he had given the right or wrong answer. Not once had they praised or corrected him; not once had they indicated the purpose of all these tests.

"That's enough," Beilin Crogh growled, when Paoul asked him for the hundredth time what it was the priests wanted. "I'm not listening to any more. I've already told you, it's for the best."

"But—"

"Another word and I'll wallop you. That's a promise."

By the fifth day, however, Paoul thought he knew. The previous morning had been spent testing his ability to remain motionless; in the afternoon, Kar Houle had lit incense and, with the examining room in near darkness and Paoul lying on a couch of layered oxhides, had asked many questions about his dreams, particularly the one at Sturt in which he had seen the trapdoor. During this, from somewhere at the far end of the vansery, Paoul had heard chanting, five or six voices in unison, and in the soothing, extended music of their song he had thought he had sensed the thing that made Kar Houle different from other old men. He had sensed that Kar Houle was searching for signs of this thing in him. Last night, in the village, Paoul had lain awake thinking, and now, this morning, as Kar Houle again entered the examining room, as his assistant again bade Paoul make himself comfortable on the layered couch, Paoul thought he knew. He thought he knew and was indignant. He considered deliberately failing the rest of the examination. But then, Kar Houle would not be deceived, and besides, what else could the future hold? If he failed the rest of the examination—not that he was sure he had passed so far—he knew that Beilin Crogh would sell him as a slave, to work in the fields, in the mines, or worse. Paoul was alone; and he was lonely. He was lonely for Tagart, for the others in the group: for Fodich and his jokes, for Tanda's little songs, for the many smells of the forest, for the excitement of arrival and departure. He wanted nothing more than to lead that life forever, but it was gone, just as Tagart was gone, just as Tanda and Fodich were gone. Of all the people he had met since that night in Sturt, there was none he could admire as he had admired Tagart; and yet, despite his tattoo and gray tunic, despite all that Tagart had said about the red priesthood, Kar Houle had come very close to earning Paoul's respect. More than once Paoul had caught himself trying to emulate the old man, wishing that he could be like him one day, wishing that he could be so calm and patient, so knowledgeable, and so wise.

"Now, Paoul," Kar Houle said, seating himself on the floor, his assistant some way behind. "You know you have no cause to be tense. Let the couch take your weight again. That's right. Like that. Are you comfortable?"

"Yes thank you, Kar Houle," Paoul said, just as he had been trained by the assistant. "I am comfortable."

"I would like to begin today by talking about your parents. Beilin Crogh has told us a little, but not enough. Your father was called Tagart, and your mother . . . Mirin. Is that right?"

"Yes, Kar Houle."

"Those are ancient names. Savages' names. Was your father a savage?"

"No."

"I beg your pardon, Paoul. Was he a nomad?"

"Once. Long ago."

"He was crippled at the siege of Valdoe, was he not? And then became the leader of a party of itinerants. The others must have held him in high esteem."

"He was a chief, chief of all the southern tribes. Fodich told me."

"Fodich being another of the nomads? I see. Beilin Crogh tells us that your mother died after drinking bad water and that you do not remember her. Did your father speak of her much to you?"

"No, Kar Houle."

"What did he say, if anything?"

"That she was kind and beautiful. That she loved me."

"Nothing more?"

"It hurt him to talk about her."

"Did Fodich or any of the others ever speak to you of your mother?"

"No, Kar Houle. My father did not want them to."

"Don't you find that strange?"

Paoul said nothing.

"I ask these questions, Paoul, because we are concerned that you do not appear to be what you are meant to be. Is it possible that your mother was not a nomad? Could she have come from one of the villages?"

"My father would not have married a village woman. He did not like farmers. He was a chief. He was Shode, the first man of the spirit. He used to be a great hunter."

Kar Houle waited delicately before speaking again. "Forgive me for asking this. Are you sure that Tagart was your father?"

Paoul answered at once: he could not have been more sure of anything in his life. "Yes."

"And you were born on Crale Day, seven years ago."

"That is what my father told me, Kar Houle."

"You see, Paoul, unless we are greatly mistaken, you are not of nomad blood. Your bones are not proportioned as a nomad's are; your skin is too fair and your eyes are not dark enough. But, most of all, the shape of your head is wrong. If I had been told nothing about your parents, I would have said that they had come from the homelands. I would even have guessed that they had probably been born in one of the provinces around the citadel. Does this mean anything to you?"

"No, Kar Houle."

"Do you remember at any time traveling across the sea?"

"No, Kar Houle."

"When was the first time you saw the Trundle?"

"I was very young. We came here for the spring fair."

"Tell me about it, please."

With only a few breaks, the questioning continued all day. This interrogation, Paoul soon realized, was much more clever and searching than had been Beilin Crogh's. Paoul answered honestly: he saw no reason to do otherwise. By dusk, or so it seemed, he had exposed his complete stock of memories to view.

"So," Kar Houle said, when he had finished. "I expect you would like something to eat."

The assistant brought Paoul a meal of fresh bread and butter, cheese, fruit, and a hot tisane, then left the room.

Kar Houle sat watching benevolently, sipping a beaker of herb tea. "Is the food to your liking, Paoul?"

"Yes thank you, Kar Houle."

"Good."

After a pause, Paoul went on eating.

"The examination," Kar Houle said, "is almost concluded. You have already guessed its purpose, have you not?"

"Yes, Kar Houle."

"Tomorrow is the last day. In the morning you will meet the Vansard. That should not take very long. Depending on what the Vansard desires, I shall then speak to Beilin Crogh. If, as is likely, we accept his terms, and if you agree, you will go to the citadel for instruction. When you are ready to return to Brennis to take up your duties, you will be offered the red tattoo. I think you have seen and been told enough in the past week to know what life here is like."

So Paoul had been right. He had guessed correctly. The priests wanted to take him and turn him into one of themselves. But, now that he was sure of it, he no longer knew how to react. Part of him, the part that belonged to the old life, was resisting strongly. But the rest was more practical. If he went along with this, he would at least be clothed, housed, and fed: and he had seen that the priests were supplied with the best of everything. If he hated the citadel, if they mistreated him, he could always run away. He could do that as well on the mainland as here, for he had no one in all the world. And despite his doubts, and the uneasy feeling that he would be betraying Tagart's memory by accepting the offer, Paoul was secretly fascinated by Kar Houle and intrigued by the possibility of learning what it was that Kar Houle knew.

"Most vanseries train their own novices," Kar Houle went on, "but as yet we do not have the facilities here. Usually our boys go just across the channel to Raighe. However, as I have said, we propose to send you to the citadel. The school there is without equal. We have been privileged to be able to send it several pupils. All were talented in their own way, or we would not have put them forward. Some are being supported by their parents; the others we are sponsoring. I examined them all, just as I examined you, just as I have examined many hundreds more, both here and in the homelands. Now listen carefully, Paoul, because you will never hear such words again, not, at least, in this or any other vansery. I should not even be saying them now. It is the Vansard who decides who shall be offered a place, not I. But, so that you may conduct yourself properly tomorrow, I am going to tell you that, in all my life, I have never examined anyone more worthy of acceptance than you. If you attend to

your teachers, you may one day make yourself equal to your
gifts. I can praise you no more highly than that. But if you are
lazy, or if you choose to ignore altogether this opportunity Gauhm
has put in your way, you will be committing an act of great
sacrilege. Do you understand what I am saying to you, Paoul?"

"Yes, Kar Houle."

"And what is your inner wish?"

"I think you already know it, Kar Houle."

The next morning was sunny and exceptionally clear. Beilin Crogh
was sitting nervously on a bench in the anteroom next to the
Vansard's chamber, wishing, more than ever, that he had not
been so foolhardy. He should never have taken this chance; he
should have left the boy at Sturt.

Through the open window he could hear the martial shouts
and cries of the priests at their weapons practice in the enclosure.

"To you! To me! Now! Strike! To me!"

With each ferocious clash of staves, with each thud of wood
on leather, Crogh wanted to cringe, to flinch, to put as much
distance as possible between the Vansard and himself. But, beyond repeatedly wiping his palms, crossing and uncrossing his
legs, and adjusting the position of his hat on the bench beside
him, Crogh did not move. He had come this far: he would have
to see things through. Besides, it was too late. He had already
woken the beast.

At last the door opened and Paoul emerged, ushered by Kar
Houle's assistant. Crogh sprang to his feet. From this angle little
could be seen of the interior of the Vansard's room: oatmeal-
colored hangings, the edge of a dais, sunshine on waxed floorboards. The assistant closed the door behind him. "Kar Houle
will be with you presently," he told Crogh. "Please resume your
seat. Paoul and I will be waiting nearby."

From Paoul's face Crogh could divine no clue as to what had
happened. Paoul looked up at him, briefly and expressionlessly
engaged his eyes, and was gone.

When Kar Houle came out he offered, with his customary,
scrupulous, and intimidating politeness, profuse apologies for the
delay. "Would you care for some mead, Beilin Crogh? We do
not take alcohol ourselves, but we like to offer it when the occasion
arises."

The chamber reserved for entertaining lay visitors was at the end of the corridor. It overlooked the herb garden and was much more richly and comfortably furnished than the rest of the vansery. On the wall hung a circular wooden plaque, finely polished and inlaid with ivory strips in the shape of a perfect pentacle. This, and a discreet but superbly made figurine of the Earth Mother in the niche below it, was the only sign that Crogh had not been invited into the private residence of some high-ranking soldier or wealthy merchant.

"The mead is excellent," he said, but in truth he was so scared that he could hardly taste it. "I don't suppose you make it here? No, well, it's delicious all the same."

Kar Houle accepted the compliment with a gracious smile and sat back, making the cushions creak. "Now," he said, fixing Crogh with a clear blue gaze. "To the matter in hand. Before we begin, however, I feel it will not prejudice our position if I tell you that we are deeply grateful to you for bringing this child to our notice. He is quite exceptional."

"I thought of you the moment I clapped eyes on him. The policy of the priesthood is . . . it's well known. Even as far out as Matley."

"Ah yes. Matley. We have been in contact with your commander. On his orders the head man was questioned and the village searched. You may be interested to know that a mass grave was found in the woods. It contained six males and four females, all adults. If we take the boy, their bodies will be sent here for examination. It seems that the good people of Sturt have devised a thrifty method of paying their debts to itinerant laborers."

Crogh did not know whether he was meant to smile.

"That, of course, concerns us not in the least. What does concern us, Beilin, is the apparent inconsistency in your version of events in the Meeting House. The boy, truthful in all other verifiable respects, is convinced that there was a secret chamber whose contents you did not want him or the serving girl to see. You, however, have already assured me that there was not. The head man, even under duress, maintains that you and not the boy are correct. By a remarkable coincidence, the floor of the Meeting House has very recently been relaid. Thus your comrades from Matley were unable to get to the truth."

This was the moment Crogh had been dreading. He had taken every possible precaution, but he had never dealt with a red priest before.

"You well appreciate, do you not, Beilin, the penalties for depriving Valdoe of its due?"

"Of course."

"And the penalties for abetting such behavior?"

"The boy had a nightmare. He wasn't himself, Kar Houle. It's not surprising when you think how they'd treated him, locked up in that shed for ten days. At least ten. Perhaps more. Then don't forget his father and all his friends had just been massacred. No wonder he was seeing things. I'd be seeing things myself in those circumstances."

"You are a clever fellow, Beilin Crogh. Somewhat of a scoundrel, but a clever fellow nonetheless."

"I assure you, Kar Houle—"

"No more assurances, if you please. Let us merely point out that our gratitude to you has precluded the further investigations that otherwise would certainly have been made. It is not every day a Paoul is brought to us. We do not wish to discourage the process by which he arrived. Nor do we wish to treat you unjustly. He may be, as you claim, mistaken about the trapdoor. But I think I need hardly remind you of the fate of those who earn an evil reputation for themselves. You need look no further than the example of Lord Torin." Kar Houle indicated the pitcher. "More mead?"

"No. No thank you."

"As to price. You suggested four toles of copper. I have discussed this with the Vansard and he feels three would be more suitable. Three toles of copper, or nine thousand first-grade scrapers or their equivalent in raw celts or worked tools."

"Copper is more portable. Yes. Copper, I think."

"Very well. Copper it shall be."

8 Paoul spent another six days at the vansery, but Beilin Crogh was no longer there to collect him each evening and take him down to the village; now he remained after nightfall with the priests, eating their food, absorbing their conversation, sleeping in his own tiny cell. Alone in the darkness, he would hug himself and weep, but at dawn, awoken by the sound of chanting, he would feel a little better and in full daylight his unhappiness receded almost completely. There was so much that was new, so much that was strange and that promised more strangeness for the future. Kar Houle and the others used these six days to prepare him for the journey and ultimately for his arrival at the citadel.

The last boat of the autumn, due to leave before the crossing became too rough, was the *Veisdrach*, a huge new vessel of nearly sixty feet belonging to the merchant Bohod Thosk. Paoul first saw it at midmorning, glimpsed among the trees and between the sheds and workshops on the Apuldram quay. The sky, softly blue, promised more fine weather; a cold breeze was keeping the ship facing generally west, riding its mooring in the middle of the channel. From time to time, the wind disturbed a drooping standard, red and black, which hung from the sternpost.

"Those are the colors of the Thosk clan," Kar Houle told him, as they came out of the trees, two hundred and fifty yards from the precincts of the sheds, where Paoul could see men busily at work. After taking formal leave of the Vansard and saying good-bye to the other priests he had got to know, Paoul had walked with Kar Houle down from the Trundle, along four miles of muddy road which ended here, at the Flint Lord's main harbor. Paoul noticed four men launching a black coracle from one of the landing stages. They began to scull toward the ship. "Bohod Thosk," Kar Houle was saying, "is an important merchant. He owns at least a hundred villages and an estate near Hohe where Lord Heite himself is often a guest. His traders cover the whole empire, even to the east. He has built many ships: the *Veisdrach* is one of the finest. You are lucky to be traveling on her."

"Yes, Kar Houle."

The quayside was strewn, seemingly at random, with stacked boxes, bales, cases of tools, bags, coils of rope, sacks, furled sails, bundles of pelts and furs, goats and pigs and sheep in wicker pens; two shag-haired gray deerhounds had been tied to the corner of the nearest shed. "Those were once Lord Torin's dogs," Kar Houle said. "Now they are to be given to Bohod Thosk." He held Paoul back as two men came past, carrying a spar. "Keep by me."

The shingle crunching under their boots, Kar Houle led him past the partly opened rear of the main building, an enormous repair shop which fronted the stone flags of the quay. Inside, looming out of the darkness, Paoul saw the stern of a small ship. A carpenter was chipping at the rudder with a curiously shaped adze. Another, on his back, was scraping at the keel.

Kar Houle found the harbor Trundleman in his quarters and was directed to the water's edge, where the ship's master, standing among some of his crew, was waiting to supervise the process of bringing the *Veisdrach* in. Three of the four men from the coracle had clambered on board; the fourth was sculling back toward the quay, trailing a length of light rope.

"Good day to you," said Kar Houle.

The whole group looked around and immediately their manner changed. The ship's master, heavy and swarthy, with a grizzled beard and a pointed leather hat, smiled and proffered his palm, which Kar Houle lightly touched. "Good day, Kar Houle."

"I trust everything is going as you wish."

"Yes thank you, father."

"When do you sail?"

"On time. At noon."

With a hand to the nape of his neck, Paoul was brought forward. "This is the child I told you about."

"Passenger for Hohe," the ship's master recalled. "His name is Paoul and he's to ask for Forzan Zett."

"Just so," said Kar Houle with a smile.

"When we've done loading I'll show you his berth."

"Excellent," said Kar Houle. "Until then, we'd better leave you to your work. Come, Paoul."

They retreated to a safe distance. The Trundleman emerged from his doorway; the overseer yelled an order and a dozen slaves came hurrying to the landing stage. Paoul watched intently as the man in the coracle flung the light rope ashore. It was attached to a heavier rope, and yet a heavier, which the slaves began hauling in. The three men on board, meanwhile, had freed the rudder and loosed the mooring cables and, gradually at first, and drifting slightly on the incoming tide, the great ship started to turn. The figurehead slowly came into view: a white dragon with half-closed wings, rising from an inferno of scarlet flame. Its tongue, protruding from jaws filled with incurved fangs, was forked and dark blue. As the prow came around the eyes swept the shore and Paoul felt a shiver of fear as he entered and left their sightless gaze. It was not just fear he felt, but anticipation, excitement. This ship, more even than the marvels of the Trundle or the workings of the vansery, embodied for him what the future held. The timbers of the hull drew their strength from the oak forests of the mainland; the precision of its curves was the product of a masterly expertise. The means to arrive at such a thing came only through total domination and through wealth: the wealth of the merchants allied to the power of the Gehans. And, as Kar Houle had told him, the Gehans were the citadel and the citadel was the Gehans. It was their inextricable heart. At the citadel resided the Prime; at the citadel lay the temple and the very center of the priesthood, and it was to the citadel that, beginning here, today, Paoul was to be sent.

These were the thoughts of a mere moment, fleeting and instantly gone. There were no words for them, only the shiver left by the cold-eyed stare of the dragon before its heard turned further and the bows were facing down the shore.

"Pull there! Pull, damn you! Pull!"

Bending long poles to keep the *Veisdrach* clear of the shallows, the three men on board maneuvered her into place. Inch by inch, the water between the hull and the landing stage narrowed and, with a creak of fenders, disappeared. Two ridged gangplanks were raised to the bulwarks; final turns were given to the cables fore and aft, and the ship was secured. The slaves immediately began fetching and stowing, in what could now be seen as a carefully planned order, the heaps of cargo from the quay.

Close to, the ship looked even larger and more impressive. It smelled almost more maritime than the sea itself.

"Do you see how the gangplanks hinge?" Kar Houle said. "As the tide comes in you'll see the ship rise. The gangplanks are made to rise with her."

Paoul nodded.

"Those two men at the bollards. What do you think their job might be?"

"To loosen the ropes as the tide comes in."

"And if they didn't, what would happen?"

"The ship would tilt over."

"Not tilt. The word is 'list.' The ship would list."

Paoul nodded again. He was becoming used to this continual correction.

"Now, Paoul, remember what I've been telling you. Keep your wits about you. This journey is the beginning of your training. I want you to keep your eyes open. Absorb everything you see. Everything." Kar Houle pointed to his own eyes. "These. These are the essence."

"Yes, Kar Houle," said Paoul, not really understanding.

The harbor Trundleman approached and invited Kar Houle to sit in his quarters to await the departure. A slave brought him fragrant tea; for Paoul there was a dish of warm milk flavored with juniper berries. Neither the milk, nor the sweet biscuits which the slave also provided, did anything to suppress the growing sensation of fluttering in his stomach. Kar Houle continued to lecture him on what to expect of the journey and how to behave when he reached the other end. At Kar Houle's insistence he opened his leather bag and checked its contents— clothes, house slippers, spare boots and boot linings, a facecloth and box of mucilage, a comb, a small pouch of flints for incidental expenses, and, most important of all, the Valdoe seal impressed with the Vansard's ring, wrapped in a square of tallowed skin and hidden in a secret pocket at the bottom of the bag. The seal, Kar Houle told him yet again, was to be given to no one but Forzan Zett.

As Paoul repacked his bag, as the loading of the ship continued, he sensed that Kar Houle, despite his carefully cultivated calmness, was also beginning to feel anxious. His anxiety went further than mere concern for the investment the vansery was risking by entrusting Paoul to the waves; it was as if the old man had conceived a genuine affection for him, a feeling Paoul had not experienced since last he had seen Tagart. Suddenly Paoul felt very close to Kar Houle. He wanted to determine to do well, to please him, to justify his faith, to repay in gratitude the sensation that someone cared about him and worried on his behalf. But, even had he known how to express himself, Paoul was not sure how his words would be received; and so he said nothing, but fastened the straps of his bag more tightly and resumed his seat.

Something of the same effect had been produced in Kar Houle. He seemed to grow slightly more distant and, when word arrived that the ship's master was at last ready to receive the passenger, he led the way down to the landing stage in virtual silence. They climbed to the bleached planking of the deck. Immediately Paoul noticed, underfoot, a vague swaying, an absence of stability. He had left the land: he was already on the sea. From here, among the clutter of ropes and gear and as yet unstowed cargo, looking out over the curved bulwarks to the worksheds, it seemed the land had lost its permanence. By aligning the rail with the far edge of the landing stage, Paoul could see that the ship was rehearsing its rise, roll, and fall, being urged by the tide to slip its hawsers and be gone. The fluttering in his stomach grew worse.

His berth was a cramped cubicle, smelly and dark, below the smallest of the three deckhouses, reached by a steep, awkward ladder which the ship's master called a "companionway."

"We were expecting his lordship this morning," the master told Kar Houle, as Paoul felt the hardness of the bunk. "He was due to look over the ship. Been no sign of him, I suppose?"

"None. But he might yet come. His tutor has instructions to show him anything of interest."

"Well, he'll have to be quick. The tide won't wait."

They returned to the sunshine; the master, seeing something amiss on the foredeck, excused himself and left Kar Houle and Paoul alone. Kar Houle guided Paoul to the rail, where there was the least chance of obstructing the crew, most of whom were by now on board, or the slaves, who had nearly completed the loading.

"So," said Kar Houle. "What do you think of your berth?"

"It is rather small."

"If you feel seasick, do as you've been taught. Come up to the air and practice the breathing exercise. Watch the land, not the waves; the shore will be in view throughout the voyage, even on the crossing itself. At night watch the stars instead. If you must be sick, do it over the side and away from the wind. Don't fall overboard. Keep out of the crew's way, especially when they're hoisting sails or rowing. Be polite. Do exactly as the master tells you. He is a good man."

"Yes, Kar Houle."

Kar Houle continued in this vein until the master told him the gangplanks were about to be removed.

"Goodbye, then, Paoul. I hope to be alive when you return." With his firm, dry, old man's grasp, he gave Paoul's hand a reassuring squeeze and moved to the head of the after gangplank. "Remember what I've told you."

"Yes, Kar Houle. I will try." Paoul felt small and helpless, more desolate than ever: Kar Houle's brief and fatherly tutelage was finished.

"Above all, remember Gauhm."

Paoul clung to the rail, no longer sure whether Kar Houle's feelings for him had been real or a clever illusion designed to make him more compliant. But he was determined not to cry—not, at least, until he reached the safety of his bunk.

Kar Houle descended to the landing stage. As the slaves took down the gangplanks, Paoul noticed movement on the road beyond the worksheds. A small sled, green and red, drawn by six slaves in green and red livery, and with an arched leather hood, was rapidly approaching the quay. Kar Houle, following Paoul's gaze, saw it too and called out to the master. "Lord Hothen is here! Put back the gangplanks!"

"There's no time! We've delayed too long already! Any longer and we'll miss the tide!"

With a good-humored expression of frustration and regret, Kar Houle smiled at Paoul and turned to greet the arriving sled.

"Cast off fore and aft!"

"Casting off!"

"Away bows!"

Three crewmen at the bows again brought poles to bear and, aided by other poles wielded by the slaves, began to push the *Veisdrach* away from the landing stage and into the current.

The sled came to a halt. A young priest, an ilven in a cloak and hat, stepped down and was followed by a fair-haired boy of about Paoul's age and size. Paoul had never seen him before, but he knew the boy could only be Lord Hothen. He was wearing very costly clothes: a blue cape and jacket and matching leggings, and boots of rich, supple hide.

Even before he had finished climbing out of the sled, however, it became apparent to Paoul that his movements were not quite right. As Kar Houle went forward, the boy brought his attention to bear and his head turned on his shoulders in a slightly exaggerated way. When he showed his teeth they looked dirty and coated with overmuch saliva; his skin seemed dry, scaly, and pale, and his blue eyes were lackluster and remote, unable to focus on anything for longer than an instant. The ilven took his hand and Paoul's own concerns were forgotten. He did not know why, but he felt a stab of sympathy for the boy. Despite his fine clothes and elegant sled, he seemed to be lost, or aimless, deficient in some quality that healthy people possessed in abundance. No one had ever had to take Paoul's hand like that.

The ilven, whom Paoul had seen once or twice at the vansery, snatched off his hat and spoke quickly to Kar Houle, obviously apologizing.

"Out oars!"

Eight of the twelve crewmen, each with a long oar dipping from sockets cut in the bulwarks, lowered their blades in unison and stood, arms out, waiting for the next order. The bows had already turned away from the shore. Paoul, near the stern, was as close to the landing stage as he could be. He looked down. The expanse of green water was widening.

Flanked by his two companions, Lord Hothen had walked to the landing stage and come to its very edge, watching without great interest the spectacle of the departing ship. No more than a few yards separated him from Paoul.

"One! Two! One! Two!"

Kar Houle raised his hand in farewell.

Paoul, meaning to wave only at Kar Houle, elicited a halfhearted response from the boy as well. With a puzzled, jerky motion of his head he sought some clue from his tutor but, receiving none, looked back at Paoul. Briefly their eyes met. In that instant Paoul was reminded of the dragon's gaze. But the dragon had been carved from seasoned oak: a human craftsman had deliberately created its air of chilling indifference. The boy's gaze was not like that at all. It was empty only because he himself was empty. He was not made of oak; he was the antithesis of oak, of the dragon and its lineage, and yet he had been given his title and dressed in lordly blue.

"Raise the foresail!"

Behind Paoul there was a squeaking of blocks and, hoisted

arm-over-arm, the tall black sail slowly climbed its mast. The breeze did not wait for it all to unfurl: the broadening fabric filled at once, bellying toward the shore, and Paoul felt the ship tighten under its impetus. They were really under way, moving out toward the estuary, leaving the land behind, leaving the forest where Paoul had been born. Some of the goats on board, frightened by the growing swell, began bleating loudly.

"Ship oars! Raise the mainsail!"

The road down from the forest, the worksheds and warehouses, the slaves on the quay, the three figures on the landing stage: the whole of Apuldram was steadily reducing in size, losing its detail. When his face was no longer distinguishable, Kar Houle returned Paoul's wave for the last time and turned aside, walking with the boy and his tutor toward the sheds and the Trundleman's quarters.

The sled team dutifully followed. The green and scarlet body of the sled, brilliant in the late autumn sunshine, provided the brightest spot of color in the scene. Paoul watched it dwindling until the course of the ship, passing the first low, tree-clad headland, obscured not only the sled, but the buildings, the landing stages, and all signs of human life.

The crewmen were busy with their work: Paoul was left alone, kept company only by a silent man at the tiller and the fluttering red and black standard of Bohod Thosk. As the ship moved effortlessly downstream, toward the broad waters of the estuary, Paoul studied the wild, wooded shore—not in hope of glimpsing anything familiar, for he knew Tagart had never taken him here, but trying to gather into his memory as much of the landscape as he could. This country was his home. He knew he might never see it again. He wanted, if nothing more, not to waste his last sight of it.

But he could not concentrate. He could not stop thinking of Lord Hothen and the peculiar, uneasy feelings he had raised in his breast. These feelings were with him still, dominating the view, coloring his last memories of the shore.

The channel widened into the brown vastness of the estuary, hazy against the sun, and Paoul knew his last chance had slipped away. Brennis, his home, the land for which he should feel only kinship, had escaped him. In all its forests and shores, in all its settlements, in all its forts, there was no one he could truly call his friend, no one who shared his blood. Brennis had killed his mother and then his father. Now it was rejecting their child.

"Look there, boy," said the man at the tiller, pointing a mile or more across the water, almost directly into the sun. "That's Eastoke Point, the harbor mouth. Get past that and we're into the open sea."

PART TWO

1 The origins of the Cult of Gauhm and the Gehan ethos were now the subject of legend as well as history. Like the citadel, like the empire, like the universe itself, the ethos began as an abstraction, a mathematical point representing only the potential for growth. All phenomena arose from this one point. The ideas it embodied were at once simple and capable of extension into realms of the utmost complexity. But, however complicated, all parts of the ethos conformed to the same pattern and obeyed the unified law of the central point. Even the elementary geometry taught in the lower temple school formed an easy introduction to the complete range of concepts the pupils would encounter later.

Gehan geometry was developed according to the basic law, in five distinct stages. The number five was sacred. It represented the four opposing elements of the universe—air, fire, earth, and water—with the addition of their sum, spirit. Each element was associated with its own level of spatial complexity. Air had no dimension, fire one, earth two dimensions, water three, and the spirit four.

The five levels of geometry corresponded to these increasing levels of complexity. First, without dimension, came the point. Secondly came another point and hence the line. Thirdly came movement of this other point and hence the circle. The line and the circle, variously combined, gave all possible geometrical figures in one plane. The fourth level, solid geometry, completed the description of static objects. The dynamic geometry of the fifth level, incorporating the dimension of time, described the phenomenon of change and was, like the fourth level, much of the third, and the advanced study of the second and first, so difficult that it was only lightly touched upon in the lower school.

The third level, and in particular the study of the circle, yielded the most fruitful source of basic symbolism. All life, all processes, behaved in exactly the same manner, following the same fourfold cycle of creation, manifestation, decay, and dormancy. The four parts or quadrants of this cycle each governed one of the four elements and each element was represented by one of the four deities. The fifth element, spirit, the motive power of the cycle, and the seed for it to continue indefinitely, was symbolized by the circle itself. Spirit could be taken as virtue, benefaction, love; in the higher philosophies it was identified as time, and then nothingness, the essence of being. By contraction the circle again became its center and the cycle began anew.

Pupils soon discovered that these were more than mere abstractions. A process as basic as breathing followed the cycle and was indeed one of the first illustrations of it to be taught. The taking of breath, the inspiration, represented creation and was in the quadrant of air, ruled by Aih the Son. The hold of breath represented manifestation and was in the quadrant of fire, ruled by Tsoaul the Father. The exhalation, representing decay, was in the quadrant of earth, ruled by Gauhm the Mother. The absence of breath, the period before the next inspiration, represented dormancy and was in the quadrant of water, ruled by Ele the Daughter. The whole cycle gave existence, being: and it was being that impelled the cycle to continue.

At a later stage in their training, the boys in the lower school were gradually given to understand that the man who had mastered the cycle had also mastered himself. By observing the eternal truths, by regulating and controlling his own behavior, he could predict that of other men and, if he so desired—if such a desire also conformed to the direction of the cycle—he could use it to his own advantage. The closer he came to living in harmony with the cycle, the closer he came to the essence of the central point. When he had reached the center he had also reached enlightenment, immortality, nothingness. His desires had coincided with the innate spirit of the cycle: his will had become one with the will of the gods.

But, just as the lowliest plant or humblest animal lived and died according to the cycle, so the pupils learned that even enlightenment, like mankind and all its works, and the world, its seasons, the moon, sun, and stars, the universe, and the cycle of universes expanding and contracting from and to the central point, the cycle of universes that made up the cosmos—everything was transient, fleeting, and illusory, governed by the inexorable progress of the essential mystery that had neither beginning nor end.

Below the lake, further down the mountainside, among lush, nightingale-filled woodland, one of the streambeds met a layer of granite and fell a few feet into a sunny pool. At midmorning the sound of the water did not penetrate far into the trees; the path, hemmed in by dense bracken, came upon it sooner than Paoul had expected.

The principal of the temple school, Forzan Zett, was leading the way. Behind him walked three other novices besides Paoul who, as the youngest, was bringing up the rear.

Although he was only sixteen, Paoul had long ago been placed in the teaching group of these older boys. They were now eighteen, some two years away from their initiation. Like them, Paoul had just passed with honor from the lower school and was ready to begin his higher training. This morning's lesson marked its start.

Slabs of rock had been placed by the pool for use as benches. They were already hot; away from the shade of the woods the heat was intense. A gaudy blue dragonfly was hawking to and fro over the water, which, after the turbulence of the fall, flowed limpidly away above a clean gravel bottom. The waterfall and its pool were sacrosanct. It was here, on this very spot, two hundred and ninety-seven years ago, that the Earth Goddess had appeared to the man who was destined to become the first Prime. She had revealed to him the nature of the ethos and the means by which the empire was to be attained.

This meeting between man and goddess, the genesis of the Gehans, formed the central legend of the entire Cycle of Songs. In its usual form the story had Atar—the man who was to become the first Prime—gazing at his own reflection in the pool and pondering on the meaning of existence. Atar was young and handsome, born into a noble family, but at twenty he had given away all his possessions, left his bride, renounced his inheritance, and withdrawn to the mountains, where he had lived in solitude for seven years. Each day he would come to the pool to drink and bathe, and afterward he would study his reflection, searching for the answer to the problem with which he had been wrestling for so long. One autumn morning he looked up to see Gauhm, the Earth Goddess, emerging from the waterfall in human guise. Day after day she had watched the young man and had fallen in love with him. Atar, overwhelmed by her beauty, allowed himself to be seduced—or perhaps it was the other way about. Their congress was the beginning of knowledge. Atar vowed to worship her and in return she imparted the secret of being, until then known only to the gods and still their jealous preserve. He begged her to stay, to forsake her consort Tsoaul and their progeny Aih and Ele; but she returned to the pool and vanished in the fall.

Besides this central Song to Gauhm, the Cycle of Songs consisted of one hundred outer legends. The first of these could also be regarded as the last, preparing the listener for his return to the center. To understand the First Song, one had to know that it was describing the physical setting of the genesis. Refraining from any mention of Gauhm or Atar, the Song, in apparently simple and guileless language, invoked the cycle of rainfall and used it as an example of the universal cycle. Water, rising from the sea, became combined with air in the form of clouds. Driven by fire—the sun—the clouds arrived at the land, the mountains, where they condensed into droplets which fell as rain. From the mountains the water flowed downhill and returned to the sea.

"Today," said Forzan Zett, once they had all made obeisance and were seated, "I wish, as you have been informed, to discuss the First Song. Buin, will you tell us what you know?"

Paoul was relieved that he had not been asked first. He knew every word of the Song; for the past week its sense had been the subject of his morning meditation, and yesterday, for many hours, he and Enco had studied its symbolism in depth. He had prepared himself thoroughly, but he knew this would no longer, in the higher school, be enough to satisfy his teachers. And he was still, even now, a little afraid of the formidable principal of the school, the man who had taught Lord Heite and who was a close companion of the Prime.

Buin launched his dissertation confidently, giving an orthodox account of the meaning of the Song. The endless flow of water in the fall represented time, the water itself the material world by which time was made manifest. The material world was composed of an infinity of droplets, weak and insignificant on their own, but capable of any achievement—even of cutting into rock—when united and allowed to function over an extended period. By inference from the Second Song, the droplets could also be compared to individual men joined together in society. Certain individuals rose, or were thrown, above the torrent as sparkling spray, making a rainbow. The droplets of the rainbow were the highest and strongest among men, those capable of transcending, however briefly, the run of white water; those who could prolong, for a moment, their passage through the world.

But even the highest and strongest of them had eventually to return to the body of the stream and hence to the sea. In other words, they had to die.

Forzan Zett received Buin's disquisition in damning silence. "If you remember, Buin, I asked you tell us what you know. You have merely told us what you have been taught. The two, you will appreciate, are not the same."

Buin blushed deeply.

"Enco, perhaps you have something original to offer."

Enco was eighteen, dark and sallow, with a square face and rather large, rounded ears. His modest, phlegmatic disposition concealed an incisive approach to his studies; of all the people in the school, he was Paoul's best and closest friend. "In the first verse," he said, "the Song speaks of the water's roar. This may be the world-noise, the gauhm."

"Did you arrive at that idea alone?"

"No, Forzan Zett."

Forzan Zett glanced at Paoul. "Very well. Continue."

"It is significant that, in the genesis, Gauhm vanishes in the fall. This reinforces the theory that the waterfall represents the substance of earth and mankind. Because it is also moving and represents time, the waterfall may be taken to symbolize not only mankind itself, but also the condition and affairs of mankind, which are in a state of constant change."

"That much Buin told us."

"The rainbow is a function of light and thus of Tsoaul. The iridescence of the droplets, besides marking them out as enlightened, is therefore also a symbol of Atar's congress with Gauhm, because, by joining with Gauhm, Atar took on the role of her consort. In worshiping Gauhm, the enlightened man takes on some of Tsoaul's attributes and so approaches more nearly to the central point. A rainbow, however, may only be seen under certain conditions. When there is no sun, or when it is not viewed from the proper angle, the rainbow disappears. From below, for example, from the viewpoint of the main body of the stream, the rainbow will be invisible. To the ordinary man caught up in the affairs of the world, therefore, the higher man does not appear to be enlightened. He appears only to occupy a higher place."

Forzan Zett restrained a smile. "Is there more?"

"In . . . in the Fourth Song the rainbow is used as an example of illusion. If a rainbow in the sky is an illusion, the lesser rainbow of the fall is doubly an illusion. Hence enlightenment is the triple illusion."

Now Forzan Zett smiled openly. "Starrad, from which Song do those words come?"

"I'm sorry, Forzan Zett, I do not know."

"Buin? Paoul, then."

"The Fiftieth."

"I was not aware that you had reached the Fiftieth."

"Ilven Melchor recited it at the summer solstice, Forzan Zett."

"So he did." Forzan Zett turned and for a moment contemplated the waterfall. The four boys looked at each other and then at their teacher, waiting for him to speak again.

Paoul was not sure whether he had blundered. The interpretations Enco had expounded were mainly of his doing, and Forzan Zett seemed to know it. Paoul also felt unhappy about the unfavorable impression that Enco's answers would have given of Buin and Starrad. But then neither of them had made any real preparation for this lesson; they were still relying solely on their intelligence to carry them through. And Starrad, risking everything, had even been slipping out at night to visit a girl in the township.

Paoul studied the Forzan's powerful shoulders and the back of his neck. Despite the sound of the fall, an intense stillness had the morning in its grip, a stillness inseparable from the force of the principal's personality. It seemed impossible that they were less than two miles from the citadel, less than two miles from the township and the garrison. It seemed impossible that these woods were not the primeval forest, but a carefully preserved and tended part of the temple grounds. Except for the intrusive slabs of rock and the evidence of the path, this pool could have been in some region unknown to man. Its vegetation was lush and apparently undisturbed; the birds nested here in peace, and still the dragonfly was hawking to and fro.

Forzan Zett treated Paoul to a moment's cool appraisal. "Now," he said, addressing the whole group. "Before your misguided imaginations carry you any further along these overgrown and hazardous paths, I feel it is time to examine this Song in a logical manner. Buin has rightly reminded us that the Song invokes the cycle of rainfall. This will be our starting point. Paoul, to which quadrant of that cycle does a description of a waterfall properly belong?"

"To the third. To the Quadrant of Earth."

"Because, Starrad?"

"Because the water is on the mountain."

"And we are studying its progress downhill. We are studying its decay. Why is this appropriate? Buin?"

"The Song is about Gauhm, master."

"We see, therefore, that the physical setting of the genesis could scarcely be more apt. It even takes place in the autumn, the third quadrant of the year. Before proceeding with this, however, I wish to summarize what you have been told in the lower school. You have been taught to perceive phenomena in terms of a multitude of concentric and interrelated cycles, each having the properties and direction of the universal cycle. Let us take an example. You are asked to describe an old widow who learns that her daughter is with child. The unborn child you would assign to the first quadrant, the daughter to the second, the widow to the third, and her late husband to the fourth. This analysis you would correctly maintain as valid notwithstanding the condition, for example, of the daughter's fortunes, which might be declining, or the state of the village or province in which these people lived. These other facts you would perceive as being governed by different, yet related, cycles. Are we agreed? Good. Now we can return to our consideration of the First Song. Buin has said that the waterfall, which, as we have seen, belongs to the third quadrant, is a symbol of the world. What may we deduce from this? Starrad?"

"The world is in a state of decay."

"Exactly. Decay. Leaving aside all secondary symbolism, this is the theme of the song. Decay. Do you understand?" Forzan Zett indicated the fall; Paoul began to feel a sense of rising excitement. It was as if he had smoothly and swiftly been brought close to the core of the ethos. "The waterfall is old. The mountain is even older, but not as old as the world itself. It was created and became manifest long ago. You know from your studies that there is no clearcut division between quadrants. Each succeeding quadrant has many properties of the one that went before. Decay continues into dormancy, dormancy into creation, creation into manifestation, and manifestation into decay. Yet there comes a point at which one can say with certainty that the properties of a single quadrant are ascendant. Consider the case of our imaginary family. The widow has lived a long life; she is old. Her

faculties are obviously failing. Her mind and body are in a state
of slow but inevitable disintegration. She is, beyond question,
proceeding toward the literal decay of her flesh. We assign her
to the third quadrant, even though she is actually every bit as
manifest as her daughter. So with the world. It is manifest: it is
all around us. But from innumerable clues we know that it is
distintegrating. Even were we incapable of interpreting such clues,
the mere fact that the world is manifest would alone be enough
to tell us that it is either approaching or has entered the quadrant
of decay. I want you to bear this idea in the forefront of your
minds. I cannot emphasize it too strongly; it is crucial to your
higher studies. These will include a basic astronomy in which
you will learn that the cycles of the planets, the sun, the stars,
and the universe itself are all passing through the third quadrant.
The cycle of the universe has been in decay for an unimaginable
period of time. It was decaying long before the birth of the sun,
the planets, or the earth. Likewise the earth began its decay long
before the appearance of mankind. The manifestation of mankind
is in fact a symptom of the earth's decay, just as the manifestation
of the earth was one of the symptoms of a dying universe. Greater
cycles contain the lesser: this is one of the first laws you were
taught. The earthly cycle contains and dominates all the lesser
cycles. Do you now begin to understand why we worship the
Earth Goddess rather than the others of her Family? Do you see
why it was the Mother who appeared to Atar and not the Daughter? Why was it Gauhm who betrayed her consort and divulged
the secret knowledge of the gods? Because man is of the earth,
and she is his goddess. Hers is decay; hers is the influence that
dominates all the lesser cycles. The earth is dying. Its wonders
and its treasures are transient. Soon they will be gone, no matter
what use we make of them. How, then, should the enlightened
man treat such a world and all it contains? Buin? Paoul?"

Paoul thought he knew, but dared not speak. The implication
of Forzan Zett's words was too exciting, too vast, too horrifying
and profound to be absorbed immediately. They had integrated
and amplified all that he had ever felt or learned; as if in a flash
of lightning he had seen illuminated the innermost recesses of
the Gehan mind.

"Starrad? Enco?"

None of the boys was able—or wanted—to offer an answer.

"Let us take another example. A man has been marooned on

a small island far out at sea. His only fresh water is in a single cask. When the cask is empty that will be the end of his water and he will die. The cask is leaking. There is nothing whatever he can do to repair it or to prevent the water from seeping away. In these circumstances, should he stint himself or should he drink his fill? Starrad, if you were that man what would you do?"

"Drink."

"Of course. And so would I. So would anyone. The leak, then, decay: this is the theme of the First Song. Metaphorically, the enlightened man should drink. He should take and use the treasures of the world. This is the essence of the message transmitted by Gauhm to Atar." Forzan Zett looked up; the sun was almost overhead. "The secondary symbolism of the Song, although of subsidiary importance, is nevertheless extremely rich and we shall be exploring it at our next meeting, which, by the way, will take place in my chambers. Before then I want you to consider a statement made by Enco. He said that the roar of the waterfall might be compared to the gauhm or world-noise. I should not need to remind you that the gauhm is the universal sound, produced by the dynamic interaction of the elements. The noise of a river is one example. Another is the sound of wind, or of a forest fire, or indeed the pulsing of blood in your own ears. Doubtless you can think of many other examples, any of which might serve as a fruitful seed for meditation." Forzan Zett arose and the boys instantly did likewise. "Now I believe Kar Ander is expecting you for taug."

Under their teacher's critical supervision, each of the novices made the signs of obeisance appropriate to leaving a holy place. Forzan Zett then made his and led his pupils to the line of white pickets which marked the boundary of the shrine.

"Paoul, shall we walk together?"

They started uphill through the green summer woods, Paoul respectfully taking the position on Forzan Zett's right. Paoul was afraid that he was going to be reprimanded for the possible irreverence with which he and Enco had interpreted the First Song; but he was mistaken. "You may have heard," Forzan Zett began, "that Bohod Thosk's new hall is to be consecrated in three weeks' time, at the Crale. Lord Heite and several members of his family will attend the ceremony, which will be conducted by the Prime. It is the custom for the temple school to be represented on such occasions by two students, one junior and one senior, to act as

lamp bearers. I have already appointed the junior student; you
are to be the other."

Paoul was speechless, overwhelmed.

"I am counting on you to live up to this distinction. Remember,
you will be the representative of the whole school. The reputation
of three hundred boys and their teachers will rest on your shoulders."

"Yes, Forzan Zett."

"Rehearsals begin tomorrow. Report to Ilven Gars at the fifth
hour of the afternoon."

"I do not know what to say, Forzan Zett."

"Then, Paoul. I advise you to say nothing."

2 The transition from the lower to the higher school had brought many changes. Most painful of these was the ending of the close relationship between Paoul and his matron, the lay woman who had been charged with his emotional development. Her name was Erta, and he had shared her with five other boys. She had never said as much, but he suspected that she kept a soft spot in her heart for him alone. When the time came for them to part he realized how much he had grown to love her and how completely he had come to regard the citadel as his home.

He had not forgotten Tagart, but the memories of his earliest life had now become diffuse and remote, as if belonging to some former existence—which, in a way, he supposed they did. Only the flavor of the Brennis countryside had remained within him unimpaired, so different from that of the mainland, so subtle and verdant compared with the dramatic scenery of Hohe.

In the years since coming here, Paoul had almost finished growing. He had attained all but an inch or two of his adult height. This, the kars had long ago predicted, would be fractionally less than the average. Under their guidance, he was in the process of realizing in full the physical potential of his childhood. Like all the recruits and trainees at Hohe, he was being fitted for a life of service to the Gehans. In the army, emphasis was placed on physical development as the basis of the military ideal; in the priesthood, it was viewed rather as the first step toward the mastery of self which alone allowed higher mental and spiritual development. For this reason, physical culture or taug was accorded great importance in the training of a novice. Its teaching was in the hands of the kars, the doctor-priests. The taug embraced all matters of health and hygiene; the treatment of injury and disease was seen as a minor part of its discipline. Its goal was the perfection and integration of the body's natural systems and processes. A man correctly trained in its techniques seldom succumbed to any but minor or accidental ailments. In the absence of an external cause of death, exponents of the taug regularly lived to be eighty, ninety, or even older. Kar Meisch, one of Kar Ander's predecessors at the taug school, was now a hundred and three. It was rare for a farmer or slave to survive beyond fifty; the longevity of priests was in itself a matter for awe and a sign of their divinity.

In this, as in most things, the Gehans played on the ignorance of the common people, or pagans, as they were contemptuously called. The methods of the taug were kept in the strictest secrecy. Even simple medical treatment was forbidden to anyone outside the red priesthood, the ruling clan, the highest ranks of the army, and the merchant class of bohods—who had to pay handsomely for the services of a kar. The ordinary people were allowed their own healers, usually chosen from the blue priesthood, but these had to work with an inadequate range of herbs and knew nothing of the taug.

The taug derived from the basic law and thus, like the human frame itself, was divided into five interdependent sections. The first of these, characterized by the right arm, was the quadrant of flexibility and control. In this the novice acquired not only extreme suppleness in all parts of the body, but also the most refined and delicate precision of movement, especially in the hands. Each of the four fingers—and the thumb—had its own symbolism; the hands were indistinguishable from the concept of control on which the empire was based. But control also implied strength, which was the province of the second quadrant. Its training produced a coordinated development of all the muscle systems and paved the way for the third quadrant, that of endurance. In this, novices were subjected to steadily increasing workloads—in walking, running, climbing, swimming, and the carrying of weights, and were exposed to lack of food and water and sleep, and to extremes of heat, cold, and humidity. The fourth quadrant dealt with diet, cleanliness, refinement of the senses, and care of the bodily organs.

The four quadrants of the taug were symbolized by the limbs and the associated areas of the trunk. Its essence was symbolized by the head. Study of the essence was concerned with the mind in relation to the body: with carriage and efficient use of the frame, control of muscular tension and the emotions, resistance to pain, self-healing and mobilization of the vital force or spirit, and, ultimately, with excellence in unarmed combat and the use of weapons. Combat, one of the necessities of control, led back to the first quadrant and the cycle began anew. Progression on the cycle of taug eventually raised the student beyond the physical and brought him to the realm of the intellect—which was the territory of other teachers besides the kars.

It was considered best to begin the taug as early as possible: a boy of five was not too young. At that age a child's body was held to be in a virtually natural state, uncorrupted by misuse or the influence of unsuitable adults. Paoul had begun his training aged seven, rather later than Kar Ander would have liked, but he had made such good progress that he had now overtaken some of the boys who were not only two or three years older, but who had started at the age of five or even sooner.

There were four main classes of priests, or nominations, each corresponding to one of the quadrants of the cycle of knowledge: the ilvens, who specialized in the arts; the kars; the phedes, who were scientists and mathematicians; and the forzans, whose field was philosophy, ethics, theology, and the law. Early in a boy's training it was clear to his teachers where his talents would be likely to take him, and the approach to his taug would be individually adjusted. Buin, for example, who had a gift for poetry, was having special training in rhythm and the voice; Enco, who was himself destined to become a kar, was making a deep study of the fourth quadrant; while Starrad, one of the cleverest boys in the school and a potential astronomer, was receiving special training of the eyesight. Paoul's taug was much concerned with the essence and with the first quadrant: he was being prepared for the duties of a forzan.

To counteract some of the disadvantages of this early specialization, teaching groups in the higher school were composed of one boy from each discipline. They shared the same dormitory, ate at the same table in the school refectory, and, whenever possible, took their lessons together.

The taug school was on the far side of the vansery grounds, adjoining the open mountain. The quickest way there from the novices' quarters would have been to cut through the cloisters and straight across the temple square. The temple square, however, was overlooked by the rear chambers of the Prime. Even when the Prime was absent, as today, it was not allowed for novices to set foot in the temple square unless accompanied by a teacher. From their quarters, therefore, Paoul and Enco had to walk past the clothing stores and laundry and—keeping strictly to the permitted paths—follow an involved route through the animal sheds and paddocks, the fruit and vegetable farm, the physic gardens, and thence into a stand of yews. Some of the trees overhung the vansery palisade, on the other side of which, from the closely built streets of the township, rose the cries of children at play.

"Do you think this is where he gets out?" Enco said.

Paoul did not know. Speculation about Starrad's nocturnal adventures was a favorite topic at the moment; Paoul preferred not to think about it. The consequences for Starrad, if he were caught, would be severe. Paoul fully shared the urges to which Starrad had given way, but it was part of his training to contain those urges and channel them into higher activities. "Come on," he said. "We don't want to be late."

This afternoon's taug, a general session, was to be attended by all of Paoul's group, together with four other groups of the same year. Most of the class had already assembled as Paoul and Enco, dressed in freshly laundered tunics and carrying their swimming gear, hurried across the sun-baked lawns and entered at the side door.

The building was cool and spacious and smelled of beeswax. The walls of the main classroom, part panelled and part lime-washed, reflected the glare of the day outside: all the storm shutters and doors to the terrace had been thrown open. Beyond the low wooden balustrade, the mountainside fell away into sheer space. There was nothing between the terrace and the next peak, Mount Sandle, twelve miles west of the river. Its very tip still bore a remnant of snow; as far down as the treeline its flanks, even at this distance, looked mostly bare, the great slabs of weathered and broken rock devoid of any but the sparsest vegetation. Then, scattered at first, the firs began, becoming densely bluish green before gradually yielding, far below, at the same level as the citadel, to the richer green of the deciduous forest which once had covered the entire Home Plain and which still covered the lower slopes of Mount Atar, up beyond Hohe and the citadel toward the fir woods of the summit.

This view of Mount Sandle, and of its companions stretching into the farthest distance, dominated the whole vansery and lent the taug school, jutting out over the lake and the canopy of trees, a feeling of airiness and light. But it was also a constant reminder for the pupils of the harshness and solidity of the mountains. In the best weather—on a day like today—and under strict supervision, Paoul and his fellows had once reached the top, a feat that had made them all the more aware of the mountains' hostility, and conscious of the achievement of some of the senior priests, who had climbed Mount Sandle many times, and not just in summer, but in the depths of winter too.

The most enthusiastic climber at Hohe was Kar Ander, head of the taug school, a quiet and entertaining man of forty-one with very pale blond hair worn in a long pigtail, a neatly trimmed blond beard, and intensely blue eyes. More perhaps than any of the other teachers, Paoul admired, and, for a time, had even hero-worshiped, Kar Ander, trying to copy his mannerisms and appearance, even to the extent of wishing that his own hair could also be blond and his eyes blue. That phase had long since passed, but Paoul still retained a profound respect for him. Kar Ander, together with Erta, had been the main influence on Paoul's upbringing. Erta was gentle, kind, and indulgent; Kar Ander was strong, resolute, and wise, the personification of the Gehan ideal. Kar Ander's body was the living proof of the taug. At weapons practice—with the bow, spear, ax, hammer, flail, net, and shield—he made even the Vuchten, the crack shock troops of Lord Heite's garrison, look clumsy and inept.

Far more impressive than any of this, though, was the intangible optimism, the positive energy made manifest in his every movement and gesture. According to the ancient doctrines that predated even the taug, Kar Ander had awoken the vital force from its deepest seat at the base of his spine. It had now infused his whole being. He could never be seriously ill. Unless injured or killed, he would grow old naturally, deteriorating at the slowest possible speed, and, at the end of the maximum term his body could sustain, he would peacefully die. Until then he would experience each moment to the full, completely and thoroughly alive; and it was this vitality that he radiated wherever he went.

The atmosphere in the room changed: the class had come subtly to attention. Paoul looked around. Kar Ander had entered.

"Good afternoon, gentlemen," he said, in his calm, even, and perfectly controlled voice. "To the terrace."

After an hour's exercise in the sunshine, the class descended to the lake. The northern end was set aside for bathing, with a changing shed for visitors, a small raft, and marker buoys for distance swimming. Normally the boys would have been brought here by another kar; Kar Ander's teaching time was too valuable to be spent on routine supervision, but this afternoon he wished to gauge their progress in person.

The lake formed part of the vansery grounds. It was open only to the priesthood and to members of Lord Heite's family and their guests. Overlooked on its northeast side by the citadel, the water was seventy or eighty acres in extent, with many wooded islands. The largest of these were in the southern end, and here nested the herons whose fate had become inextricable from Hohe's—for enshrined in the legends was the belief that if ever the heronry failed so would the citadel and the whole empire. The lake had become the herons' sanctuary. Much of the shore had been left wild; the northern end had been partly screened with a magnificent grove of beeches—planted, according to legend, by Atar himself. In front of this Founder's Grove a close sward, kept specially short by the early morning grazings of the lakeman's three white goats, extended to the water's edge and to a small clump of ornamental cut-leafed alders.

When everyone had undressed, Kar Ander started the class in relay. One by one the weaker swimmers reached their targets and dropped out, leaving the rest still churning through the cold, clear water of the lake. Paoul's target for today was seventeen laps of the two-hundred-yard course; he was one of the last to finish. Climbing out at the end of his swim, he felt again the familiar fatigue, as if his flesh had been softly but repeatedly clubbed, that meant he had exceeded his previous maximum by the required amount. The sensation was not unpleasant. Paoul liked swimming, especially at this season, even when the load was being steadily increased. Most of his classmates liked it too. Having been judged by Kar Ander and with his permission, they were now lazing on the sward or, laughing and fooling about, had plunged in again and swum out to the raft. There would be no more lessons today.

Paoul picked up his chamois leather and dried his face and arms.

"Your style is still too formal," Kar Ander told him. "And you are still snatching a little at your breath. Let the air come naturally, in harmony with your stroke."

"Yes, Kar Ander."

"Otherwise, your progress is satisfactory."

"Thank you, Kar Ander." Paoul rubbed at his hair, prolonging the moment before he was dismissed. All through his swim he had been unable to stop thinking about this morning and the waterfall. Could it be that Forzan Zett's words had really been such a revelation to him? Or had he invented those feelings because he so much wanted to understand, to do well? Was he deceiving himself? But, even more than the lesson itself, what the Forzan had told him afterward had thrown his mind into ferment. To bear a lamp at a consecration attended by Lord Heite and conducted by the Prime—surely there could be no greater honor in all the school! The honor was made greater still by the fact that Paoul was so young. He did not want to admit it to himself, but this was a source of pride, and pride was specifically disapproved of by his teachers. And so, even though he was bursting to tell Kar Ander what had happened, he did not know how to do so without seeming boastful. It had occurred to Paoul that he surely knew already: as one of Paoul's teachers, he must have been consulted by Forzan Zett and the Prime.

But if he knew, Kar Ander was not letting on. Paoul's hopes that he would raise the matter were left unfulfilled. The next swimmer to finish was already wading ashore.

Before he had left the water, however, Kar Ander's attention was attracted by movement among the smooth gray boles of the beech trees. Paoul followed his gaze and saw a man and a woman on the path, being followed by two slaves carrying bags, and a squad of ten soldiers dressed in the green, red, and gray of Lord Heite's personal guard. Although the man and woman were not actually touching, the way they were walking conveyed an unmistakable sense of intimacy. The man, tall, fair-haired, of middle age, and dressed casually in a pale tunic, was indeed none other than Lord Heite himself. The woman Paoul had never seen before. She was dark and young and, even from here, looked extremely pretty.

Kar Ander clapped his hands. The two swimmers still on the circuit broke off their practice; those on the raft dived into the water, and they all made for the shore. By the time the newcomers had arrived, the whole class was standing in formation behind Kar Ander.

Paoul understood little of the ensuing conversation between Kar Ander and Lord Heite. Despite the terrifying proximity of the Gehan of the Gehans, Paoul scarcely looked at him or heard a single word he said. From his position in the second rank, he could do nothing but fight the urge to stare without restraint at Lord Heite's companion.

She was the most beautiful woman he had ever seen.

3 The three syllables of her name made the loveliest sound in the world. In his bed, letting them infuse his thoughts, Paoul repeated them over and over again. Atane, Atane, the Lady Atane. Lying awake long after midnight, listening to the dogs barking in the township, he could not keep his mind from her face and her voice and the shape of her body. He could not keep his mind from the wonderful events of the afternoon.

Put logically, coldly, they were simple enough. She and Lord Heite had come down to the lake for a swim. They had arrived, inadvertently, at the end of the lesson. Kar Ander had immediately offered to leave; Lord Heite would not hear of it. Kar Ander was one of his personal friends. Lord Heite insisted that he and his class should remain just as long as they liked. Wasn't this, Lord Heite had asked, the class that had just entered the higher school? And wasn't this the class that was to provide the senior lamp bearer for Bohod Thosk's consecration? Whereupon Kar Ander had been persuaded to point out the chosen one and, for the first time in his life, Paoul had been addressed face to face by Lord Heite. "So this is the special young man from Brennis. The Prime has spoken to me of you, Paoul." Lord Heite had said other things too, all equally intoxicating. Paoul still felt dizzy: he could not really remember them now. He had been intensely aware of the Lady Atane in her green-gray robe and sandals, her soft and shining dark hair worn loose about her shoulders, her amused, intelligent dark eyes taking everything in, responding to every word spoken. Then, later—after she had emerged from the changing shed in an off-white garment which had contrasted with the smooth, slightly olive, southern perfection of her skin —Lord Heite had challenged Kar Ander to a race, out to a birch-covered island and back. Kar Ander, of course, had beaten him easily, but Lord Heite had been expecting this and had merely laughed. And then Lord Heite had suggested that Atane should race someone. With an enchanting smile she had tried, in vain, to refuse. "You must race, if only to restore honor to the military!" Laughter. "But not Kar Ander—he's too good for anyone." Then—who was a good swimmer in the class? No one? Surely not. What about the lad from Brennis? What about Paoul? Would Kar Ander permit it? "He's just swum all but two miles, my lord." "Then the competition will be slightly more equal!"

There were two things Paoul remembered most about the race. The first was the fact of being in the water with her, of sharing the same sensuous, all-encompassing medium; the second was his appreciation of the need for delicacy in his tactics. For it had been instantly obvious that she had neither strength nor skill in swimming. Thus, rather than win by too great a margin—or, worse, shame her by deliberately losing—Paoul had contrived to finish only a few yards ahead.

"Well swum," she had said, once back on dry land. "I'd hate to race you when you're fresh." She had understood his stratagem and, in this exquisitely private and elegant way, had chosen to thank him. Trapped in her dark glance, Paoul had been tongue-tied, powerless, and she, sensing it, had lowered her eyes. Then she had looked up at him again, boldly, as if he were a man and not a boy. An instant later the slave had enclosed her in a wrap and she had danced away toward Lord Heite, ignoring Paoul, and in the few minutes left to him by the lake she had scarcely glanced at him again. But that look, that one look, had been more than enough.

"Enco," Paoul whispered. "Enco. Are you awake?"

Paoul heard the neighboring mattress creak as Enco turned over, growling disagreeably. "What is it?"

"I'm thinking about the Lady Atane."

"What about her?"

"How old do you think she is?"

"Twenty. Twenty-two. I don't know. What's it got to do with us?"

"Do you think she's been at Hohe long?"

"Go to sleep."

Starrad's quietly jeering voice came from the corner. "Paoul's in love."

"But not with a fishmonger's daughter," Enco said. "At least he doesn't sneak over the palisade every second night."

"Who says I sneak over the palisade? And even if I do, who says I'm in love with her? If I go, it's for one thing, and one thing only. The same thing Lord Heite gets from the Lady Atane. He's probably between her legs right now."

Paoul sat upright. "No!"

"If not her, then one of his others. Even Lady Heite. They're all the same."

"You'd better shut your filthy mouth, Starrad."

"Or else what? You're young, Paoul. You don't know a thing. Why do you think those two came down to the lake exactly when they did? They knew we'd be there, that's why. It gave Lord Heite a thrill to see us all gaping at forbidden fruit. She even played along with it, the bitch. Look at that thing she was wearing. She's just a courtesan, Paoul. Don't make a statue of her."

"They're all forbidden fruit to us," Enco said. "You'd do well to bear that in mind, Starrad."

"What on earth do you mean? I've no idea, to be sure."

With that, the conversation came to an end. Paoul resisted the impulse to say anything further. He did not want to admit it, but he felt betrayed. He knew that Starrad, the worldly, perceptive Starrad, had almost certainly been right. What Paoul, in his innocence, had taken to be the spontaneous expression of mutual attraction was now revealed as nothing more than sordid coquetry. He had forgotten, momentarily, the teaching of the taug and allowed himself to be swayed by carnal desires. Such behavior was appropriate outside the vansery palisade—it was worthy of the common people, the rabble, the pagans. But it was not worthy of a future forzan, of someone who had been noticed by the Prime. But then—had Lord Heite's praise also been a part of his game? How much of it could be believed? Perhaps the whole episode had even been staged by the kars; perhaps it had been a test which Paoul had miserably failed. He had let himself and Kar Ander down.

For a long time he stared into the darkness, feeling cheated and confused. Most disturbing of all had been the conduct of Lord Heite. For the Gehan of the Gehans to behave in such a way was unthinkable. In the eyes of the world—including, Paoul had naively imagined, Starrad's eyes too—he was almost a god, the secular representative of the Prime, the enactor of the holy decrees, the leader of the army and the ruler of the empire. He was nobility itself, above petty temptation. But now he had shown himself to be weak and depraved, just as other men were.

No. It was simply not possible. Starrad was wrong. He had imputed his own values to a man beyond reproach. The Lady Atane, young and beautiful as she was, had acted naturally, in

faith with her heart. In recent weeks and months Paoul had
received certain glances in the street which had made him wonder
whether he might be attractive to girls. Might the Lady Atane
merely have shared their opinion? Yes: that was it. His first
impression had been indisputably correct. None the less, it had
been wrong to forget himself like that. He would learn from the
incident and take it as a warning. His admiration of Lord Heite
remained undiminished.

Still trying to convince himself of this, he slipped at last into
a shallow and uneasy sleep.

The next morning's routine began in the usual way. Paoul and
the others woke to the sound of a wooden gong. In the early
twilight they sluiced themselves with cold water and dressed in
the black leggings and tunics which denoted their lowly rank.
After participating in the dawn litany at the temple—attended
by nearly all the priests and pupils and conducted today by the
Prime—they went back to their quarters for breathing exercise
and meditation. Then came breakfast, of milk, steaming oatmeal
porridge, rye bread, raw fish, fruit, and the soft cheese for which
Hohe was renowned.

This was one of the mornings set aside each week for handicraft.
In theory a part of the taug—for they belonged in the region
where art and science merged—these lessons were not normally
given by kars, but, depending on their exact nature, by ilvens or
phedes, or sometimes by ilvens and phedes working together.
The projects undertaken by their pupils ranged from minute
carvings on ivory to the construction of full-scale buildings. The
buoys, raft, and changing shed at the lake had all been made by
the school, as had various structures in the citadel at large.

In the lower school the pupils were brought to a certain level
of skill; once in the higher school, the teaching became less formal
and there was more scope for self-expression. Paoul, who was
both musical and had an aptitude for fine work in wood, was
planning to try his hand at a scharan, a big-bellied stringed instrument with a sweetly melancholy tone of which he was especially fond.

Before starting on this, though, he was required, as were his
classmates, to make a set piece commemorating their arrival in
the higher school. The set piece was always the same: a circular

plaque with an inlaid pentacle in contrasting wood, made to the highest standards of accuracy and finish.

The geometry of polygons formed part of the simple mathematics taught in the lower school, but the precise technique of constructing the pentagon and its derivative pentacle was shown to a novice only when he had reached the higher school. The secret was imparted by the chief phede at the confirmation ceremony. The confirmation plaque, as it was called, had a special significance in a novice's career. If good enough, the plaque would be sanctified as a talisman. If not, it would be burned and the novice would have to try again.

For his plaque, Paoul had chosen applewood and yew. On previous mornings he had selected seasoned logs from the lumber sheds and, with ax, adze, scraper, and finally with sandstones of decreasing coarseness, had produced two smooth, knot-free blanks. These he now took from his locker and carried to his place in the workshop, where he shared a bench with Enco.

The morning was already quite hot. The sun, beating on the timber walls and sloping roof of the workshop, seemed to heighten the smell of the bubbling gluepots and the agreeable odor of freshly worked wood. Except for the quietly authoritative voice of Ilven Gars, and the occasional comments one to the other of the boys, the room was silent but for the sound of tools.

"Ready?" Enco said. He was halfway through marking out his own plaque, and now it was time for him to help with Paoul's.

The diameter of the plaque, excluding the frame, was to equal the span of the maker's left hand at full stretch. The size of the pentacle was determined by the size of the notional pentagon at its heart: the sum of the five sides of this pentagon was also to equal the span of the maker's left hand.

Aware that he was about to take part in a symbolic tradition almost as old as the Red Order itself, Paoul laid his left hand on the clean beechwood surface of the bench and spread his thumb and fingers to their utmost extent. Enco opened a pair of calipers and meticulously measured the span. Paoul, craning over, confirmed that the measurement was correct, and Enco's part in the proceedings was over.

Using a large tablet of geometry clay, Paoul ascertained the dimensions corresponding to one half and one fifth of his span. Locking first one and then the other blank in the bench holdfast, he took his best and sharpest flint scribe, his boxwood compass and hornbeam straightedge and, remembering what he had been told by the chief phede, marked on each blank the seven arcs and nine lines that generated the sacred figure.

When he had finished he painstakingly checked all the measurements against the original setting of the calipers and, satisfied, stood upright. The two pentacles—that on the applewood enclosed by a faintly scribed circle—lay side by side, waiting to be cut and worked and transformed by a mystical fusion of art and science into the finished piece. If Paoul had heeded his teachers, if he performed well, if he used his mind and body to control the difficult and fragile flint chisels, the yew would eventually slot precisely into the applewood, male into female, a fit so snug that Ilven Gars would be able to invert the plaque without it parting. And, having passed that test, Paoul would smear the merest trace of fish glue on the jointing surfaces, fix the frame, treat the whole to many coats of thin varnish, then to a final, somewhat thicker, coat, and lastly to repeated waxing and polishing. And if, after all this, the Prime judged his work true, if the shine, like the surface of a still pool, made an uninterrupted and undistorted reflection, then Paoul would know that his entry to the higher school had been justified.

At Paoul's request, Ilven Gars came over to inspect his setting-out.

"You'll have to watch the grain here, Paoul. And here."

Ilven Gars was silver-haired, of middle height, one of the senior teachers of joinery as well as an accomplished sculptor. He was also in charge of much of the ceremonial organized by the vansery. It was to Ilven Gars that Paoul was to report later today, to start rehearsals for the ceremony at the Crale.

Ilven Gars did not mention the fact. "Yes," he said, nodding at the blanks in approval. "Begin."

When he had gone, Paoul selected a chisel. As he made the first cut, some quirk of sensation or feeling put him in mind of a half-forgotten scene from his early childhood and he remembered standing with Kar Houle on the quayside at Apuldram, watching the *Veisdrach* turn. Like a herald from the mainland, the dragon of the figurehead had given him notice of what was to come. He had watched it with a mixture of awe and fear: awe that mere men could make something so splendid, and fear of the knowledge that enabled them to do it.

Paoul now possessed some of that knowledge. In outline, at least, he would know how to set about building another *Veisdrach*. And more: his learning went far beyond the simple skills of a shipwright. He could no longer count himself a part of the ignorant, amorphous mass of ordinary people from whose ranks he had risen. He had become more priest than layman. By their rite of confirmation, by bringing him into the higher school, his teachers had in effect told him this already.

On the eve of his confirmation, Paoul had been warned to consider the consequences very carefully. Once in the higher school, he would have learned too many secrets and there could be no turning back. But he had no doubts: he believed in the faith, in the ethos, with all his heart. More than anything he yearned to prove himself worthy of his training; he desperately wanted to continue on the arduous journey toward his initiation, toward the day when he finally became a real priest. The pentacle of his talisman would then be not of yew, but of crimson pigment tattooed into his flesh.

A corner snapped off the chisel and Paoul checked his hand. In his enthusiasm he was forgetting the most elementary rule of all. He was letting his thoughts race ahead, failing to maintain the single point of concentration where all success lay.

Pausing to take breath, he discarded the broken chisel and chose another from the rack.

4 Three weeks later, just before the Crale, the fine weather came to an end. Crale Day itself, the day of the ceremony, was cloudy, with sporadic drizzle and a noticeable chill in the air: the autumn equinox was only a month away.

The Crale was a festival of the agrestic calendar of the farmers, and thus was not officially recognized by the Red Order, which divided the year into four seasons and not six. There was nothing unseemly, however, in the choice of the Crale for the consecration of Bohod Thosk's new hall; and the celebrations afterward would be fully in tune with those taking place in the township and throughout the countryside. The festival marked the end of High Summer and the beginning of Harvest. It also happened to be the day, seventeen years ago, on which Paoul had been born.

It seemed to Paoul, standing alone and apparently unnoticed by a window, that dusk was falling quickly, prematurely, draining the outside world of color. The tall trees, the evergreen shrubs and topiary of the formal gardens had become so many fantastic and sinister black shapes; the lawns and terraces, the stone ornaments, the lily pads on the carp pool, were now a uniform gray and becoming gloomier by the minute.

Inside, though, all was brilliance. The half hour after the ceremony and before the banquet was giving the guests a chance to admire in detail the splendor and workmanship of the new hall. Individually and in groups they were congratulating their host. Those of inferior rank were surreptitiously trying to get closer to the Prime, to Lord Heite, or to members of his family. Of the Lady Atane, Paoul had noted, there was no sign. He had not seen her since that day at the lake. Instead Lord Heite this evening was accompanied by his wife, two sons, three daughters, one of his brothers, and a concubine whose name Paoul did not know. Slaves in the red and black livery of the Thosk clan were passing to and fro with trays of wine and essence. Alcohol was eschewed by practitioners of the taug; abstemious as ever, the Prime had even refused fruit juice. Paoul was also empty-handed, mainly because no one had thought to offer him anything. It was not his place to ask, or to do more than remain on the sidelines of such a glittering gathering. The other lamp bearer, the boy of twelve who had represented the lower school, had already returned to the citadel, but Ilven Gars had allowed Paoul to stay and, as part of his education, had secured him an invitation to the banquet. Ilven Gars was elsewhere at the moment, however, and Paoul had been left to his own devices.

"Excuse me. Would you like something to drink?"

Paoul looked around to see a girl in an embroidered robe, the same rather pretty girl he had noticed at yesterday's dress re-hearsal, the same girl whose presence he had been conscious of during the ceremony itself. She was about his age or a little younger, with dark blond hair tied back, a creamy skin, and brown eyes. She seemed shy, which he found hard to understand, because she was Bohod Thosk's daughter and must have been exposed to court life from an early age. Last night he had caught himself thinking about her and wondering whether she would be here again today. Then he had heard Starrad stealthily leaving and had angrily dismissed the matter from his mind.

"The slaves seem to have forgotten you," she said. "They're very busy, I'm afraid. I know you can't have wine or anything, but would you like some grape juice?"

"No. Not for me."

She shrank back and Paoul realized he had spoken curtly. It had cost her an effort to approach him; her motives had sprung simply from kindness, and now he had let down the good name of the school. "Really, I'm not at all thirsty," he went on, un-truthfully, trying to rescue the situation. "Besides, there'll be plenty to drink at the banquet." He smiled and engaged her eyes. She certainly was pretty: not like the Lady Atane, of course, but attractive in a more lasting and less obvious way. In other cir-cumstances, in another life, perhaps, he might have let himself admire the color of her eyes, the shape of her mouth, or the whiteness of the enamel on her small, neatly formed teeth. Drawn there by the tiny pink and blue flowers of embroidered forget-me-nots, he might have allowed his gaze to stray briefly over the youthful swell of her bodice. He might have noticed her fem-ininity, the softness of her voice, the delicate make of her hands; and he might have acknowledged to himself how gentle and graceful she was. Instead he made himself smile again and said, "My name is Paoul. I have the honor to address the daughter of Bohod Thosk, I believe."

"Yseld. That's my name."

Her name was modest, yet also the sort of name that a hopeless suitor might breathe to himself in unrequited passion. It fitted her perfectly. Paoul wanted to tell her so, or, at least, to say something else, but, despite what he still imagined to be the coolness of the composure bestowed on him by the taug, he found himself lost for words. He had never conducted such a conversation before.

"Was that lamp as heavy as it looked?"

He was about to say "Not really," but that would have been another lie. "Heavier."

"It made a horrible smell."

"I know."

"Almost as bad as the Prime's censer."

"If the incense is disagreeable to you, my lady, please speak to your father, for it is he who imports it."

Paoul had tried to temper his reply with a smile; he was expecting one in return. It did not come, and for the first time he realized, with alarm, how disconcerting he found her. And more: he realized that his feelings were reciprocated. "I'm . . . I'm so sorry," she said, still speaking, he supposed, about the incense. "I didn't mean—"

She was unable to finish. Her father's voice sounded close behind Paoul's back. "There you are, Yseld."

Disturbed beyond measure, Paoul tried to calm himself, to pretend that nothing had happened. It was as if he had been struck a physical blow, taken the full impact of one of the heavy sandbags swinging from the ceiling of the taug school. What had just happened was impossible. A moment ago, before meeting her, he had been in possession of his will. Now he had lost it, surrendered it, and, it seemed, she had done the same.

He knew that on no account must he betray himself or give her cause to imagine that he saw her as anything more than the daughter of his host. And so he moved aside, as though intimidated by Bohod Thosk's importance. Bohod Thosk was, indeed, on close terms with Lord Heite. But most of all he was father to the Lady Yseld, her proprietor and controller. For a moment he turned his smoky brown eyes on Paoul and it seemed as if he had guessed everything. But his expression remained utterly bland, concealing all emotion, all opinion, all thought and feeling. "Ah. One of the lamp bearers. Paoul, isn't it?"

"Yes, sir."

Had it not been for Yseld, Paoul would have taken this as it had probably been intended, as a cue to depart. He would also have felt amazed and flattered to think that Bohod Thosk should have known or remembered his name: they had not met until now.

"Forgive me for interrupting your conversation." There was no trace of irony in Bohod Thosk's tone. He turned to his daughter. "Yseld, it is nearly time to go in. Do you forget that Lord Mond is here?"

This was the younger of the two sons Lord Heite had brought to the ceremony, a well-favored youth of eighteen who had inherited his father's looks and manner. Immediately Paoul scented the odor of a marriage contract, of politics and intrigue. For the daughter of a rich and ambitious merchant, what could be more inevitable than a union with the ruling clan? Paoul wondered at last whether he was expected to slip away: his conversation with the Lady Yseld had, after all, hardly warranted the name. But he stayed where he was, reluctant to leave her, and fascinated, too, by the opportunity of studying at close quarters one of the most famous and influential men in the empire—in the known world.

His study was short-lived. Even before another word was spoken there came, from the great doorway of the dining hall, a flourish of pipes and horns, followed by a measured beating of the drums. Bohod Thosk took his daughter's elbow. "You will excuse us," he told Paoul.

As her father drew her away, Yseld half turned her head and gave Paoul a parting look.

This look, all the more eloquent because she had yielded it involuntarily, quite unlike the Lady Atane, haunted him until the guests had almost finished taking their places for the banquet. Walking behind Ilven Gars and three other priests, Paoul entered at the end of the procession and was shown to a lowly position near the door, a long way from Yseld and the main dais. Ilven Gars was standing beside him, waiting, like all the guests, for the Prime to enter and bless the meal. As the guests waited they marveled at the blue and white opulence of the dining hall, gazing up in wonder at the intricate carvings of dragons, storks, and eagles on the ceiling. None of it registered with Paoul. He could think only of the Lady Yseld. So little had been spoken, but so much said in the language of the eyes. It was irrational, illogical, mad, contrary to all his past experience, to base such certainty on such slight apparent cause. They had been together for no more than a minute; he knew nothing about her, nothing except one undeniable fact: that, in his excitement, he was sure that he must meet her again, touch her, stay with her, and confirm beyond all doubt that she felt just as he did.

The Prime entered, larger than life in his cream and scarlet brocade, his voluminous train dragging the floor as he mounted a podium near the main dais. The hall became silent. Briefly the Prime's gray eyes surveyed the gathering with a benign yet distant expression. Grasping the rail with his lean, supple hands, he then inclined his head deeply, revealing the close-cropped, whorled denseness of the pure white hair of his crown. This was a moment for individual contemplation: the guests also bent their heads, raising them only when the Prime began to speak.

"Great Gauhm." His voice did not seem loud, but penetrated with astonishing clarity every corner of the hall. "From the fruits of your womb we accept now this bounteous harvest."

The words of the blessing were familiar to Paoul. He had heard them in the refectory each day for almost ten years. As line succeeded line, Paoul, despite the presence beside him of Ilven Gars, found himself overwhelmed by the need to turn and seek out Yseld's face, certain that she would also be turning to seek out his. But she was obscured by others and could not be seen.

As soon as the blessing was over, however, the guests began to sit and Paoul glimpsed her settling into her place next to Lord Mond, on the right side of the dais. The head of the dais was occupied by the Prime, flanked by Lord Heite and Bohod Thosk.

From here, diagonally opposite her and about forty feet away, Paoul had a clear view of her face. She cast several glances over the assembly, but did not seem to single him out, even for an instant. Neither did she avoid looking in his direction.

The first dish was announced and brought for the food tasters to try. While this was happening, Lord Mond leaned toward her, away from Paoul, and spoke. She smiled modestly. Lord Mond spoke again and her eyes widened. With a new and wholly unfamiliar pain, Paoul watched as she put her hand to her mouth as if to suppress a laugh. Lord Mond, the effortlessly superior rival in a contest which Paoul could not even enter, had already won his spoils. She had already been assimilated by his future: she was already part of his vast inheritance. He leaned toward her again with another amusing remark, made no doubt at the expense of those in the body of the hall. The change it produced transformed her face. When she smiled like that she was more than passively pretty. She was beautiful.

"Paoul!"

Paoul looked around. Ilven Gars was regarding him closely.

"Did you hear me? I asked you a question."

"I'm sorry, Ilven Gars. I humbly beg your pardon."

"Do you know the etiquette of eating capercaillie?"

"Yes, Ilven Gars."

Ilven Gars frowned. "Are you feeling ill, Paoul?"

"No, Ilven Gars. I am quite well, thank you."

"Are you sure? There's still time for you to leave. You may go to your chamber if you wish."

The prospect was tempting. Paoul had been looking forward to the evening, but he no longer had the stomach for a large and extended meal, or for giving his polite attention to the small talk of the guests. Most of all, he no longer wished to sit here, in plain view of Lord Mond's companion. To leave now, though, would be an intolerable admission of defeat.

"Thank you, Ilven Gars, but I'm quite all right."

Paoul consoled himself with the thought that he would not have to stay for very long. At midnight or thereabouts, soon after the food had been eaten, he would be able to withdraw to his room upstairs. Because Bohod Thosk's residence was some distance from the citadel, too far to be safely traversed in the dark —it was situated near the Lower Township, the river port—and because the gates of the citadel were anyway locked at nightfall, accommodation had been provided for the guests. Paoul had been given a tiny room, barely large enough to take a bed, next to the chambers occupied by Ilven Gars and the other priests. They too, like the Prime, would be leaving the banquet at midnight. Only then, Paoul guessed, would the true celebrations—the ancient, unruly observance of the Crale—begin.

The food, in small portions, was exquisitely prepared and served, and Paoul made himself eat every scrap, as good manners required. As course succeeded course and toast succeeded toast, he managed to keep his eyes as much as possible away from the main dais. But, when the Prime and with him the whole assembly arose, when it was time for the priests to leave, Paoul's concentration lapsed.

He turned and in that instant she did the same. When she saw him she hurriedly looked away, at Lord Mond, at her father, at the Prime, and, with an embarrassed intentness, watched and listened as the Prime took his leave.

Once Paoul had escaped from the dining hall—his eyes fixed firmly on neutral territory—and once he had washed himself and was in the privacy of his room, he climbed straight into bed, unable even to consider starting the routine of breathing exercises which preceded the nightly meditation. For once he would be undisciplined and let his meditation go. The exercises would calm him, he knew, and let him examine his experience more objectively, but that was theory and the Lady Yseld was fact. And so he immediately snuffed the lamp and pulled the sheepskin cover across his shoulder, lying not on his back, as he had been taught, but on his side. The mattress felt lumpy and prickled his naked skin; the bedclothes exuded a stale, faintly nauseous smell. From below, through the thick planking of the floor on which his mattress lay, came the sound of the banquet. He was not directly above it, but at a slight remove. Nevertheless he could hear the music and, by using his hearing as the kars had shown him, by narrowing its field and singling out individual sounds, he could distinguish several of the feasters' voices: he could hear Lord Heite proposing a toast. She would be hearing it too, not as thin, distant abstraction, but loudly and with all the richness of presence.

In the next chamber Paoul heard Ilven Gars moving about. Soon the noises ceased and Paoul knew he had assumed the meditation posture. He had begun his breathing, counting in heartbeats for each phase of the fourfold cycle. The first three cycles were performed to the count of three, the next five by the count of five, on through the series of sacred numbers: seven, nine, and for the experienced, eleven. In the adjoining chambers, the other priests would be doing the same. Sitting very still, breathing very quietly, eyes half closed, they would no longer be here, now, in Bohod Thosk's hall, but everywhere and nowhere, set free from their bodies and the constraints of time. Paoul wished he shared their ability. He wished his training had already taken him further. He wished he were older and able to exert total self-control. Then he would not be so weak and vulnerable and uncertain.

By the time he again heard slight sounds from the next chamber, Paoul had relived the evening over and over again. He could remember each word she had said, each inflection of her voice, each nuance of meaning, and he realized that, by complaining about the smell of the incense, she had spoken of the Prime with a hint, however veiled and guarded, of disrespect. Her behavior had been forward; had she not approached Paoul and spoken first? Starrad would see no difference between her and the Lady Atane or the fishmonger's daughter.

Paoul knew so little about girls, however, that he was prepared to accept that he had read her wrongly. He thought he had sensed in her manner something forced, uncharacteristic, almost desperate, overlying a deeper sincerity to which he had intuitively responded. Even before the exchange of names, it now seemed, their eyes had confirmed and begun to explore a mutual attraction which yesterday had existed only in Paoul's wildest conjectures. But he was already betrothed, and to the sternest possible bride. The Lady Yseld had acted, as he had, without thinking. Their instincts were dangerous and misplaced. She had understood this, but too late. Her remark about the Prime might have been an attempt to bring their encounter onto safer ground.

All that, though, however much he wanted to believe it, was contradicted by her demeanor at the banquet. There she had shown him quite plainly that she found his reaction embarrassing. Her approach had been meaningless, empty, and flippant. Lack of contact with young women had made him overserious and too susceptible to their charms. That final glance had told him everything. Her prank had misfired. What fun to flirt with a trainee priest! How entertaining to giggle about it with her friends tomorrow! Starrad, after all, was right.

And because he was right, Paoul could not help thinking of her as he had thought of the Lady Atane. What would it be like to touch her, to caress such skin, to receive a kiss from such a mouth? To . . .

Abruptly he threw back the cover, glad of the chilly night air on his body. In the darkness, impervious to the sounds from below, he faithfully executed the cycles of breathing and, much calmed and comforted, managed to achieve a few minutes' peace.

He returned to bed and lay supine, relaxed. Before composing himself for sleep he put into concise terms the lessons of the evening. He saw that he belonged here, above the music, side by side with Ilven Gars and the others. This was his life. Not only was he reconciled to it: he loved it. There could be no greater privilege than acceptance by the Red Order. Temptations put in his way served merely to strengthen his resolve and teach him how worthless and transient were the treasures that ordinary men held dear.

Paoul shut his eyes. His relaxation deepened and he purposely fragmented his thoughts, darting from one unconnected image to another, inducing the state that was already drawing him down. The last thing he knew was the sound of a whisper. It had nothing to do with him, it came from beyond, from outside; but, in the instant of falling asleep, he knew the whisper had also been the sound of her name.

5 At the end of the next morning the novices went back to their quarters to get ready for the afternoon session. They had just endured a long tutorial with Forzan Zett. Even though it was the Crale and work in the rest of the citadel had come to a halt, the schedule of the vansery was continuing unchanged.

Earlier, on returning from Bohod Thosk's estate, Paoul had gone straight to Forzan Zett's chambers. He had apologized for and explained his lateness and, taking his place, had thought little of the fact that Starrad was absent. Very soon, though, he had sensed that something was badly wrong.

"No one knows anything," Buin had said, on the way here through the rain. "No one dares ask. All we know is that he didn't come back last night."

Water was dripping sparsely from the wooden canopy above the window. The damp and the midday gloom made the dormitory seem even smaller than it was; Starrad's tidy locker, his bed—straightened in his absence by Buin and Enco—and the neatly appointed shelves above it all appeared to be waiting in vain for their master's return.

"Buin thinks he's been caught," Enco said, taking out his best tunic.

"Or robbed. He might have been attacked."

To Paoul's ears this sounded most unlikely. Inside the citadel robbery was almost unknown, and anyway Starrad knew how to defend himself, as did all the higher school pupils.

"They must know where he is," Paoul said, "otherwise they'd have asked you questions when he didn't show at the litany. Whatever else may have happened, we can take it he's been found out."

There was little time for further discussion. They had to get changed, and quickly. In a few minutes the whole class was expected at the temple, for this was the day of their first confrontation with the Prime: this was the afternoon when he was to examine their confirmation plaques.

Somehow Paoul had been expecting such an important day to

be sunny. He had awaited it eagerly, but the news about Starrad had overshadowed his pleasure and now all that remained was a dread of failure, tinged with a fear of facing the Prime. And there was something more: a residue of unease from the events of the previous evening.

Buin straightened his cap and they were ready to depart; but, at that moment, the curtain at the doorway was pulled aside and Ilven Fend stepped into the room. One of the least strict of the teachers, Ilven Fend was relatively young, in his thirties, with reddish hair and freckles. He was a favorite of most of the pupils. There was no smile on his face, however, as he said, "Which is Starrad's locker?"

"That one, Ilven Fend."

The contents of the locker and the objects on the shelves were alike tossed onto Starrad's bed and, with the bedding, gathered unceremoniously into a bundle which Ilven Fend took in his arms. He turned to go. "I am permitted to tell you," he said, addressing the three boys equally, "that Starrad has, by his bestial conduct, brought shame to the school. He has defiled its reputation and you will not be seeing him again. He has left Hohe. From tomorrow it will be forbidden to utter his name anywhere in the citadel. Until then you may pass this information on to your fellows." Ilven Fend moved to the doorway, treating Buin to an especially withering glance. "The complicity of his roommates in this matter has not been overlooked."

Buin respectfully held back the curtain: the ilven pushed past him without another word.

The three boys looked at each other, stunned as much by the force of his anger as by his revelation that the worst—the very worst—had befallen their friend. To be expelled at this stage of the training was unimaginable. After so much work and self-sacrifice, Starrad, for a trifle, had thrown away the chance of life as a red priest—in his case, as a high-ranking phede, perhaps even an astronomer. He had been ruined, dishonored, ignominiously thrust from the gates of Hohe. His punishment was appalling, yet each of the three was also privately fascinated to be involved, however peripherally, in such a serious affair; fascinated, and relieved and thankful that it was not he who had shared Starrad's fate.

Buin had known him best. "Where did he come from?" Enco said, already speaking of Starrad, Paoul noted, in the past tense.

"I'm not sure. A province in the east. His father is a bohod."

"I didn't know that," Paoul said. Once inside the citadel, it was considered irrelevant and ill-mannered to talk about one's origins.

"So he's not sponsored?"

Buin shook his head. "He can't ever go back. What could he say to his father? What could he possibly say?"

"We'd better get moving," Enco said, reminding them sharply of the next session, of the temple and the Prime. "You heard what Ilven Fend said. We're in enough trouble as it is."

"Your plaque is now a talisman," the Prime had told Paoul quietly, under the echoing vault of the temple, the rest of the class sitting in ranks on the far side of the floor, either waiting to be judged or already knowing the verdict. Most had looked elated; some, their plaques rejected, had looked downcast. "Like most of your work, it is of the required standard. However, the Principal tells me your progress recently has been giving him concern. He had intended to speak to you personally, but the events of this morning are so grave that he has asked me to intervene. Buin and Enco I shall deal with in due course. As for you, come to my chambers tomorrow at noon."

Paoul arrived early, having left a mathematics lesson partway through to spend half an hour grooming and dressing. His state of dread could not have been more complete. He had hardly slept; nor had Buin and Enco, whose interviews were to take place later in the day. At breakfast he had been unable to touch his food, and in class he had been severely reprimanded for his lack of concentration.

The chambers of the Prime formed part of the upper story of the temple and were reached from the cloisters by an enclosed staircase which Paoul now climbed for the first time in his life. At the top was a small landing and a pair of elaborately carved doors. He paused before raising the knocker, shut his eyes, and tried to swallow. He could not. His mouth was too dry. Beside him, set deeply in the wood and clay wall, a circular window gave a view over glistening roofs toward the herb gardens and the vansery palisade, beyond which he could see the rain-soaked streets of the township. A few stray particles of drizzle blew in and clung to the sleeve of his robe.

He was admitted by an attendant—a young forzan in the cream

robes of the Prime's personal staff—who took him through one door and then another, along a dark corridor, and showed him into a waiting room furnished with a low, padded bench.

Paoul was too agitated to sit. He went to the window. To keep calm he tried to identify some of the roofs, shingled or merely boarded and caulked, which spread out below. He had never seen the vansery like this before, or realized how big it was; higher up the mountain, looking down on the citadel, the vansery tended to merge with the township and the barracks. The view from here was much like that from the landing, except that more of the gardens could be seen. Paoul noticed that one or two of the yew boughs, where they had overhung the palisade, had been freshly lopped. In his imagination he saw Starrad dropping from the branches in the darkness, landing badly, perhaps spraining his ankle, unable to climb back, trapped in the township. Or perhaps the lopped branches were unconnected with Starrad's disgrace: perhaps he had been betrayed by one of the townsfolk. The girl's father? The girl herself?

The midday gong sounded dolefully in the temple square.

Paoul turned from the window, deciding to use his remaining moments more sensibly. Fully expecting to be interrupted, he sat down, closed his eyes, and began a breathing routine. He was able to finish: no interruption came. The Prime, it seemed, was keeping him waiting, either deliberately or, much more probably, because Paoul and the matter in hand were so insignificant.

In the corridor outside he could hear the continual passage to and fro of the servants and officials of the Prime's staff. To this suite of chambers were directed scores of messages, inquiries, and petitions a day. Some were relatively trifling; others raised profound questions of religion or state with far-reaching consequences on the lives of tens of thousands of people. Each petition had to be carefully considered and an answer sent to the offices of Lord Heite for enactment. For, although the Gehans controlled the army, the real power lay with the Prime. He was the very hub of the empire, the still point at the center of the circle: through him came divine guidance from the Earth Goddess. He was her mortal representative, in absolute command of the empire—through the two priesthoods, the Gehans, and the merchant class, which depended for its survival on his favor. The common people regarded him as a god. With very little encouragement, Paoul reflected, they would also worship him as such.

Paoul looked about him. In the Prime's suite even a humble waiting room was finished with matchless skill. The walls were paneled to chest height with bas-reliefs of the four seasons which, continued in fresco, rose to the ceiling where they merged with a subtly clouded sky. The door, varnished and veneered with reed-leaf laminate, hung on five hinges and made a flawless fit with its frame. The copper-lined oak lever and hook of the latch had become worn, but still engaged sweetly and were probably original, installed over eighty years ago. The whole temple, of which the Prime's chambers formed an integral part, had been rebuilt then, following a fire. Its site—and hence the site of Hohe, the "High Place"—had been decreed by Gauhm: easily defended, easily reached from the Great River, and surrounded by the rich farmland of the Home Plain. The precise position of Mount Atar also had symbolic properties with respect to the earth's surface and the celestial dome. Its latitude and its relationship with the solstitial positions of the five major constellations and the paths of the five planets produced a unique web of coordinates which fixed Hohe as the only possible location for the temple. The distance between the temple altar and the waterfall, furthermore, was exactly one five thousandth of the equatorial axis or, measured in standard bars, three thousand one hundred and twenty-five— or five raised to the power of five. Paoul had also been told that the temple altar, suspended as it were between heaven and earth, was exactly one fifth of this height above sea level.

For those sensitive to such influences, the citadel had a special, spiritual feeling about it, weakest in the outlying parts of the township, stronger in the vansery, stronger still in the temple, reaching its purest concentration at the altar stone itself. The Prime dwelled directly above the stone, sharing its focus of co-ordinates, absorbing Gauhm's power. This power he radiated outward and downward through the ranks of his priests. Paoul could feel it even now, just as he had felt it yesterday in the temple, and just as, to a lesser extent, he had felt it in the Prime's presence at Bohod Thosk's hall.

The door opened. The attendant had returned. "The Lord Prime will see you now. Quickly."

Paoul followed. After being made to pause in a panelled ante-chamber, he was escorted through a pair of tall doors and found himself in the Prime's huge day room. The doors shut behind him: he and the Prime were alone.

"Be seated," the Prime said, indicating a broad, leather-covered stool in front of him. "I shall not keep you waiting very much longer."

Wearing a cream and dark-green robe, he was sitting at a walnut writing table, his back to an alcove on the right-hand side of the room. On a smaller table beside him was a sheaf of swan quills, and several parchments covered with columns of neat black hieroglyphics.

Most of the far wall was taken up with a line of deeply canopied windows which overlooked the formal grounds and, beyond the billowing treetops of the Founder's Grove, the greeny-gray water of the lake. As Paoul crossed the room he noticed a heron far below, gliding over the trees.

He sat down, his eyes irresistibly drawn by the quiet scratching of the Prime's pen. With rapid, confident strokes, the Prime was adding comments in red to the columns of black. Upside-down, and from this distance, Paoul could make out none of the words but, observing the movements of the nib, he was able to guess at some of the characters being formed. "Borders." "Province." "Blue priesthood." "Gehan." "Petitioner." And again, "Gehan."

Despite his terror of the approaching interview, a corner of Paoul's mind was left free to be intrigued by the sensation of sitting here in the sanctum of the Prime, of being able to observe closely the weave of his robe, the pattern of the braid edging on his cuff, the shape of his fingernails and his neatly manicured cuticles, the way the veins on his left hand were just beginning to distort the shape of his tattoo; and, most intriguing of all, displayed on the polished surface of the table, two small objects which were evidently personal possessions: a flint penknife in an ivory holder and, no more than three inches high, a limestone figurine of the Earth Mother. For these few seconds Paoul was privileged to witness what none of his friends had ever seen: the Prime at work, attending to the minutiae of his awesome office.

"Now," he said, setting down his pen, and Paoul felt his heart in his throat. "Tell me what you know of this Starrad business. From the beginning."

"Last spring, my lord, I understood he met a young woman in the township."

"Do you know her name?"

"No, my lord."

"Then do you know anything else that would serve to identify her?"

The Prime's tone was so ominous that Paoul made the mistake of hesitating before answering.

"Your reticence does not please me."

"She is a daughter of one of the fishmongers, my lord. I do not know which."

"Continue."

"Starrad . . . Starrad was conducting improper relations with her. Once or twice a week, sometimes more frequently, he would visit her at night. We believed he was getting over the palisade near the physic gardens."

"By climbing the yew trees?"

"That is what we thought, my lord. But we were never certain. He always denied everything. I never saw the girl or heard anything but rumor and speculation. That is all I really know, my lord."

"You were aware of his absences, of course."

"Yes, my lord."

"Then why did you not report them to your teachers?"

Paoul was unable to reply.

The Prime sat back, subjecting Paoul to the full force of his searching gray eyes. "Tell me, young man, why do you think you are attending the temple school?"

"To . . . to learn the ethos, my lord."

"And what is the ethos? How do we describe it?"

"Gentleness through strength."

"From where does that strength derive?"

This was a line from an elementary catechism. "Perfection of the self, obedience, and loyalty."

"Loyalty to whom?"

"To Gauhm, my lord."

"Yet you prefer to give yours to a liar and a fornicator." The Prime paused, allowing his words their maximum effect. "Did it never once occur to you that you were doing Starrad a disservice by failing in your proper duty? If this matter had been brought to light at the start, the outcome for him may not have been so serious. By your connivance you contributed to his weakness and must be held partly to blame."

"Yes, my lord."

"You understand, do you not, the damage that such an incident can inflict on the Order? What may appear to you as no more than an infraction of vansery law may have profound and unforeseeable consequences. If we are to serve Gauhm, our reputation must remain unassailable. Do you understand?"

"Yes, my lord."

The Prime's gaze relented slightly and he seemed satisfied that the lesson had been taken to heart. "It is customary," he went on, "for offending novices to be dealt with by the Principal. However, in order to impress upon you and the whole school the gravity of what has happened, Forzan Zett has asked me to conduct the investigation myself. That is one of the reasons you are here. Another is the question of your recent progress, which, as I informed you yesterday, has been giving him cause for concern. He wished me to have an opportunity to speak to you in circumstances which would arouse neither the suspicions nor the curiosity of your fellows, and nothing I am about to say is to be transmitted by you to any third person."

Paoul did not know how to respond to this enigmatic statement and could do little but nod in compliance.

"Your part in this Starrad affair is perhaps indicative of what the Principal means when he tells me your work is disappointing. Since you are no longer a child, I can speak to you bluntly, without fear that you will mistake my words for praise or derive from them any grounds for conceit. I trust you will bear this in mind when considering what I am about to say next."

Again Paoul could only nod.

"Judged by normal, commonplace standards, your work has always been excellent. In the ten years you have been at Hohe you have developed well. Your progress has been so rapid that you are now at least two full years ahead of your age and on course to becoming one of the youngest initiates the Order has ever known. By commonplace standards, you would be considered an exceptionally able pupil. In your case, however, the commonplace does not apply. Your gifts are such that you cannot be measured against your peers. For your work to be merely excellent is not enough. It should be exemplary. You should not be two years ahead, but three, or even four. Do I begin to make myself understood?"

"Yes, my lord."

"The decision to advance you into the higher school was taken some months ago. Since then, Forzan Zett has had occasion to question his own wisdom. He sees that you are becoming content to adopt the pace of your fellows. He sees that you appear to defer to them, that you seek at every turn to spare their feelings, that you thereby waste time on tolerating inferior debate. Perhaps this is understandable. You are unassuming by nature. The age difference inhibits you still further. But, while making full use of the advantages your teaching group has to offer, you should not become subservient to it. You must be more assertive. Do not be afraid of making yourself unpopular. Such unpopularity is the product of small and envious minds and must not be allowed to hold you back. This is what the Principal fears, Paoul, that you are holding yourself back. Gauhm does not choose her servants lightly. You have no right to squander her gifts in this way. They are not yours to dispose of as you see fit."

For a moment Paoul remained silent. He could see that Forzan Zett was right: he had been failing his teachers for some months past. Quietly he said, "I am very sorry, my lord."

"You are resolved to take your rightful place in the school?"

"Yes, my lord."

"Good. Well and good." The Prime contemplatively reached out and made a tiny adjustment to the position of the figurine. Gauhm's broad hips and narrow shoulders were inverted and vaguely duplicated by the reflection that descended into the illusory depths of the tabletop. Her face could not be seen from here: she had her back to Paoul. "More may hinge on your resolve than you might guess. You have eighteen months more at Hohe. Then, of course, you will embark on your six months of travel. If you acquit yourself well you will return here to take the pentacles. You will then leave us and go back to Brennis. That is only proper, for Brennis is where you began and you have a debt to repay to the vansery at Valdoe. It is not, however, a foregone conclusion that you will spend the rest of your life in Brennis. As you must be aware, the Order is constantly searching for men of special promise. For such men, the opportunities are almost without limit. I trust this is something else you will bear in mind."

An air of finality in the Prime's manner hinted that the interview had come to its end. The Prime's expression confirmed it: Paoul stood up, his head swimming.

The Prime remained seated. "Do you have any questions, Paoul?"

"No, my lord."

"Good." The Prime picked up his pen. "Do not forget what has been said here this afternoon."

As if anyone could forget such words! "I won't, my lord."

"The attendant will escort you to the stairs. Good day, Paoul."

"Good day, my lord. Thank you, my lord."

Paoul found himself crossing to the doors. He opened them and, turning to back out, looked up, half expecting the Prime to be watching; but he had already taken another parchment from the small table beside him and, his pen held ready, was again immersed in his work.

6 The mathematics lesson would be finishing by now: there was no point in going back there. And besides, he needed a few minutes on his own. He needed to think, to compose himself.

Scarcely aware of the treads beneath his feet, Paoul descended the staircase and entered the cloisters, slowing only in deference to the three or four priests he passed. From the cloisters he went straight to his dormitory and pressed shut the door.

Too stunned and excited to think of changing his clothes or preparing for the next session, he made himself sit down on the edge of the bed and tried to make sense of his feelings.

His world had been shattered and remade. He had suddenly been freed from the many small doubts, each insignificant on its own, that he now realized had been weighing him down. At their root—which the Prime had so perceptively uncovered—was a doubt that the horizons of Brennis were broad enough to contain his future. From slight beginnings a sureness had been growing within him, a confidence that he would one day be of service to the Order and thus to the empire and his fellow man. How, he was not certain, but he knew he could not serve best in isolation, and Valdoe was no place for an ambitious forzan: it was for phedes, astronomers, an observatory of a very high standard, but of little interest to him. Whatever nostalgia he had felt for Brennis itself, he believed, had long since glimmered and died. His life there had ended with Tagart's death, with the horrible scenes he still sometimes relived in his nightmares, with Dagda and Bocher and Beilin Crogh. Without even being aware of it, Paoul had been assuming that he was somehow sentenced to a lifetime in Brennis, and that he would soon have to leave forever the place where he felt he belonged. The citadel had become his home, and the Order had become his family; more than a family. It had been better and kinder to him than any parent could have been. And all the time, while his doubts had been growing and proliferating and bearing strange fruit—such as his encounter with the Lady Yseld—his teachers had been planning for him and wisely guiding his course.

They wanted him for something more than a provincial forzan. It all seemed to fit into place: first, his early elevation to the higher school; second, his selection as lamp bearer; third, the remark that Lord Heite had made at the lake—"the Prime has spoken to me of you, Paoul"; and fourth, most important of all, the circumstances of the interview and the things the Prime had said.

He would have to spend some time in Brennis, the Prime had made that clear. But after that? Would he be coming back to Hohe? It seemed likely, perhaps even certain: why else should the Prime have spoken as he had? Why else should he have told Paoul, in so many words, that his opportunities were "almost without limit"?

Paoul could not imagine what form those opportunities might take. Just to be in service here at Hohe would be more than enough. Would he be offered a post in the temple? Or in the school, as a teacher!

But then it struck him that he was meant for an even higher position than that. Perhaps, after many more years' study, he would be put in charge of a minor vansery of his own, become a vansard! Or would they train him for the High Council? Would he sit with Lord Heite and become an adviser on the Prime's staff?

It was all too dazzling to contemplate. The Prime, indeed, had tried to slow down this line of reasoning, to reduce its final impact, by explaining his motives for conducting the Starrad inquiry in person. It was inconceivable that the Prime, even by the subtlest omission, should ever be guilty of falsehood; but nothing could get away from the fact that, in the past, breaches of school discipline, however serious, had always been dealt with by the school Principal. There was surely a reason for the Prime's intervention on this occasion, and Paoul could think of only one. Was it possible? Was it possible that the Prime—the Prime himself, and not just the Prime acting on behalf of the Principal—could have wanted an opportunity to speak to Paoul alone, arousing "neither the suspicions nor the curiosity" of his fellows? Was it possible that the Prime thought so highly of him, was so interested in his career, and was so anxious to impress upon him what was at stake? Incredible as it seemed, there could be no other explanation. The rest naturally followed. And it also followed that, in the plainest terms available to him, the Prime had warned Paoul that he was in danger of risking whatever it was that had been planned for him. "More may hinge on your resolve than you might guess." Were those not the very words the Prime had spoken not half an hour since?

Paoul arose. He had decided, as a man decides. His determination to heed the Prime's golden advice would not be sudden, dramatic, or flimsily contrived. It would be slow to build, strong, immovable. There would be no immediate or superficial results. His reform would come from within, from the core of obduracy at his center, a gradual change in his habits and outlook that would slowly but irreversibly increase his capacity for work. His mind was made up. He would not fail his teachers or the Prime; he would not fail Gauhm.

Calmly, unhurriedly, he took off his robe and hung it in its place. From the wicker basket by his bed he selected a clean taug tunic and his swimming things. As he was washing, Enco and Buin arrived.

"Well?" said Enco.

"Yes," said Buin, also fearful about his own interview later in the afternoon. "What did he say?"

Paoul told them all they were allowed to know.

During the next eighteen months each of the boys spent progressively more time in specialist classes: Paoul with the forzans, Enco with the kars, Buin with the ilvens, and Relle—Starrad's replacement—with the phedes. As their basic training drew to a close, they were being prepared for their vows and for the years immediately after initiation.

They were also being prepared for the six months of travel which completed every novice's training and gave him a chance to see at first hand the way the empire worked. The novices, in pairs, were always accompanied by a teacher to act as guide and mentor. The exact itinerary was left to his discretion. There was not time to see more than a small part of the empire, which, counting the extensive tracts of uncivilized mountain and forest outside the settled regions, covered some three quarters of a million square miles. Of this vast area, only a fraction was under the direct administration of the Gehans or their subordinated, blood-related clans—the Abendgehans, the Felsengehans, the Nordengehans, and the others. The remainder, especially in the south and west, was the original territory of a legion of chieftains large and small who had been conquered by the Gehan clans and paid them yearly tribute. This process of expansion was still continuing, with the fiercest wars being fought in the chiefdoms of Iberia. Along the borders of the north and east, however, there was no expansion, only an unremitting struggle to hold back the invasive tribes of barbarians whose warlords, if ever they became united, would be a formidable threat indeed.

Such regions were not visited by touring novices. They kept to the heartlands, to villages where they were sure of a suitable welcome. Journeying between the villages could itself be hazardous enough. Even today, in the marshes and mountains and unclaimed forests, there were plenty of bandits. Some, perhaps, were the remnants of the aboriginal tribes of hunters; most were disaffected or dispossessed farmers and their descendants. The novices would learn to deal with other hazards too—with wild animals, the vagaries of the weather, and all the other hardships of the road.

There was a certain amount of freedom in the boys' choice of traveling companion, and when Paoul and Enco expressed a wish to travel together this was not refused. Their mentor, traditionally chosen from another discipline, was named as Ilven Fend. A week before they were due to leave, when muddy torrents of meltwater were already roaring down the mountain and the ice in the lake had largely broken up, Ilven Fend decided on the final route. On a cloudy afternoon, with a cold east wind blowing sleet across the temple square, he called Paoul and Enco to his chambers.

Opening cylinders and scrolls, spreading skin and reed paper maps on the floor, he took up a hazelwood pointer and indicated the course of their journey. It was to be a thousand miles long, beginning with a river passage north from Hohe, through the home provinces and thence into the country of the Felsengehans. At the port of Coblenz they would leave the river and head generally west, moving toward the channel coast. From the important seaside settlement of Raighe they would turn south, exploring the farming villages of the Kluh and the Courfen Plain and, eventually, by following the River Loire for part of its course, descend into the valley of the Rhône. After a brief stay in the fort at Chaer they would, by skirting the High Peaks and following the course of the River Doubs, make their way back through the homelands and so to the citadel.

"We will visit only three vanseries and a single fort, the one at Chaer," said Ilven Fend. "I want you to see as much of the country as possible and to spend your time among the simple people. Our route will not be easy, and we shall have to maintain a good speed if we're to be back here for the equinox. But I think you'll enjoy it." He glanced at the earthenware kettle which, on its bed of heated rocks, had nearly come to the boil. "I've elderflower and spearmint, nettle, or thyme. Enco, will you make the tea?"

Paoul sat quietly as Enco prepared the three beakers. He felt subdued. He was pleased, very pleased, that Ilven Fend was to be their mentor, but he was still slightly in awe of his teachers and could not get used to the way they were beginning to regard and treat him almost as an equal. To be invited informally into the chambers of an ilven still had a flavor of novelty and privilege.

And there was something else on Paoul's mind. This morning he had accidentally heard, from another novice, that Lord Mond was soon to be married. The bride was to be a distant cousin from a subordinate clan. "Not Bohod Thosk's daughter, then?" Paoul had asked, as casually as he could, for the news had affected him strangely. Quite often in the past eighteen months, ever since their first and only meeting, he had been unable, despite the most rigorous efforts, to stop remembering the Lady Yseld. He had long ago forgiven her for her conduct: such behavior was implicit in the mysterious and unattainable symbol she had become. For Paoul she represented everything his vows were designed to help him renounce. She was the alternative to his calling. Whenever, among his friends, the subject of women arose, it was her face and form he put to the hypothetical example being discussed. But so soon as the talk became coarse, as it occasionally did, he protected her image from defilement, replacing it with a composite derived from a dozen girls he had seen in the township. The same was true of his dreams. Her rare appearances there were invariably fleeting and innocent. Sometimes, to his alarm, he suspected that he also dreamed of her in other ways or, perhaps, more frequently than he knew. It was as though, deliberately excluded from his waking mind, she was managing to surface elsewhere. Yet he was convinced that he had no real feeling for her—how could he, after such a brief and unsatisfactory meeting so long ago? Had he not been a trainee priest, had he been exposed in the normal way to any number of marriageable girls, he would surely have soon forgotten the Lady Yseld, just as, without question, she had forgotten him.

Not that she concerned him anyway. Her only function was to serve as a symbol. Nonetheless, it had helped to know that she was betrothed to Lord Mond and thus truly out of bounds.

Perhaps their betrothal had been called off long since. Or perhaps it had never existed, except in Paoul's imagination. Perhaps she had already married someone else. That was more than likely. To be unwed and eighteen and the daughter of Bohod Thosk was an improbable combination. Yes: she was already married. Paoul knew next to nothing of court life. Its events only touched the vansery when ceremonial was required. He would not have heard of her marriage. It had undoubtedly taken place; and, even if it hadn't, what possible difference could that make to him?

Irrational as it was, the matter had been intruding on his thoughts all day. He had not been so disturbed since the ending of the Starrad affair, when another boy had told him that, shortly after Paoul's interview with the Prime, one of the fishmongers in the township had disappeared. The fishmonger's wife and two unmarried daughters had disappeared also, and when soldiers had come to dismantle his shop and empty his house of possessions, his neighbors had been told that he had been ejected from Hohe for evasion of the tithe.

Nobody had known the name of Starrad's conquest or which of the three fishmongers in the township was her father. There was no more than the flimsiest circumstantial evidence linking the two events. It was both profane and ridiculous to suggest that the Prime, using the army to distance himself from the affair, should have stooped to punish a guiltless girl and her family—for they had committed no recognized offense. Rumors even arose that the family had not merely been expelled, but executed. Execution was the normal punishment for evasion of the tithe, but always in public and before a large crowd. If the rumors were taken to their logical conclusion, it followed that the authorities had not dared to expose the fishmonger to an audience and so had secretly murdered him and his family.

Naturally, no one believed this for an instant. The rumors were idle speculation, supposition, the kind of extravagant gossip which circulates in the wake of any drama. There was no cogent reason for the girl to be silenced, even less for her family. But Paoul had still found the rumors distressing, because it had been he, and Enco and Buin, who had given testimony which could conceivably have been used to identify the girl. For a short time the rumors had even threatened to shake his faith in the Prime and weaken his resolve to work harder.

Like all such affairs, though, this one had soon been forgotten, and Paoul had emerged from it virtually unchanged. He had kept his resolution. A fortnight ago, in the academic tests which qualified a novice for the tour and marked the end of his formal training, Paoul had surpassed the highest standard in all but two subjects, and in those he had been commended with honor by his examiners. Together with Enco, Buin, Relle, and most of his friends, Paoul had been pronounced fit to enter the Pathway of the Tracts. The next morning, therefore, attended by an ilven and a kar, the first stage of his tattooing had begun.

The tattoo of a red priest was applied with needles of blue flint, fashioned by the phedes and heated to boiling in vessels of sanctified water. Elaborate ritual attended the preparation of the pigment, which was sent from Hohe to all vanseries where priests were trained. The pigment base, found only at one site on the slopes of Mount Atar, was a red earth yielding a deep crimson when mixed, in aqueous solution, with the fresh pulp of ripe barberries—fruits sacred to Gauhm and gathered for this purpose only on the day of the autumn equinox, from a consecrated grove below the citadel. To this was added an infusion of marjoram in water from the shrine falls, and, to promote healing, a decoction of madder root. The whole was reduced by heat to the consistency of blood, and stored in airtight jars until needed.

The symbology of the tattoo was extremely complicated. The pattern consisted of exactly three thousand puncture marks, forming a pentacle on the left instep and another on the back of the left hand, connected by three lines, or tracts, extending up the leg and flank and down the arm. The pentacle on the foot symbolized contact with the earth, source of the power which was channeled through the tracts to the hand. Of the three tracts, one, the major, was thicker than the paired minor tracts; the position of the major, whether to the right or left of the minors, varied according to a priest's nomination. A major adjacent to the outer edge of the forearm denoted a phede or ilven; one adjacent to the inner edge denoted a forzan or kar.

The apex of the pentacle represented spirit. Each of the four lower points, proceeding sunwise from the apex, represented one of the four quadrants—creation, manifestation, decay, dormancy—and hence one of the four nominations: ilven, kar, phede, forzan. The major tract ended at the point on the hand corresponding to the priest's nomination.

The pentacles of phedes and kars were upright, with the apex pointing toward the digits, while those of ilvens and forzans were inverted. Thus the three tracts began and ended in a different way in each of the four types of tattoo. The arrangements and connections of the tracts and pentacles formed a kind of language, intelligible to the initiated, which could be read as an account of the unifying and distinguishing characteristics of the four nominations. And there was a fifth nomination, that of the Prime. In his tattoo all three tracts were of the same thickness, the minors being reworked as a sign of the new Prime's accession.

A novice's tattoo was applied in stages. First, before the tour, he entered the Pathway of the Tracts. The Pathway began at the instep and ended at the hand. On each day save the last, over a period of eleven days, he received fifteen times fifteen punctures; each set of fifteen had its own special prayer, song, or chant, forming a narrative, recited by the attending ilven, who also marked out the course for the kar to follow with his needles and pigment. On the last day there were only thirteen sets of fifteen. Then, six months later, on returning from the tour, the two pentacles—each of two hundred and fifty punctures—were made. Lastly, at the full initiation ceremony, the pentacles were connected to the tracts with a further fifty-five punctures.

Paoul had almost finished the Pathway and heard the whole narrative: he had been tattooed as far as the upper arm. He was finding the process more uncomfortable than painful. An herbal styptic, a fragrant white powder sprinkled by the kar from a perforated box, stanched most of the residual bleeding. At night the most recent punctures pained him slightly, but it was a pain of which he was intensely proud, and he was studying with fascination the regular, beautifully even progression of the three tracts toward his wrist, each evening comparing his tattoo with those of his friends.

Sitting here now, sipping nettle tea and listening to Ilven Fend making plans for the tour, Paoul was pleasurably conscious of the ache which from time to time made him adjust the set of his upper sleeve. Only three sessions remained before his Pathway was complete. Each session was carrying him further toward his goal. With today's news about Lord Mond, Paoul saw that each session was also carrying him further away from the danger posed by his image of the Lady Yseld. He was glad. Soon he would be safe forever. And he was glad that next week he would be leaving on the tour. His departure was coming just at the right time: travel would remove him from her in person as well as thought.

Paoul finished his tea and, asking a question about the route, sat forward and gave Ilven Fend his undivided attention.

7 Arriving at Chaer Fort in the cool of evening, Ilven Fend made himself known to the sentry high in the gatehouse. A minute later Paoul heard first one bar and then another and another being pulled back: a small doorway, just wide enough to admit one man, opened in the heavily timbered expanse of the gates, and Ilven Fend, followed by Paoul and Enco, stepped through.

They were met by a soldier wearing the braided wristband of a unit leader. "Good evening to you, father," he said, with the same note of deference that Paoul had found everywhere so far on the tour—in all the villages and settlements, at the ports and ferry stations, and in the tone of almost everyone they had encountered on the road. "And to the young men, of course. Welcome. I'm sorry the gates were locked, father. There's been some trouble today."

"What sort of trouble?"

"Brigands, father. Please come with me. I'll take you to the commander."

The settlement at Chaer was the largest in the province, with extensive field systems in the fertile soil of the river valley. The road to the fort passed near the village, which was one of the more prosperous Paoul had seen, its people apparently healthy and its thatched houses and barns in generally good repair. The fort stood on level ground a quarter of a mile or so from the village, guarded by a high palisade and a deep double ditch lined with a fearsome array of spikes.

Except for the citadel, and the Trundle at Valdoe—which he could remember at best only indistinctly—Paoul had never been inside a fort before; neither had Enco. This visit was intended to improve their knowledge of the day-to-day administration of the provinces, a process in which the forts played an indispensable part. Paoul had already seen at first hand something of the function of the forts. Their main purpose was to supervise the farming population, keeping order, enforcing the edicts and the judgments of the provincial commanders. They also controlled the labor gangs of slaves who maintained the roads, bridges, ferries, and other communal works. Their third duty was to defend the empire's interests from those who refused to recognize its authority—barbarians beyond the border, or bandits within. Paoul had seen little of this aspect of provincial administration, except, and the scene remained disgustingly vivid in his mind, at a village farther north where the mutilated remains of three robbers, caught stealing livestock, had been hung from a gibbet outside the gates. This sight, more perhaps than any of the harrowing scenes of poverty and neglect he had witnessed on the tour, had brought home to Paoul how vast and how puzzling was the discrepancy between the plenty of the countryside and the lot of its inhabitants, all its inhabitants: for it seemed to him that the bandits and robbers were themselves only people who at some stage in their history had been displaced or dispossessed. For reasons he was not sure about, Paoul had decided to keep these feelings private. At the gibbet Ilven Fend had declared that there could be no room for weakness when dealing with such criminals.

The physical structure of the fort spoke of anything but weakness. The palisade, ramparts, and the buildings of the central stronghold were all constructed of dark timbers, more or less massive, and the roofs, unlike those of the village, were not of reed thatch, but of overlapping planks—perhaps a precaution against fire attack. From a slanting pole above the gateway of the commander's quarters hung the familiar green and red pennon of the Gehans: a few days ago, Ilven Fend had led his two charges out of the country of the Abendgehans and back at last into the territory of the ruling clan. The few soldiers on the ramparts were clad in Gehan armor and helmets; those in the enclosure or visible at the windows of the barracks were, like the unit leader, wearing hot-weather tunics and leggings. A smell of new bread was coming from the long, low building Paoul took to be the cookhouse, and he wondered how much longer he would have to wait before eating. Since dawn, when they had left the village of Vinzy, he and his companions had covered thirty-five or forty miles. Ilven Fend had insisted on reaching Chaer by nightfall. Paoul was footsore, thirsty, and hungry: the food the head man had given them on leaving had not lasted long, and Ilven Fend had not allowed them to stop to catch or pick anything from the wild, as was their custom on the road.

The unit leader showed the group into the official receiving room, a ground-floor chamber four yards square, furnished more to civilian than military standards. The window overlooked a little limewashed courtyard where, on the far wall, a trellis was laden with a profusion of honeysuckle foliage and blooms. Darkness was approaching: the unit leader fetched a taper to light the oil lamps, and made as if to close the shutters.

"Leave them open, please," said Ilven Fend.

"Gladly, father, but the insects—"

"Yes, of course. Do as you must."

Commander Yahl came in. He was a spare, resilient-looking man of early middle age, with brown eyes, graying hair and beard, and a nose that looked as if it had been broken long ago. "Please be seated," he said, once the introductions had been made. "Kuber, take these bags to the guests' quarters and see that fresh water and bedding are made ready." He turned back to Ilven Fend. "Was your journey uneventful?"

"Should it have been otherwise?"

"Perhaps. I am surprised but also very thankful to see you all safely here. I sent smoke to Vinzy, warning you not to set out. Was the message not received?"

"It merely warned us to be on our guard."

"Then, somewhere along the way, it was misread. You were lucky, father. Several travelers have been attacked by brigands on that stretch of road. Did you see anything unusual, anything at all?"

"No, Commander. Nothing."

Yahl sat forward. "Yesterday the brigands became more ambitious. They burned a village three miles upstream. This morning we finally managed to locate their camp, but the patrol was discovered. Two of my men were brought back dead, one has died since, and another is dying even now. One of my best." The commander gave a harsh smile in which Paoul detected great anguish and bitterness.

"Would you like me to attend him?"

"No, father, I cannot ask you that. You must be tired and in need of refreshment."

"Not so," Ilven Fend stood up. "Take us to him."

The wounded man was in a small chamber in the barracks. The first thing Paoul noticed, even before entering, was a strong smell of excrement. That, or the smoky light of the rush lamps, had attracted an assortment of insects: lacewings, beetles, flies, small moths, dashing themselves against the lamps and the freckled limewash of the low, uneven ceiling.

The man had been laid on a straw-covered pallet by the far wall. Behind his head, keeping watch, was another soldier, and beside the pallet, offering water from a wooden bowl, was an old man in coarse garments, a civilian. Paoul did not realize at first that the old man was a village priest, not until he saw the tattoo on his right hand and forearm, the blue tattoo with its three thin, wavering tracts and its crudely drawn pentacle. The old priest, noticing the newcomers, arose and moved aside.

The room was silent but for the insects and the congested passage of the man's breath. Ilven Fend squatted by the pallet, allowing Paoul and Enco to take a closer look. Paoul felt his stomach twist. The brigands had used an ax.

"What is his name?" Ilven Fend asked the priest.

"Reisen, master."

"What prayers have you said for him?"

"All the prayers for the dying, master."

The man was still conscious: he could understand perfectly what was being said. He recognized Ilven Fend's robes and tattoo and the agony in his eyes was relieved for a moment by gratitude. His mouth opened more widely, but no sound emerged.

"No, my son. Be quiet."

He seemed to be about Paoul's age, no more, dark and strongly made, his skin deeply tanned and his hair streaked with grime and blood and with fragments and stalks of straw-colored vegetation. The stump of his left arm had been clumsily wrapped in chamois. The terrible wounds in his chest and abdomen had been uncovered and thickly sprinkled with what looked like fine wood ash.

"What is this?"

"From the altar in the village, master. A sacred offering."

"Burned bone?"

"Yes, master."

Ilven Fend lightly shook his head. Bone ash: useless, worse than useless, an ignorant, stupid, pagan superstition. Paoul felt his pity turning to bewilderment and then to anger. He had seen wounds before, and pain, and corpses: it was part of Ilven Fend's brief to show him and Enco these things. He had seen suffering before, but never quite like this. Here, in this squalid room, on this red-soaked pallet, was the reality of the administration that Paoul had previously learned only as lofty and distant theory. This foul, mangled mass of flesh had this morning been the noblest pinnacle of the earth's creation: a man. He had been strong and healthy and vibrantly alive, the same age as Paoul, with the same scantiness of memory and experience and the same hope and eagerness for the future. And now, through his trusting service to the Gehan ideal, to Lord Heite and the bohods and all the frivolities of the court, to the Atanes and the Yselds and all their kind, he was finished, cut down; his life was almost over.

This morning, perhaps, the moment he had been brought in, he might have had a chance. If instead of this old fool he had been attended by a kar—by Kar Ander—he might have been saved. But now it was too late. Enco offered to clean his wounds; Ilven Fend refused. The young soldier was already slipping away.

Ilven Fend began to recite the beautiful words of the Seventy-fifth Song, the Song of the Voyage, the song of death.

Commander Yahl bowed his head and the others did the same. Paoul bowed his head too, but as he listened to the verses unfolding they began to take on a horrible and unfamiliar aspect. They began to sound like something hollow and contrived, a clever piece of mummery to beguile the credulous and keep them subservient to some ulterior cause. Paoul remembered the starving villagers he had seen; he remembered the gibbet; he remembered the luxury of Bohod Thosk's new hall; he remembered Lord Heite with Lady Atane at the lake, and it seemed to him in this moment that the words of the Song were meaningless, a travesty of the brutal truth of this young man's death, robbing it of its dignity: and the worst part was that the dying man was deceived to the very last. He was wrong to be comforted by Ilven Fend's presence, wrong to be reassured and grateful that a red priest should have appeared, as if by divine intervention, at the scene of his final agony.

"He is dead."

Paoul was unsteady on his feet, light-headed and close to collapse. Suddenly, eagerly, he realized that this was more than enough to account for his hallucinatory perception of the Song. He was faint from hunger, from exhaustion, from the heat. He was in no state to think, to form opinions, or to withstand such profound emotional distress.

None of this could he reveal to Ilven Fend. As much as anything else, the tour was a practical test of endurance and fortitude. If he failed it, Paoul would not be accepted for his initiation. And so, as Ilven Fend shut the soldier's eyes and rose to his feet, Paoul imperceptibly braced his shoulders and assumed the impassive, self-contained expression of strength that was second nature to any man who belonged to the Red Order, who was dedicated to it and served it body and soul without question.

"Will Reisen be buried here?" Ilven Fend asked the commander.

"Yes. Tomorrow morning."

"I will officiate, if that is your desire."

The retaliatory raid on the brigands next day was described by Commander Yahl as a complete success. Of the two hundred soldiers in the fort, a hundred and eighty took part, led by the commander in person. The brigands' new camp—two miles from the last, which, as expected, they had vacated following its discovery by the patrol—was surrounded and each of its sixty-three occupants, women and children as well as men, was captured or killed. Children under the age of about nine were routinely dispatched as worthless; the others, and all the surviving adults except one, who, being lame, was therefore dispatched also, were bound and fettered and brought back to the fort.

They arrived late in the afternoon. Once the prisoners had been sorted they were interrogated. As a result of the interrogation—which had involved torture with burning brands and with tourniquets wound around the forehead—Commander Yahl decided that two more of the men, leaders and troublemakers who would anyway be unlikely to make suitable slaves, should be given to the soldiers for disposal as they saw fit, bearing in mind the murder of Reisen and his comrades the previous day. Lastly, most of the younger women, and some of the older ones, were taken to the barracks for the evening to be used in any way the soldiers pleased.

"You were very quiet at supper, Paoul," said Ilven Fend, studying him closely.

They had just left Commander Yahl and had returned to

the guests' quarters. Before retiring, as was their habit, Ilven Fend and the two novices had sat down to discuss the events of the day.

"Yes, Ilven Fend. I was."

"Nor did you eat very much. That was a discourtesy."

"I am sorry, Ilven Fend."

For the instructive experience it had promised, Ilven Fend had accepted the commander's invitation to take Paoul and Enco out with the soldiers on the raid. There had been little danger, for both the novices were proficient in the use of weapons and had gone armed; and Ilven Fend had in any case kept them well back from the fighting. They had been close enough, though, to observe everything that had happened; and afterward, at the fort, they had watched the interrogation and seen the execution of the two leaders. And, during supper, Paoul had from time to time heard laughter and vile shouting from the barracks.

He knew in theory the justification of the policy that countenanced the soldiers' behavior, just as he had known the theory that had brought Reisen to his death. Gentleness through strength: that was the key. By the application of strength, peace was maintained. In this peace, this "gentleness," the empire was able to flourish. It was the same in nature. The weak submitted to the strong, resulting in beauty and harmony. The empire was indeed not to be distinguished from nature: it was merely one part of the manifestation of the universal and therefore continuous with Gauhm's will. Any and all actions taken in defense of the empire were thus a form of worship. Had the brigands not been stopped, they would have burned another village, and another, until the whole province was in ruins and its people without food.

This was the irrefutable proof of a theory which was easy enough to understand in the safety and comfort of a tutorial chamber, but a different matter entirely out here. The brigands' ramshackle tents and shelters had been inexpertly concealed among dry scrub on a hot and barren hillside; the camp had seemed to Paoul less like the stronghold of dangerous criminals than the pathetic refuge of a tribe of frightened destitutes. The brigands themselves, most of them, had been pitiful creatures, like vagrants and outsiders almost anywhere. If they had met the same hostility in the valleys as had once been shown to Tagart and his group, then it was not surprising that they had been reduced to such straits of evil and despair.

What Paoul had seen here had also affected him in another way. Until today, the existence of slavery had been a fact of his life which he had not thought to question. Nor had he wondered about the source of its raw material. If asked, he might have said that the slaves had always been so, and, surely, replaced themselves in the usual manner.

Now he knew otherwise. And, since he himself had once been part of a band of vagrants, since he had in effect been captured by the ruling clan, what was he if not a special and unusual kind of slave? And if that were so, to whom exactly was he enslaved, when it was the Red Order that, by guiding and confining the actions of Lord Heite, was in reality the controller of the empire?

And further: it appeared to Paoul that the controller of any system must be responsible for the conduct of all those in its administration. If the soldiers committed atrocities in the name of Lord Heite—and hence in the name of the Prime—then surely the Prime, by failing to punish or forbid these acts, was equally if not more to blame. And, because it was the Prime who made the laws, who ultimately controlled the apportionment of land and titles and favor, then it was also the Prime who was to blame for the conditions which produced the misery of such people as the brigands.

Paoul felt he had not yet comprehended the full implication of these thoughts, but already he knew they must be wrong. The idea that the Prime could ever be considered blameworthy in any way was clearly a preposterous contradiction in terms. It had to be. The reason Paoul felt so shaken, so disturbed, he told himself, had nothing to do with the Prime. It was the simple result of heat, fatigue, and exposure to scenes of violence and brutality. On the hillside it had taken all his strength to prevent himself from being physically sick. It had been the same during the interrogation and the executions that had followed.

He had tried to keep his feelings hidden from Ilven Fend, but without, it now seemed, much success.

"And you, Enco," said Ilven Fend. "You too are guilty of discourtesy to our host."

"I am very sorry, Ilven Fend."

Ilven Fend straightened the folds in the front of his robe and laid one hand upon the other in his lap. "I must say I had been expecting greater insight and self-control from you both. Have you already forgotten the most basic principles of your training? In a few weeks you are due to be taken into the Order. To all intents and purposes, you should already be behaving like red priests. Yes, Enco?" he said, even more sharply. "Do you have a comment to make?"

"No, Ilven Fend."

"Doubtless you imagine that what we have seen today is both monstrous and wrong. By the standards expected of a man of refinement, it is monstrous. Of course it is. But not wrong. The conduct of Commander Yahl and his men has been in complete accord with the teachings. That is why I am so glad we came to Chaer when we did, for you have been allowed to observe what few of your fellows will ever see: the most extreme example of the ethos at work." He lifted his hands. "Well. You are young. Perhaps I am being harsh. I remember my own tour. I too had never been beyond the citadel, not, at least, with intelligent eyes. But I think you are old enough now to understand the ethos not as an intellectual abstraction, but as an emotional reality. I think you are mature enough to understand why the soldiers act as they do. Enco?"

"I confess to being shocked," Enco said, and Paoul watched, fascinated, as his friend seemed to swell with the pride of being able to accept Ilven Fend's compliment. "I had never seen such things before, but now I understand. I meant no discourtesy to Commander Yahl, nor did I mean to criticize him."

Ilven Fend nodded, pleased with Enco's answer. "And Paoul?"

In all his years of training, Paoul could not remember ever once having told his teachers a conscious lie. Falsehood was wrong, contrary to the ethos. And besides, he had always imagined that lies were instantly found out, that the liar always betrayed himself, if not by blushing or stammering, then by some change in voice or expression that would be apparent to his elders. He had not guessed how easy a lie could be, especially when it was a lie only by omission: for what Ilven Fend had asked him was whether he understood the ethos as Enco did, and to this Paoul could give what was in fact a truthful answer.

"Yes, Ilven Fend," he said, "I too understand."

But, no sooner had he spoken, no sooner had his lie, so glibly framed and delivered, found its mark and done its work of deception, than Paoul realized he had taken an irrevocable step toward alienating himself from everything he had aspired to be. With these few words he had begun to set himself apart, to dissociate himself from the Order. A cold and yet enticing feeling rose within him that had lain dormant since his early childhood, since the time when he had been orphaned and sold and sent across the sea.

It was the feeling of being alone.

8 The vessels plying the Great River between Coblenz and Hohe were of many different kinds and sizes. Larger even than the seagoing ships of the Gehans and bohods were the sturdy, blunt-prowed riverboats, designed to carry heavy cargoes of merchandise and passengers from port to port and from landing stage to landing stage along the way. They carried little sail; going upstream, they were drawn with long ropes wherever there was a towpath, or propelled by their crewmen with poles and oars.

It was on a boat like this that Paoul and the others had begun the first stage of the tour, alighting at Coblenz. Now, for the last twenty-five miles to Hohe, Ilven Fend had decided, with uncharacteristic leniency, to take passage rather than walk. He had said that they all deserved a rest, and at first light they had boarded at the village of Imber.

The ordinary passengers traveled in the open, among the goats and sheep and sacks of grain, and were expected to lend a hand with the towropes when required. For the others, though, there was usually a cabin, which provided a degree of comfort and somewhere dry to sit. On the first trip, nearly six months ago, Ilven Fend had chosen to travel on deck; but today, on hearing that the cabin was vacant, he had gone to the expense of hiring it.

The cabin on this boat was built high on the afterdeck, and was about eight feet square, with bench seats giving a view of the river to the rear and to either side. The flag at the sternpost, Paoul had noticed, was red and black: the colors of the Thosks, and he reflected that it had been a Thosk ship that had first brought him here from Brennis. Rain had been falling for much of the afternoon; Paoul had watched the flag gradually becoming darker and more soaked, and now, as the light began to fail, it was no longer even moving with the breeze, but hanging dejectedly against its pole.

They were nearly at Hohe. Already, once or twice, they had glimpsed the citadel; after three more bends, three more bluffs of gray, fir-grown rock, the lamps and smoke and jetties of the landing place, the merchants' sheds, and the houses of the Lower Township would come into view. Staring out across the water, he could see several rafts and black coracles trailing nets and lines, and beyond them the huts and houses of one of the outlying villages. A cormorant was fishing too, its back almost awash and its neck and head protruding from the water at an angle, like a bent piece of burned wood. With a shallow leap the cormorant dived: Paoul saw its webbed feet and the oily, dark feathers of its rounded tail, and it was gone.

"Not far now," said Ilven Fend. "We should be up at the gates before locking-up. They usually wait for the last riverboat."

Enco was eating raisins. He offered the bag to Paoul who, for Ilven Fend's benefit, accepted a few and ate them. It would be better not to stare at the river anymore, better to make a more convincing job of hiding his despondency. So far he had been very careful to give no grounds for suspicion. He had applied the techniques of the taug, and since Chaer had learned to be more guarded, even with Enco; he was sure that neither Ilven Fend nor Enco had guessed what was going on in his heart.

Not that Paoul himself really knew. Looking back on the tour, he could not truly name the point at which he had realized that he no longer felt the same about the priesthood. Since Chaer he had wanted, several times, to broach the subject with Enco and more than once with Ilven Fend. His inner counsel, however, had cautioned him to keep silent. He had already received most of his tattoo; he was not fitted for life outside the Order. The only practical course now would be to accept the rest of the tattoo, to take his initiation, and to wait and see.

This was logic speaking, the voice of philosophy and of the mind, his own special field. His emotions spoke differently. With each passing mile, with each yard gained against the river current, he wanted less and less to return to Hohe.

"Look there!" cried Ilven Fend. They were rounding the second bluff, the crewmen straining at the oars, while the rain slanted down across the deck passengers and the animals and the bales of skin-covered cargo, making the planking gleam. An area of thinner cloud, a rift of brightness, had appeared in the southeast, behind the lower flanks of Mount Atar, spreading its watery light down into the valley and across the river, illuminating the inside of the cabin. At its apparent heart, at its source, lay the familiar silhouette of the citadel gates and palisade, the township, the barracks, and, above them all, the roofs of the vansery and of the temple.

"Farewell, then, Enco. Or 'Kar Enco,' I ought to say."

"No. Let me always be plain 'Enco' to you."

There was very little time left. Paoul looked once more around the small dormitory room that had been his home for almost two years. All but Enco's shelves and locker were bare; all but Enco's bed had been stripped and the bedding neatly rolled and tied. Buin and Relle had already left Hohe, gone to vanseries in the south, and this afternoon Paoul was due to board the Gehan ship taking the annual commission of inspection to Brennis. Only Enco, at the special request of Kar Ander, was staying on: he would soon be given his own chambers in the kars' quarters, where he would be employed as an assistant to the Chief Herbalist. The announcement of this honor had come as a surprise to nobody but Enco himself.

A week had passed since then, since the day of the autumn equinox and the last in the series of solemn ceremonies that had transformed Paoul and eighteen others into initiates of the Red Order. At the final ceremony Paoul had been allowed to touch the Vessel of the Forzans, and the Prime, as vansard, had supervised the completion of his tattoo and heard his vows of obedience, celibacy, loyalty, and faith. Then the Prime had touched his forehead and he had arisen as a priest.

After the rite of initiation, Forzan Zett had called each new priest to his chambers to tell him what and where his first post was to be. The vansery at Valdoe had sent word to say that, if Paoul's initiation were confirmed, and if his services were not required at Hohe, then he would be expected to begin his duties with a period of one year as a teacher in the school at Valdoe Village. His pupils, Forzan Zett had explained, were to be the sons of the military and civilian officers at the Trundle. When the year was up, he would either have to continue at the school, or, more probably, he would join the astronomers working under the new Vansard, Phede Keldis, whom he would eventually serve as a theological adviser. "However," Forzan Zett had added, in an oddly cryptic tone that had immediately put Paoul on the alert, "However, I doubt whether you will spend much longer in Brennis than is needed to repay Valdoe for their sponsorship. In something less than five years you are likely to return to the citadel.

This is a delicate and strictly confidential matter to be discussed with you by the Lord Prime, and you are invited to present yourself at his chambers tomorrow at the third hour of the forenoon."

The substance and import of that interview had thrown Paoul into a turmoil from which he thought he might never recover, a turmoil of conscience in which, by the cruelest irony imaginable, his doubts had become deeper and more numerous. And yet, even if he had not been ordered to keep silent—he had been empowered to divulge only the details of his duties in Brennis—he would still have felt unable to discuss the least of his doubts with his best and closest friend.

"I must be going, Enco."

"I could come with you as far as the gate."

"Better not."

Enco held out his hand. Paoul took it.

"Farewell. Paoul . . . I hope this is not the end of our friendship."

"So do I."

Paoul walked alone to the vansery gate. He had already taken leave of his teachers, of Erta and the other lay staff, and of the rest of his contemporaries. There was nothing left but to summon the gatekeeper and say good-bye to him also.

Once through the township, once through the main citadel gates, Paoul hefted his heavy leather bag onto his shoulder and started down the steep road to the river and the Lower Township. The afternoon was warm and bright, with a solid azure sky above the yellowing birches that lined this part of the road. Each twist and turn kept him facing more or less toward the southwest, and as he walked, passed now and then by respectful peasants and townsfolk heading uphill, he knew exactly how the appearance of the citadel behind him was changing. With the sun at his back, the darkness of the palisade would just be visible through the trees, and above it, to the right, the south face of the temple and the balconies of the Prime's quarters. There would be smoke rising from the township, perhaps three slate-blue pigeons circling in the air. And here, further down the road, the temple would have disappeared, its place taken by the twin towers of the western gatehouse, each bearing at its pinnacle a tall staff flying the personal standard of Lord Heite—an emerald-green serpent on a scarlet ground. These two flags, brilliant against the autumn sky, would be the last of the citadel that he would see before reaching the river.

The temptation was to turn and look, to permit himself a trace of sentiment. But that presupposed his continuance as a priest, his adherence to an order which he now felt he had entered dishonestly, with fraudulent vows of loyalty and obedience. And it presupposed he could live with what the Prime had told him almost a week ago.

No. He had to look. He would never see this place again.

But when he turned, he saw that the two standards had also disappeared. The citadel lay completely hidden, like Paoul's falsehood, like his reaction when he had been informed that, five years from now, he was destined to be brought back from Brennis, brought back, and entered on the long and grueling course of preparation that, one day, might end with him becoming Prime.

PART THREE

1   "Forzan Paoul! Are you here to take tea with me again? What a delightful surprise! Do be seated. Yes, there. Tell me, are they working you too hard down at that school? You mustn't let them, you know."

"I won't, Kar Houle."

It was Paoul's free afternoon. Bringing a gift of Kar Houle's favorite oatmeal-and-hazelnut biscuits, he had left his lodgings at the settlement farm and, well protected against the snow falling on Valdoe Hill, had climbed up to the vansery to visit once more the priest who, twelve years ago, had first examined him. Even then it had seemed to Paoul that Kar Houle was impossibly ancient; but, although now becoming rather frail, the old man was still quite active, taking regular walks on the hillside, practicing his daily routine of martial exercises, and working each morning in the physic garden or in the herb room indoors. His skin was liver-spotted and beginning to acquire the texture and color of the finest parchment; he had lost two or three teeth and his white hair was not quite so thick, but his eyes were just as clear and perceptive as ever. He was in his ninety-seventh year, the oldest inhabitant of the vansery, and indeed of Valdoe and perhaps the whole domain.

Paoul liked him. But there was another reason for today's visit. On the way up here, Paoul had been trying to find the words that would enable him to seek Kar Houle's advice without seeming to do so. He wanted above all just to talk freely, to find a listener who might shed light on the paradox that had taken control of Paoul's life: the paradox of distrusting the aims of the priesthood and yet revering its individual priests. Until this was resolved Paoul could not decide how to deal with the astounding revelation that they were planning to prepare him for the highest office of the empire. He did not know how many other candidates there would be, or how many different posts would intervene before the final question of his accession. But, given the opportunity, given that he was spiritually suited to such a position—and this, surely, they already believed—then he knew he had the ability to succeed. This was a fact he had demonstrated to himself over and over again. If he chose to become Prime, if becoming Prime depended solely upon himself, then, no matter how long it might take, he felt he could do it.

The Vansard, Phede Keldis, should have been the recipient of a young priest's questions, but Paoul, living as he did away from the vansery, had only conversed with him twice. Besides, to ask fundamental questions of that kind would surely be regarded as an act of heresy.

Yet Paoul had to unburden himself. He had to talk to someone. Kar Houle, with his slightly irreverent manner, his vast experience, his wisdom, and his apparent special fondness for Paoul, would be unlikely to report the contents of a dubious conversation to Phede Keldis; Kar Houle was himself the senior kar at Valdoe and a member of the vansery board. And, alarmed, fascinated, and also peculiarly reassured to discover in himself a self-protective streak of chilling and ruthless realism, Paoul had not overlooked the fact that Kar Houle did not have much longer to live.

As the servant brought the tea and arranged Paoul's gift of biscuits on a carved willow platter, Paoul framed his opening remark and decided he would speak as soon as the man had shut the door.

At last the door closed; the peg of the latch dropped into place, and Paoul felt his tenseness giving way to the act of forming the first word.

Suddenly, one of the logs in Kar Houle's hearth, whitish gray and all but consumed, collapsed and projected a smoking cinder onto the mat. Kar Houle rose and quickly threw the cinder back, and, pulling fresh logs from the basket, made up the fire. "One of the few privileges of age," he said, once he had sat down again, and nodded at the hearth. This chamber, on an outside wall of the vansery, was one of the few private rooms to have a fireplace rather than the customary cradle for heated rocks or, what was more usual still, no heating at all. "Have your lodgings improved, Forzan Paoul? Last time we spoke I sensed you were not entirely comfortable."

"I did not mean to give that impression, Kar Houle."

The old man smiled. "Well, the least we can do is give you a hot cup of tea." He handed Paoul one of the two beakers and proffered the biscuits. The gesture, the faintly sweet smell of oatmeal and honey and chopped nuts, the aroma of clover-blossom tea, reminded Paoul of the Kar Houle who had waited with him in the harbor Trundleman's quarters, who had sipped the same kind of tea and eaten the same kind of biscuits while the *Veisdrach* had been loading. For an instant Paoul was transported back there, to the moment on the ship when he had doubted Kar Houle's affection for him, and he realized that he was still no nearer knowing whether Kar Houle or anyone else in a priest's tunic was to be trusted. That providential little cinder might have spared him from what could have proved a fatal mistake.

"Tell me, Kar Houle," Paoul said, once they had drunk their tea, "how thorough is the archive we keep here? At Hohe everything that is written is put into store."

"The same applies at any vansery. Is there something specific you wish to know?"

"Not really. I was just curious."

But later, as darkness was falling and Paoul left Kar Houle's chamber, he decided to make his way to the library, not quite sure what it was that he hoped to find. From the sleeping-quarters he passed through narrow corridors lined with polished wood and lit by stone cressets, through the refectory and past the taug room, and came to the double doors of the library. After a moment's hesitation, he went in.

On the day of his arrival, Phede Keldis, conducting Paoul around the vansery, had given him the freedom of the library and had briefly shown him how the shelves and pigeonholes were arranged. The shutters had been open then; it had been sunny, and three or four priests had been at work at the low, sloping tables; another had been illustrating a copy of one of the legends, adding clustered berries to the honeysuckled border of the scroll with deft strokes of a fine squirrelhair brush dipped in crimson ink.

This afternoon there was only a single priest present, on the far side of the room, a young phede who Paoul remembered was one of the leaders of Phede Keldis's team of astronomers. His table illuminated by two freestanding lamps, he was engrossed in the uppermost of a heap of large parchments, a sky map showing the celestial dome as a circle and the stars and constellations as points of black, red, yellow, green, and blue. A measuring-rod and pair of compasses lay across the parchment and he was busily making notes on a small tablet.

He looked up as Paoul entered, acknowledged him in the informal manner, and, after making an offer of assistance which Paoul politely declined, went back to his work.

Lighting a portable lamp, Paoul approached the end of the room devoted to the archive, twenty racks extending from floor to ceiling and almost from wall to wall, so closely spaced that there was barely enough room to pass between them. Either side of each of the first fifteen racks was divided into five hundred compartments, each a hand's-width square. Many of the compartments were as yet empty; in each of the rest, tightly and concentrically rolled, were stuffed several parchments. The other five racks, differently divided, held clay tablets, sheets of wood or reed-paper, and the more precious parchments, which were stored in capped cylinders.

Some of the hieroglyphs labeling the rows of compartments were flaking away; it took Paoul a while to deduce their meaning and to trace the section containing the records of induction. These were arranged in chronological order. Finally he found the parchments covering the Year of the Blue Hare, the two hundred and eighty-seventh of the Gehan era, and pulled them out.

Of all the secrets preserved by the priesthood, writing was one of the most powerful and the most arcane. In its higher forms it was even denied to the ruling clan. The notation was based on pictures of the object to be represented, refined and augmented with a stylized version of the smoke-signaling system evolved by the army. The characters were written with a pen or brush, vertically, in columns from left to right. Paoul had been taught the latest Hohe script: Kar Houle's hand, full of old-fashioned flourishes and lacking many of the contractions that Paoul used, was nevertheless very neat and readable, and Paoul had no difficulty in finding the parchments relating to himself.

Kar Houle's report was exceedingly thorough. Paoul read it to the end. The part describing himself at seven was uncanny, so unfamiliar and yet recognizable was the embryo of his adult self. It was curious to see how much and how little he had changed, and how incompletely the boy he had known himself to be had been perceived by the kars. But the account of the search at Sturt, the interrogation of the villagers, Kar Houle's interviews with Beilin Crogh, and, most of all, the detailed examination of the ten corpses recovered from a grave in the woods and brought back to Valdoe, all this—and especially the description of an "aboriginal male in fourth decade, subject's putative father, incapacitated by old spear wound, killed by severe blow above right ear," the impartial, clinical, inch-by-inch dissection and measurement of the body of Tagart, Paoul's father, Shode, leader and chieftain of the southern tribes—all this he read with a surge of pain and adult understanding, realizing now something of what Tagart must have endured and trying to imagine him as he must once have been, in the days when he had been whole and proud and free. The knives and probes and note-taking of the kars were not the last indignity he had suffered, nor was the callous disposal of his remains, like so much refuse, "by fire": for, throughout the report, Kar Houle again and again expressed doubt that Paoul was Tagart's son. Only at the very end did he relent. "Without confirmation of these suspicions, the child's word has been accepted on this matter."

The library was empty when Paoul had finished reading: the phede, leaving one of his lamps burning for Paoul, had gone. Paoul slowly rolled up the parchments and returned them to their place. The rest of his personal records, dealing with his career at Hohe and his arrival at Valdoe, would be in the Vansard's quarters. Even if he had been free to see them, he was sure they could have told him nothing, any more than he had learned from the archive here. He still did not even know what he had wanted to find.

From the common room he could hear a five-voice chant, the contrapuntal Benison of the Night, a chant he himself had sung at Hohe. The words then had seemed moving and profound. Now they seemed to have no more warmth or solidity than the snowflakes falling so thickly outside.

Resolving to go back to his meager lodgings at the farm rather than take supper here, Paoul left the library in darkness and quietly shut the doors.

Paoul had been at Valdoe for just over three months, and he had yet to settle in or feel himself at home. The place, or his memory of it, had changed almost beyond recognition. Under the firm administration of General Teshe, the domain had prospered. Valdoe Village had grown in size, with many new buildings; but the house where Paoul had once stayed, the house of Beilin Crogh's father, had been taken over by another family. Both the father and the mother, however, were still in the village, living, Paoul

discovered, with their son, who had long since left the army and
built a commodious dwelling on the outskirts, with a large plot
in which he kept sixty or seventy beehives. He owned more
beehives in surrounding villages; Crogh had become the foremost
producer of honey in the district. He was now an important
freeman, with a place on the village council. This entitled him
to send the youngest of his sons, a lad of thirteen, to the school
where Paoul taught each day.

Classes were held in the schoolroom, part of the ornate Meeting
House, and attended in all by forty or fifty of the sons of notables
from the Trundle and from the village. The pupils varied in ability
as much as they did in age, from five to fifteen. The curriculum,
determined by Hohe, was strictly limited to the simplest treatment of practical subjects—craft, agronomy, applied mathematics, language, a little of the more accessible philosophy as it directly
affected the blue priesthood and the beliefs of the farmers. Paoul's
two fellow teachers, a middle-aged phede and the old ilven who
was in charge, seemed content with the drudgery of their lot,
but, for Paoul, only the knowledge that his position was temporary enabled him to continue. Often, though, when he was
able to treat the boys as children rather than pupils, when he was
able to forget that he was equipping them to perpetuate the rule
of the Gehans, he derived enjoyment, even delight, from his work.
The ilven had hinted that he was pleased with Paoul's influence
on the school.

One afternoon almost a month after his visit to the archive,
Paoul was approached between lessons by the ilven, who, vaguely
alluding to the fact that he would be "sorry to lose him," handed
Paoul a sealed note from the vansery. The note ordered Paoul to
report to the Vansard the following day. No reason was given for
the summons, but from the ilven's reassuring manner Paoul guessed
that there was nothing much to fear. On the contrary, it looked
as if his promotion had come sooner than he dared have hoped.

The course of the interview, though, soon took an unexpected
turn. "I have received impressive accounts of your aptitude as a
teacher," the Vansard said, once the formalities were over. He
was seated at his high-backed chair, the raw light of a late winter
morning falling across the neatly ordered parchments and tablets
on the broad surface of his desk. His brown eyes, more than ever,
seemed to be inquisitive, assessing, secretly ironic, watching Paoul
from deep sockets set under a wide forehead and closely cropped

black hair. Today he was wearing his official tunic, with a stiff, high collar which, each time he moved, rasped against the freshly shaved skin of his chin and throat. The collar was fastened with a copper pin; on his breast was a minute copper brooch, the emblem of the phedes, a serpent devouring its own tail. "The boys are better behaved," he went on. "The older ones, in particular, are less unruly. They look up to you and have become keen to learn." He held up his hand. "No, Forzan Paoul, do not protest. I speak no more than the truth. You have shown yourself an asset to the vansery, and I am most reluctant to deprive the school of your services. A week ago, however, I received a request from the Protector and, in subsequent discussions with him and with the vansery board, your name emerged. You are ideally qualified by age as well as temperament for the delicate and difficult task that General Teshe and I would like you to undertake. So uncongenial is this work that we think it only fair to offer you the chance to decline it outright as well as at the end of a probationary period." Phede Keldis gave what Paoul could only interpret as an awkward smile. "Have you been introduced to Lord Hothen?"

"No, Phede Keldis."

"I thought not. Have you seen him?"

"No, Phede Keldis. At least . . ." Paoul began, remembering once again the pathetic, deficient child he had seen all those years ago from the rail of the *Veisdrach*. "At least, not since we were small boys, and then I only saw him once and at a distance."

"What stories have you heard about him?"

"I know that he comes of age next autumn, and that some doubt attaches to his chances of being allowed to accede."

The Vansard grunted. "Have you heard about the latest incident?"

"Very little news reaches us in the village, Phede Keldis, especially where the inner enclosure is concerned."

Choosing his words with care, Phede Keldis then proceeded to explain what he wanted of Paoul. Ten days ago, Lord Hothen had beaten one of his servants so badly that he would never be able to work again. It was partly an accident: the servant had fallen down some stairs. In the normal way, of course, this incident would not have given rise to undue concern, but it was only the latest, and the worst, in a long series of outbursts. Lord Hothen was developing very badly. Becoming even more circumspect, Phede

Keldis implied that a large measure of the blame belonged to Lord Hothen's mother, the Lady Ika. She had continuously undermined General Teshe's efforts to provide him with a suitable education. She had so spoiled her son, so indulged his whims, that now General Teshe could scarcely exert effective control. But it was not as straightforward as that. Sometimes Lord Hothen could be remarkably cunning. He had manipulated his mother just as much as she had encouraged him. He was playing her off against General Teshe, perhaps in a misguided and futile attempt to have General Teshe sent back to Hohe. It was still the desire of Lord Heite that Lord Hothen should, eight months from now, be declared Brennis Gehan Sixth. Unless there was a profound change in Lord Hothen's behavior, though, Lord Heite would be disappointed and—just at a time when the domain was achieving peace and prosperity—some degree of political upheaval would be sure to result. This would reflect most unjustly on General Teshe, who was an able administrator and had borne his responsibility toward Lord Hothen with prodigious patience and restraint. In desperation, then, General Teshe had sought the Vansard's help. The idea of a new tutor for Lord Hothen, a companion, a calming influence, someone his own age who would not be seen as a threat, had come from the General himself. Paoul was the youngest priest in the vansery, only two months older than Lord Hothen, with whom he had had no contact; and his flair for teaching suited him perfectly for the job. In addition, he had been warmly recommended by Kar Houle.

The post would last only until Lord Hothen came of age. It would necessitate taking quarters in the residence, so that Paoul would be on call at all times, though one day a week would be left free for his private use. After one month—assuming, of course, that Lord Hothen had not already taken a dislike to him, or that the arrangement had not failed in some other way—Paoul would have the right to resign if he wished, without any recriminations whatever.

"Indeed," Phede Keldis continued, "you can turn it down here and now. I would not blame you if you did. It is likely to be thankless work. You only have to say."

"No, Phede Keldis," Paoul said, astounded that he should have been chosen, and already wondering what it would be like and how he would manage to deal with the delinquent Lord Hothen. He was also thinking how relieved he would be to get away from Valdoe Village, from the school, and from his lodgings at the settlement farm. "I am truly flattered. If you feel that I can be of service, I will do my very best."

"Splendid!" The Vansard put his hands together. "That is just the way Kar Houle said you'd react." He stood up. "I believe General Teshe is in his chambers at this very moment. Let us go there at once and introduce you to him. Then, this afternoon, we can go and meet your charge."

2 Rian had no idea why, but she felt a great and immediate affinity for this gentle, quietly spoken young priest. He was almost absurdly good-looking, she thought, and, it seemed, completely unaware of the fact. Even at her age she still felt a weakness when regarded by such a pair of dark eyes, and his beautiful manners, his impeccable politeness, noteworthy even by the standards of the priesthood, had won her approval from the first moment he had stepped through the threshold this afternoon. The contrast between him and Hothen could hardly be more pronounced; but—and Rian could not rid herself of the sensation that something mysterious was at work in her imagination—it also seemed that Forzan Paoul and Lord Hothen shared an uncanny, shadowy, physical resemblance.

"I'm relying on you to guide me through the first few days, Mistress Rian. I don't want to upset any customs of the household. You must tell me what is expected."

"You should not call me 'Mistress,' Forzan Paoul," she said, unable to bring herself to address him as "father": he was simply too young, barely older than Hothen himself, and not the least bit like any of the other priests she had met. "I am a slave."

"But are you not the Lady Ika's companion?"

"I was once her body slave, and my Lord Hothen's nurse, but I have no title now. I just belong to the household."

"I see," he said, brusquely, for the sake of a servant who was passing them on the corridor, but from the earnest way he looked up at her again she saw that he wanted her help still. She saw that he made no real distinction between a slave and a free woman, a servant with the right to the courtesy title "Mistress," and Rian felt herself becoming more drawn to him than ever. She could not remember when she had last been accorded the dignity of being treated not as an object, but as a human being: not since the old days, not since the days of the Lady Altheme.

It was early evening, an hour after dark, and his baggage had just arrived from Valdoe Village. He was unpacking, laying out his clothes and his few possessions in the room he had been given, a small chamber on the north side of the gallery, between the guest quarters and one of the pantries. The room, allotted to him earlier by the chamberlain, had been used as a temporary store for some of Ika's unwanted things. Rian had been in the process of removing them when Forzan Paoul had arrived. She had offered to unpack for him, but, declining, he had engaged her in conversation instead. Now she was standing in the doorway, in her arms a bundle of embroidered robes.

"Would Forzan Paoul like some flowers?"

The room seemed very bare and cold; his possessions, thinly spread on the shelves and on top of the cupboard, made it appear bleaker yet.

"Surely, at this time of year . . ."

"Dried flowers, I mean, and teasels and grasses."

"You are very kind, Rian, but please do not trouble yourself." He pushed his leather bag out of sight, under the bed. "What I would like, though, is to know what sort of dress is worn at the night meal."

"Formal, Forzan Paoul. General Teshe makes it a rule."

"Will he be there?"

"This evening I believe the General is entertaining guests in his own suite downstairs."

"And you, Rian, will you be there?"

"Yes, Forzan Paoul. I am always with my Lady Ika when she needs me." Rian suddenly remembered the weight of all the robes in her arms. "I think I ought to go to her now."

"Of course," he said, reverting to a sharper tone, for another servant had just emerged from the kitchen door farther along the gallery, releasing the odors of cooked food reaching the final stages of preparation.

The night meal was always served in Hothen's quarters, in the Flint Lord's Chamber. At one time it had often been attended by General Teshe, but no longer. Nowadays he ate there as seldom as his long and ingenious list of excuses allowed. This did not worry Rian: she feared and disliked General Teshe, and without his presence there was a better chance of surviving the meal without a tantrum. As it was, there were quite enough hidden difficulties to consider, quite enough uncertain and constantly changing likes and dislikes to remember and keep in check. Rian wondered how Forzan Paoul would fare. She had lost count of Hothen's tutors. Most had lasted only a few months, some only a few weeks, and one, whom Hothen had deliberately wounded at archery practice, had lasted only four days. All the other tutors had lived in the vansery. Forzan Paoul was the first to be given quarters here. Perhaps he was more than an ordinary tutor; after all, Hothen was getting beyond the age when there could be hope of his responding to conventional teaching.

Watching Forzan Paoul as he took his place by the dais, however, Rian began to fear for his chances. He looked too innocent, too inexperienced, despite his red tattoo and his spotless tunic of priestly gray. In the suffuse light of the pole lamps, the resemblance between him and Hothen seemed yet more marked. It even extended somehow to Ika, who, this evening, an avid listener to her slaves' gossip about the new young priest, had made a ludicrous effort to present herself at her best. At forty-three, with the tops of her arms beginning to sag, with a lifetime's inactivity recorded in the laxity of her flesh and on the coarsening grain of her skin, she should not have put on that robe; nor should she have worn those earrings or told her body slave to apply quite so much powder to the wrinkles around her blank, deformed, and sunken eyes. In fact, Rian realized with a start, Ika had made herself grotesque. Until tonight Rian had not noticed how stealthily and persistently the years had been destroying Ika's youth. It had all gone: Ika was middle-aged.

"Are we to be kept waiting yet again?" she said, as the three servants, having spread out the cloths and distributed the spoons and bowls in readiness for the meal, went out once more to the kitchen. Ika was sitting in her usual place, near the door from her chambers—from the suite reserved for the Flint Lord's lady, the rooms that Ika had no right to occupy—and Rian, as always, was sitting beside her. Hothen, the nominal head of the household, was sitting with his food taster at the dominant place, his back to the east window. Forzan Paoul was on his right. The place opposite Forzan Paoul was still vacant.

"I cannot imagine what Forzan Paoul must think of us," Ika said.

"It is early yet, my lady," Rian said quietly, hoping that Hothen's interest had not been aroused: he was sitting in his slumped, disagreeable way, making a minute and prolonged examination of the intricate carving on the handle of his spoon. Forzan Paoul was watching him calmly, as if deciding on a course of action.

Hothen had virtually ignored his new tutor. "And there was no water for her bath," Rian added.

Ika pretended not to have heard. "I believe, Forzan Paoul, that there is still one of us whose acquaintance the kindly General spared you this afternoon. She was indisposed, was she not, Hothen?"

At this moment the door from the gallery opened and, to her relief, Rian saw that Yseld had finally arrived. She looked harassed and upset; the skirts of her stone-colored robe were crumpled and a few tendrils of her hair were still damp and disheveled from her late and, undoubtedly, lukewarm bath.

Forzan Paoul rose smoothly to his feet.

"My daughter of sorts has deigned to join us, I take it," said Ika, turning toward the noise of the opening door. "Forzan Paoul, allow me to present you to the Lady Yseld."

"We have already met, my lady," he said—and Rian was not sure which one he was addressing, for his eyes were fixed on Yseld. "Two Crales ago, at the consecration of Bohod Thosk's hall."

"You have the advantage of me, I'm afraid," Yseld said. "I don't remember." But, from the faint reddening of Yseld's cheeks, from the dissembled expression of alarm and astonishment with which she had set eyes on the young man, it was plain to a woman of Rian's experience that she remembered him very well. "I must apologize. My father introduced me to so many people on that occasion."

"We spoke only for a few moments, my lady. I was merely one of the lamp bearers." And it seemed to Rian that Forzan Paoul's memory was also better than he pretended. His expression, though, remained utterly unperturbed.

Two Crales ago: that must have been shortly before the Thosk clan had begun negotiating the purchase of Yseld's marriage into this branch of the Gehans. She would have been sixteen then, and Forzan Paoul about the same, or a little older. Looking at him as he sat down again, Rian could still not believe that anyone so youthful could be a red priest, with all the knowledge and wisdom that the title implied. Yet he had the composure of a full-grown man, and the way he had acquitted himself so far was leading Rian to suspect that he could easily be underestimated. And there, on the back of his hand, was the proof, the five-pointed star that showed he had been accepted into the Red Order; and not at any vansery, either, but at Hohe, at the citadel itself.

Yseld had come from somewhere near there: her father's estate, she had once told Rian, on one of her more confiding days, was often visited by Lord Heite. Presumably she and Forzan Paoul would have known several people in common and might have been expected to exchange polite inquiries and reminiscences, but, although sitting directly opposite him throughout the whole course of the meal, Yseld preserved a cool, disinterested aloofness which, while confirming Rian's suspicions, also made her feel even more sorry for the girl. The "few moments" during which the two of them had spoken had clearly left a lasting impression on the young Lady Yseld. She had recognized him immediately. And if it had been impossible then for her to show her feelings —and not just because he was of the priesthood, although that in itself was more than reason enough—how must she be feeling now, under these circumstances, when she knew she would be seeing him every day?

As for Forzan Paoul, Rian could not deduce what he was thinking or whether he had even noticed Yseld's odd behavior. During the meal he had managed to parry Ika's remarks in such a way that each one had fallen spent before it could do any harm. As a result, Hothen had been unusually quiet and tractable. He had eaten consistently: crab soup, whiting with juniper sauce, roast woodcock, venison, raspberry clabber, dried fruit, and cheese, and as he had eaten his skin seemed to have taken on a complacent gloss which extended to the blond roots of his hair. His glittering blue eyes, set in his somewhat fat, pink face, had darted occasional glances at Forzan Paoul in which Rian had detected a combination of admiration and fear. Was it possible that, at last, Hothen was trying to win the approval of one of his tutors?

After the meal, once the dishes had been cleared and all but one of the servants had retired, Hothen, reviving a custom he had let lapse for some weeks, called for his scharan and began to play a tune. His tongue protruding wetly from the corner of his mouth, he crouched over the instrument, supporting it in his lap, and clumsily fretted the long neck of the fingerboard while his other hand drew mournful notes from the strings. Then, softly, be began to sing. He had learned the song from the under falconer, the story of a peregrine that had "raked away" and escaped. The words were maudlin and sentimental, and, although Hothen took them quite literally, it was not a peregrine the song was about, but the singer's wife.

Hothen was not very proficient at music. This attempt to show off in front of his new tutor was making Rian feel embarrassed and uneasy. It was the certain forerunner of trouble. She knew the signs of old. Yseld knew them too. She was looking down at her hands, her teeth lightly pressed into her lower lip. Forzan Paoul, however, was unabashed. He was watching Hothen, studying his technique, on his face an expression of guarded approval, as if for the effort rather than the performance itself. Strangely, while he was singing Hothen never stammered, and while he was singing Ika was always entranced.

At the end of the song her praise and applause were, as usual, the loudest and the most extravagant. Goaded by a defiant stare from her husband, Yseld quickly joined in, as did Rian, the food taster, and the serving-maid. Everyone in the room was discovering new ways to congratulate the future Lord Brennis on his artistry and skill. Everyone, that is, except the one person for whose benefit the song had been performed.

He had neither moved nor uttered a sound. He was sitting quite still, on his face exactly the same expression as before.

Becoming aware of this, Hothen turned to him and the room fell silent; even Ika had sensed that something was wrong.

Forzan Paoul waited a moment longer before speaking. Then, pleasantly, he said: "If you want my opinion, my lord, I think your playing leaves much to be desired."

The silence in the room suddenly grew to tremendous proportions. Rian felt herself pinned to the floor, helpless, horrified, and yet also curiously intrigued and detached, like someone who was both the witness and the victim of an impending natural disaster, a disaster of inconceivable ferocity and power—an avalanche, an earthquake, the end of the world. Hothen's face was registering the difficulty he was having in comprehending the enormity of what had been said. As the play of emotion intensified, as it approached and rapidly passed through all the stages she knew so well, as it gathered momentum and entered a new and most dangerous region whose existence Rian had never even suspected before, she looked away and mentally braced herself, preparing for the onslaught of his rage.

Just at the very instant she expected it to break, she heard Forzan Paoul speaking again. His voice was reason itself, blandly

courteous and kind, seamlessly impenetrable to any suggestion
of bad feeling or hurt pride. "If my lord will permit, I will show
him where he is going wrong."

Hothen had been disarmed, dumbfounded. Rian could not
believe her eyes. Neither, it seemed, could Yseld. As for Ika, she
was too surprised to react.

Forzan Paoul was holding out his hand, ready to receive the
scharan, which, meekly, and to Rian's continuing amazement,
Hothen passed across the dais.

The young priest easily and naturally adapted the long-necked,
big-bellied instrument to his grasp and, producing a few sample
notes, adjusted the pegbox to his satisfaction. In this he was quite
absorbed: it was as if the other people in the room had ceased to
exist. Then he looked up. "The first thing, my lord, is to make
sure it's in tune. Next, you must hold it properly, not bent over
it, not crouching or tensed, but like this. Your scharan should
be part of you. Its music should come as easily as thought. You
cannot think straight if you are uncomfortable. So: left hand like
this, the elbow free, the right hand held here. Do you see?"

Hothen nodded.

"Let us take the first phrase of your song. You were careless
with your fingering. You must touch the strings lightly, but precisely. I'll play the opening chords slowly so you can see. There.
And again. Now a little more quickly. Now more quickly still."

In Hothen's eyes was growing an enthusiastic light Rian had
never seen before. He was following the instruction with an intentness of which she had not imagined him capable. Until now
his scharan-playing had been regarded in the household as yet
another bad joke. No one had suspected that he might have a
real feeling for music or that through music he might be reached.
And yet it already seemed that Forzan Paoul had discovered
Hothen's vulnerable point. The notes he was playing bore only
a skeletal resemblance to the sounds Hothen had made. This was
a fragment of real music, pure and serene, and Hothen knew it.

"Now you try."

Hothen's first eager effort, however, although an improvement,
was not good. Forzan Paoul moved to his side, took the instrument, and demonstrated again. He corrected Hothen's grip and
posture and, at the second attempt, Hothen managed to produce
some chords that were a passable imitation of his teacher's. He
grinned in delight, and Rian was fleetingly reminded of the little

boy she had once sat up with and cared for. Her vigils then had occasionally been rewarded with just such a flash of pleasure. "That's good," he said, as Forzan Paoul resumed his place.

"You've made a promising start, my lord. I'll show you the next phrase tomorrow, and with it the rest of the tune."

"No. Show me now. I want you to show me now."

"You are forgetting the ladies, my lord."

"What?"

"This is not the time for a music lesson. I fear we have already trespassed on their patience more than we ought. We have been most discourteous." He turned to Yseld. "Do you accept our apologies, my lady Yseld?"

He had deliberately addressed her first, naming her, giving her precedence—the legal precedence to which she was entitled—over Ika. There could be no doubt about it. He had thrown down the challenge. He was prepared to make an enemy of Ika, if that was what it was going to take to help her son.

Yseld did not appear to know how to answer.

Rian had already decided as much, but now she was resolved to do what she had planned earlier: to put a beautiful arrangement of dried flowers in the Forzan's room.

"And my lady Ika?" he said. "Do you forgive us?"

"Yes, of course," she said, harshly. "What is there to forgive?"

"Never mind about them," Hothen said. "If they don't like it they can go to bed. I want you to show me now."

As if he had not heard, Forzan Paoul arose. "I have had a long day," he said. "With the permission of the company, I will go to bed. It is very late, my lord, and I suggest you do the same. That is, of course, if you want to be up in time for the morning's music lesson." With that, acknowledging Yseld, Ika, and the speechless Hothen, and nodding in turn to Rian and the two servants, he retired.

3 "I beg your pardon, my lady," Paoul said, on finding Yseld alone in the ground floor day room where he was accustomed to giving Hothen his morning lessons. "Is my lord not yet here?"

Until this moment Paoul had kept alive the hope that he was mistaken about her. He had hoped that her avoidance of him, which during the last four weeks she had developed almost into an art, was engendered by dislike rather than by a reciprocation of the feelings which, although he had tried to deny the fact to himself, he now realized had been growing steadily in his heart. Since that first evening, when he had been all but struck dumb by the shock of seeing her again, he had thought of little else but Yseld. She was no longer the Yseld he had met so briefly and inconclusively in the homelands and on whose image he had built such a flimsy and elaborate construction of adolescent ideals; but each addition to his sparse stock of seconds and minutes and hours spent in her company—from chance meetings on the stairs, in the corridors, in the gallery, or, where he could drink his fill of her presence, at the nightly meals—had confirmed that, at their first meeting two and more years ago, something had been exchanged that was in essence both durable and true.

She was seated by the window, where she had been looking out into the early spring rain, listening perhaps to the blackbird that was pouring out its song from a wayfaring tree in the garden of the inner enclosure. In her lap, forgotten, lay a small frame containing a half-finished embroidery in muted colors. Paoul guessed that she had been sitting here for some time, anticipating his arrival, deciding what she would finally say to him. She looked around. Her face, pale and anxious, divulged everything and he knew there could be no further hope of self-deception.

"He has gone hunting, Forzan Paoul. He did not ask me to, but I have come to offer apologies on his behalf."

Paoul came farther into the room, the floorboards creaking. His hearing told him that no one was about. This was a rare moment in the residence, rare on the ground floor, and virtually impossible upstairs, where slaves or servants were always present and there could be no such thing as a truly private conversation. Yseld had picked her time and place most carefully. Paoul thought he already knew what she was going to say, to imply, to demand of him, and he was already prepared to give it.

"I am afraid you are not helping my husband very much," she began. "At first it looked as if you were, but just lately he appears to do exactly as he pleases. This is the second time in three days that he has gone hunting without your permission."

Still she was avoiding him, avoiding his eyes. Her hands, demurely holding the embroidery frame, peeping out from the sleeves of her ocher and russet robe, could, on scrutiny, be seen to be minutely trembling. These were not the reactions of the flirt he had once imagined her to be. Her behavior at her father's banquet had anyway become understandable when viewed from the perspective of her marriage to Hothen. Evidently her father had been unable to snare Lord Mond, but she had seen it as her duty to help him try. She was not free, but a marketable commodity; her conversation with Paoul, the lamp bearer, had been a mistake, a lapse, a foolish impulse to which, for one reason or another, she had given way. The attempt to buy her into Lord Heite's immediate family having failed, Bohod Thosk must have been compelled to set his sights lower and her dowry had ended up here.

In theory she was the future Lady Brennis. In fact, as Paoul had observed, she was subordinate to her husband's mother, and had been relegated to the guests' quarters. At first Paoul had believed—listening at night from his own chamber, which nearly adjoined hers—that she was Hothen's wife in name only and that Hothen was content with the services of the two concubines who singly or together visited his bed. On the fourth night, though, Paoul had heard her summoned to his room.

Paoul had never really known jealousy before. Despite all his training, it must have affected his attitude toward Hothen: there could be no doubt of that. To begin with Paoul had found Hothen a pitiable creature, dominated by a mother who only made his difficulties worse. He had seemed more stupid than cruel, constantly baffled by the workings of a reality he would never be able to understand. Within a week, however, Paoul had come to understand the view of the slaves and servants. Rian, in particular, had unwittingly revealed how much she detested Hothen and sympathized with his lady. What Rian would never know, and what Paoul had not been certain of until now, was that his own continuing presence here would make Yseld's position not just worse, but intolerable.

"This afternoon, my lady," he said, sparing her from having to broach the subject further, "I am due to see the Vansard and General Teshe. We will be discussing my place as Lord Hothen's tutor. Today marks the end of my month's probation." This, he was sure, she already knew. The subject had arisen the other night at the meal. Although she had appeared inattentive at the time, she must have been listening: why else would she have come here this morning? "If I so request," Paoul went on, "I will be relieved of my duty and sent back to teaching at the village school. I can tell you now, my lady, that I have already decided to make that request."

"Indeed." She did not raise her eyes to his. "That is rather a shame, Forzan Paoul, but in the end I think it is probably for the best. My lord is getting too old for a tutor. He has never responded well to discipline."

The blackbird stopped singing. In the unexpected silence, unbroken even by the soft descent of the rain outside, Paoul realized he was in all likelihood speaking to her for the last time. In the future, if he saw her at all it would be in company, at some official function. He would never have the opportunity to be with her like this again.

But, as she had said, it was probably for the best. He was a red priest, and a red priest was not allowed to feel this way. He was not allowed to ache when he looked upon the girl whose memory he would forever carry in his closest thoughts. He was not allowed to long to touch her or even simply to call her, just once, by her unadorned and birth-given name.

"Does my lady know where he has gone?"

"To the woods at Lavant, I believe. They left about an hour ago."

"If you will excuse me, then, I ought to go and seek him out."

With a small and somehow fatalistic movement of her head she indicated her acquiescence and Paoul, trying to remain outwardly calm, passed through the door and left her alone, still sitting at her place by the window.

"Kar Houle is worse," the Vansard said, from behind his desk. "Did you know?"

"No, Phede Keldis. I did not."

Paoul could not really comprehend what was being said. It was all he could do to maintain his composure in front of the Vansard and General Teshe. His request to leave the residence and get away from Yseld, to leave her and go back to the village, had just been, in so many words, flatly refused. They had said that the remarkable improvement in Hothen was directly attributable to him and could not be allowed to end. They had praised him and urged him to reconsider. Then, when he had pressed the point and tried to insist on his right to resign, the Vansard's manner—veiled, as always, with the punctilious correctitude that was one of the most effective weapons in a red priest's armory—had become rapidly less pleasant. He had all but accused Paoul of acting against the interests of the empire. The penalty for that was invariable and swift.

Paoul was shocked. He could not believe that such a trifling dispute should have immediately called forth the full weight of the Vansard's authority. But he was even more surprised by the Vansard's lack of scruples. He had not imagined any red priest, least of all a vansard, capable of this kind of behavior. The Vansard had been supported in his dishonesty by the silent, worldly approval of General Teshe, massive in his gray armor and cloak, legs crossed, fingertips meditatively raised and touching, observing Paoul and from time to time pursing his lips as if mildly amused. Cynicism, lies: these were his stock in trade. He cared nothing for the integrity of the Order. If one of its priests did not willingly bend, he would have to be forced, no matter what damage that did to him or to his future development.

In these few minutes, Paoul had grown up. Just as he had clung to the belief that he was mistaken about the Lady Yseld, so had he been clinging to the last remnants of his vision of the priesthood as something noble and rare. Between them, General Teshe and the Vansard had broken his hold. They had revealed the Order for what it was, an integral part of the world of politics and expediency. The laws of that world applied to him too. Somehow he had believed himself immune. Somehow he had not expected to give an account of all the years and resources they had invested in his training. They had made him. Now, for the sake of the few remaining months of Hothen's education, they were prepared to destroy him. No matter that Hothen would never be what they wanted: it was the will of Lord Heite that the effort should be made. No matter that Paoul was capable of higher service, no matter that he had been selected as a potential Prime. If he were ruined, disillusioned, rendered unable to aspire, there would be plenty of others to take his place.

"Kar Houle?" said General Teshe. " 'Worse'? Do you mean he's ill?"

"He has been ailing for some time. A fortnight ago he collapsed in the refectory. Kar Vever diagnoses no particular cause; the real culprit is age. Kar Houle is a very old man indeed."

Paoul said, "Is he still comfortable?"

"Yes, I believe so."

"Is he receiving visitors?"

"Certainly, Forzan Paoul. He would be pleased to see you, I'm sure. But check with Kar Vever first."

"Yes. Yes of course."

As Paoul was about to rise from his seat—for, plainly, he had now been dismissed—a fanciful idea which had occurred to him after a difficult morning with Hothen a week ago, returned to him in a more serious guise, not as a means to deal with Hothen's problems, but as a chance of being reunited with the only person in whom Paoul felt he might, at last, be able to confide, and whose advice, for the sake of friendship, would perhaps be impartial and sound.

"Phede Keldis," he said. "I have been giving further thought to the question of Lord Hothen."

The Vansard raised his eyebrows. As far as he was concerned, the whole subject was closed.

Paoul prepared himself for a rebuke, but pressed on anyway. "Before leaving the citadel, Phede Keldis, I chanced to hear about some remarkable work the kars are doing now. I have a friend who has been appointed an assistant to the Chief Herbalist. We took the tattoo together."

"And?"

"He told me about a new treatment they are developing for disorders of the mind. It uses new herbs, brought from the east. In certain cases, the results are said to be spectacular."

The Vansard glanced at General Teshe.

"I do not know whether Lord Hothen might benefit, but it seems possible, even likely. I wonder if Kar Vever . . . I wonder if he is aware of it."

"We receive all the usual bulletins from Hohe. I imagine Kar Vever is fully conversant with the latest developments in his art."

"The treatment is very new, Phede Keldis. It may not have reached the bulletins yet."

"What is the name of your friend?"

"Kar Enco."

"Are you suggesting that I ask for him?"

"He is very highly qualified, Phede Keldis, but the final choice would of course be Hohe's."

Phede Keldis gave an icy smile and Paoul wondered whether he had gone too far. "I will speak to Kar Vever about this." Paoul arose. "Thank you, Forzan Paoul. Your suggestion may well prove helpful—whomsoever Hohe chooses to send. And thank you for agreeing to continue with Lord Hothen. It will not be forever."

Not forever: but it might as well have been. Hothen would be twenty, officially, on the first day of the eleventh moon, seven months hence. That meant he would not come of age until at least two hundred more days had elapsed, or, as Paoul calculated on the way to Kar Vever's door, some one hundred and seventy working days, each of which might produce any number of encounters with the Lady Yseld. He did not know how he would manage even the first. What could he tell her? How could he explain what had happened? She would surely never believe that the Vansard had gone back on his word.

But, once he had gained permission to see the patient and was on his way to Kar Houle's room, Paoul became aware that the source of his agitation was not simply anxiety for Yseld's sake, but this mixed with pleasurable anticipation and fear. He was ashamed to discover that he was secretly glad to be returning to the residence.

Of course, absolutely nothing could come of it. Not the slightest hint of his feelings could ever be allowed to escape. It would be too dangerous, disastrous for them both, a crime not only of the grossest and most unthinkable impropriety, but a treasonable offense. And they would be certain, eventually, to get caught.

And yet—was it not possible, even now, that he was wrong about her feelings? Was it not a great presumption and a conceit to imagine that his presence or absence could make any difference to her? What, after all, did he know about matters of the heart? What had he learned about men and women, except for the austere, factual teachings of the kars and the ill-informed sniggerings of his classmates at Hohe?

Even so, he felt ashamed. He had broken his promise to her. Through cowardice, he had not resisted the Vansard as strongly as he ought. For the sake of honor, he should have refused outright to continue, no matter what consequences that brought on himself.

4 As the spring advanced toward summer, Kar Houle's condition correspondingly declined. Paoul visited him as often as his duties with Hothen allowed, and so was not fully conscious of the magnitude of the changes that less frequent visits would have made plain: the wasting of his flesh, the dulling of his eyes and their gradual withdrawal into the sockets, the worsening pallor and grayness of his skin. At an earlier stage in his illness, Kar Houle had been able to get up for short periods, to sit by his fire or even, on sunny afternoons, to bask in a sheltered corner of the physic garden among his beloved plants; but recently even that had been denied to him and he now remained permanently in bed. His old hands lay limply for hours on end in one place on the counterpane. The color of his tattoo seemed itself to have dulled as much as his gaze, which was usually directed at a point some scores of yards or miles or years beyond the whiteness of the far wall. Whenever Paoul had come in, though, he had always managed to greet him, however feebly; he had always managed to absorb and enjoy Paoul's tidbits of harmless gossip; and, before he tired, he had always managed to smile at least once.

Until today. Today it had taken him some time just to recognize his visitor, and Paoul knew at last, for himself, that what Kar Vever had first said six weeks and more ago was right: Kar Houle was dying. At breakfast, interrupting his own preoccupations, Paoul had received a message from Kar Vever and had come straight from the residence to the vansery. "He's been asking for you," Kar Vever had said. "I don't think he can last much longer."

"Is he in pain?"

"No. But I suspect the end will come as a relief."

A week ago Paoul had been told that the Chief Herbalist had granted Phede Keldis's fraternal request: Enco had been released to treat Hothen. He would arrive by the next merchantman from Hohe, the ship following the one that had brought the news.

Enco was coming. Any day now, he would be traveling the road from Apuldram up to the Trundle. He was coming, and Paoul had made it happen. By tweaking the Vansard's vanity,

Paoul had managed to manipulate the organization of the Order to suit his own ends. The thought filled him with astonishment, with disbelief in his own impudence.

Much more than this, though, was occupying his mind. Deny it as he might, he was now certain of Yseld's feelings. After two more months in the residence, two more months of night meals and conversations in which only the words spoken were superficial and impersonal, he was certain. Worse: he was afraid that some of the entourage—particularly Rian—were beginning to suspect how matters lay.

His growing certainty about Yseld had been matched by his growing unhappiness with the Order and what it stood for. His qualms had started long ago—as far back as that night after seeing the Lady Atane at the lake, when Starrad had explained Lord Heite's motives for taking her there. His misgivings had greatly increased on the tour; the steady accumulation of disturbing sights had finally overflowed, perhaps, in that small room at Chaer where Reisen had died; or, if not there, then at the brigands' camp and during the ensuing scenes at the fort. And, here in Brennis, Paoul had found his doubts crystallizing into something which, for want only of proof, would become a firm conviction. If that happened, he would no longer want to be a priest. He would no longer wish to be part of the conspiracy of religion and military power that fed upon the weakness of the common people and kept them in a permanent state of deprivation. The tour had taught him that the empire relied for its continuance on a single truth: that farming, demanding a relatively settled way of life, alone created a fixed population which could be cheaply dominated and controlled. The farmers got very little back for their taxes; it seemed to Paoul that the Gehans were nothing but a highly successful version of what those brigands had tried to be. The Order bestowed on the ruling clan a spurious sheen of rectitude, of divine right springing from a deity that the Gehans had themselves invented. Like much of the faith, the Gehans' place in the scheme depended on circular argument. They were the ruling clan and hence occupied the dominant place; because they occupied the dominant place, Gauhm had fitted them to be the ruling clan.

This was heresy of the first magnitude. Except in his bleakest moments, Paoul still could not bring himself to believe it might be true. Yet, in recent months—especially since his visit to the archive—he had found himself thinking more and more often of Tagart and of the stories Tagart had told him about the old times. Although Paoul had been so young, he knew that Tagart had loved him with a father's love, perhaps the only genuine love he had ever received. He was beginning to see how important it had been. Tagart had laid the foundation of Paoul's character and given him an independence of spirit that now threatened to be his undoing. Paoul recalled that Tagart, who had been right about so much else, had condemned the farmers and farming itself as intrinsically unnatural and therefore evil. And had not Tagart also warned him to beware of the priests, the red priests with the five-pointed stars on their left hands? Had he not called them worse than the soldiers, worse even than the Flint Lord himself?

Paoul was profoundly perplexed. It would be so much easier to forget his doubts and hold to the faith as a true ideal, to accept that it was the only conceivable way of describing and explaining the world. Indeed there was much in it that was undeniably true. It would be easy and safe to accept it all and play his allotted part in the hierarchy. He could never hope to leave: they had marked him for life. His tattoo announced to the world that he had taken his vows and was to be regarded as a servant of the Earth Goddess. But, by doubting, he had already broken those vows and forfeited the right to wear the red pentacle.

He did not know what to do. He was young and inexperienced; he was prepared to believe himself mistaken. More: he was eager to believe himself mistaken. He longed to receive some evidence of it. That was what he wanted from Enco, and that was what he wanted from Kar Houle, but had always been afraid to ask.

Above Kar Houle's bed, hanging from a peg against the roughness of the wall, was an oak and boxwood plaque, perhaps his own confirmation plaque, made seventy-five or eighty years before. This was the only permanent decoration in the room; but on a wicker table beside him, next to Paoul's chair, someone had placed a patterned bowl containing a cluster of freshly picked moon daisies.

"Kar Thurman brought them," Kar Houle said. "That was kind of him."

The heat of the morning sun, falling on the canopy at the window, was making the timbers expand and gently creak. From the outer enclosure, beyond the vansery grounds, came the irregular clinking of the flint knappers at work, the sound of parading soldiers, the bleating of goats, and, from somewhere nearer at hand, the repeated cadences of a singing chaffinch. All these sounds, the commonplace sounds of an ordinary day, seemed to stop short at the window and enter in a more respectful form, as if reluctant to intrude; but the light, the intense, wholesome sunshine of late spring, entered fearlessly and found itself transformed by the white walls and ceiling into a diffusion that found its way among the pale shadows cast by the petals of each daisy and penetrated even to the recesses of the yellow disc of florets at the heart.

Paoul felt as if he were standing at a threshold. Behind him was the cold and desolate room where no one could be trusted. Ahead was another room which might be different. He had no way of knowing, except by taking one more step. With that step he might begin to learn the truth, but taking it might alarm and distress Kar Houle, and that would be unforgivable. Unless he spoke now, though, Paoul knew he might never be presented with another chance.

The bowl of flowers had become the exaggerated focus of his attention, sparing him from looking at Kar Houle. The daisies had become strangely peaceful and sharply defined, at one with the natural world. In a few hours they would begin to wilt. Tomorrow they would be thrown away.

"Is something troubling you, Paoul?"

There was no expression in Kar Houle's eyes, no clue to his feelings. Surely he knew he was dying. What thoughts were passing through his head, what memories of his long years of rich yet abstinent life? What did he see when he looked at Paoul? Himself as a young man?

"Kar Houle, I would like to ask your advice."

"I am listening."

"Kar Houle . . ." he began, and then the words were coming of themselves, "is it right that one should question the faith?"

Still there was no expression in Kar Houle's eyes. "We should always question. Questioning is all we ever do."

"Then . . . is it right to question the aims of the ruling clan?"

"Be more specific."

"Is it right to ask whether the Gehans exist as a force for good?"

Kar Houle did not answer; his eyes registered no reaction, but he moved his left hand on the counterpane, opening it toward Paoul in an invitation which Paoul instinctively accepted. Kar

Houle's grasp was feeble. It was no longer the firm and confident grip with which he had bade Paoul farewell on board the *Veisdrach*. Now it seemed to convey an urgent warning that could not be put into words, a fear for Paoul's safety.

Kar Houle turned his head on the pillow. "How beautiful they are," he said. "The flowers. You would not think we use them as an irritant. They promote the flow of blood. In the skin. Everything has its place, you see." He looked back at Paoul, and for a moment it seemed as if he had said as much as he dared.

Then, suddenly, his whole expression changed. Yes, he knew he was dying: there was no longer any reason to keep silent or to let anything artificial remain between Paoul and himself.

The grip of his hand tightened. "They're evil," he said, almost in a whisper. "All of them. I'm sorry for what I have done to you." He let Paoul's hand go. His head seemed to sink deeper into the pillow.

"Kar Houle—"

"No." Kar Houle weakly shook his head. "No more talk. I am feeling very tired, and you must return to your duties."

"Shall I come to see you later?"

"Yes. Please do. I would like that."

The temple at Valdoe had been built not in the vansery, but on a slight and partly man-made eminence on the southern slope of the hill, between the Trundle and the flint workings. The temple doors, facing south toward the sea, commanded a panoramic view from the newly built fort at Bignor in the northeast, right around to Bow Hill in the northwest. The structure, thirty-four feet across at the widest point, was of imported stone, with a pitched and deeply eaved roof. In plan view it occupied an unequal pentagon with its long axis running from east to west. The altar ran the length of the west-facing wall. It consisted of a wide slab bearing the four figures of the Family of Gods. On the right, on the northern side, stood Tsoaul the Father, the spirit of manifestation and of summer. On the left was Ele the Daughter, ruling spirit of winter and dormancy. In the center, the largest and most striking of the sculptures, Gauhm the Mother, was depicted in the act of giving birth to Aih the Son.

On the hill forty-five yards away to the east was a curving stone wall, the height of a man and with a small aperture at its center. The aperture aligned exactly with a vertical slit in the eastern corner of the temple at the junction of the two longest walls, in such a way that, at the moment of sunrise on the day of the equinox, a beam of light illuminated the figure of Gauhm. The two ends of the curving wall were also aligned with the slit, and defined the furthest travel of the point of sunrise between the summer and winter solstices. Thus, in the absence of cloud or fog, the altar was illuminated four times a year, the beam striking the figure associated with the forthcoming season.

"Yes, my lord," Paoul said. "I saw it myself, at the spring equinox."

Hothen was peering through the slit. "What about the winter solstice? Did you see it then?"

"No. That day was cloudy."

Paoul had brought him here this morning as part of a lesson illustrating the potential of accurate construction. The visit was not going well. It had been specially arranged in advance through Phede Keldis; otherwise, Paoul would have cut it short and gone back to the residence. Hothen was in an awkward mood, and Paoul felt in no condition to control him. Since leaving Kar Houle's room, Paoul had been in a kind of daze. There was no unusual sound in his ears, but his thoughts were immobilized as though by a deafening roar of surf. He could not comprehend, not yet, not really, what Kar Houle's reaction meant to him.

Hothen raised his hands to shield either side of his head. "It's very dark in there."

They were standing on the glaring shingle that extended from the temple walls to the surrounding yew hedge. The hedge was now waist-high, consisting of seedlings taken from hallowed ground on Mount Atar and grown along four of the five sides of the temple court. The rest of the temple precincts, two acres in all, were enclosed by a line of chalk boulders. On the south side the turf had been marked out for a new tumulus; the old barrow of the Brennis Gehans had been destroyed by Torin Hewzane. On the north side was the vansery burial mound, already occupied by three priests who had died in service here. In the precincts and beyond, across the face of the hill, were many pairs of notched posts, short or tall, temporary or permanent, which the phedes used for the study and measurement of the heavens. A few of these posts had even been planted among the spoil heaps and shaft heads of the flint mines, farther down the hill. Paoul had once wondered what the luckless slaves there made of them or of the ceremonies enacted at the temple itself.

Hothen said, "I want to go inside."

"I am afraid that is not possible, my lord. The doors are locked."

"Unlock them, then."

"I do not know how. Besides, we have no business inside. We should not even be looking through the slit. Phede Keldis gave us permission only to examine the exterior."

"Phede Keldis, Phede Keldis," Hothan said, becoming ominously more fluent. "That old turd. He doesn't own the hill. I do. That means I own the temple as well."

Paoul said nothing.

"Open the doors."

"My lord, that is impossible, as I have explained."

Hothen looked over his shoulder, toward the place where his bodyguards—a team of five men in black and gray armor, hand-picked by General Teshe—were waiting outside the hedge. "Are you disobeying my orders, you stuck-up little bastard?"

This was the way he usually addressed his slaves, or anyone who displeased him; he had never spoken to Paoul like this before. He had always treated Paoul with a certain timidity, deferring to his person as well as his rank. That had now vanished: in its place was a hot, sudden surge of resentment. Impossible as it seemed, Paoul could not help but think that behind it all was Yseld, as if Hothen unconsciously knew what had happened and remained unspoken between his wife and his priestly, supposedly incorruptible tutor. For a curious moment Paoul thought Hothen was going to throw a punch. Hothen was taller and heavier, but he was also clumsy and soft, and he would know that Paoul, that any red priest, was adept in an invincible and exasperating system of self defense that turned the adversary's every move against itself.

Hothen unclenched his fists. He looked over his shoulder again. "Guards!"

The five bodyguards, each armed with a shield and a short spear, jumped over and through the hedge and, boots crashing on the shingle, ran to Hothen's side. The team leader, Hace, a dark, powerfully made man of thirty, gave his crispest salute. "My lord!"

However good his unarmed combat, no single man was any

match for a team of spear-wielding soldiers, least of all a team chosen in person by General Teshe. Paoul was unable to quell a twinge of fear. The way they had leaped the hedge showed how little they cared for his authority or the sanctity of the temple. Hothen was so unpredictable that he might order these men to do anything, and there was no absolute guarantee that they would not obey.

But he did not tell them to attack Paoul. "I want you to go to the flint workings," he said. "Get an ax. Better still, get something heavy. Really heavy. A tree trunk, or something. Then break down the temple doors."

Hace managed to conceal his surprise, but let slip an apprehensive and questioning glance at Paoul which filled Paoul with relief.

"There's no need to look at him! You get your orders from me!"

"I'm sorry, Team-leader," Paoul said. "Lord Hothen is jesting. He knows it is more than your life is worth to damage the temple. We just wanted to test your readiness and see how you would react to such an impossible command."

Hace visibly relaxed. "Very good, my lord. Will that be all?"

Without making himself seem ridiculous, Hothen could say nothing more. He had been thwarted. His anger, thus turned in on itself, became more heated than ever, and Paoul saw a flash of genuine hatred in his eyes.

"No, Hace, that will not be all. I'm going back to the residence. Without him." He turned obliquely toward Paoul, but took care not to address him directly. "I've had enough of this shit for one day."

At Hohe, whenever one of the newer pupils had thrown a tantrum, he had been appropriately chastised by his teacher. The technique had proved effective. Not a few of the boys, those perhaps from wealthier homes, had at first shown signs of being spoiled which had been quickly eradicated. Hothen was not too old to benefit from the same treatment. Indeed it was remarkable that he had escaped it for so long, remarkable and strange, even suspicious. For, although Phede Keldis had outwardly given Paoul wide discretion in his approach, Paoul sensed that a request to use the most obvious form of control would be refused.

As Hothen turned his back and walked away, Paoul considered bypassing the Vansard and acting on his own responsibility. But this was not the time to do it, when Hothen was with his body-guards, and nor was it the place. The temple had already been defiled enough, by Hothen's intrusive inspection of the interior, by his behavior and bad language, and by the boots and weapons of his guards.

Watching Hothen and the guards climbing the slope, letting them go, Paoul acknowledged that there was something else making him hold back. He saw that he wanted to punish Hothen not from any high-minded motives of correction, but from personal animosity that had its origins with Yseld. Had it not been for her, Paoul would have been able to view Hothen and his failings properly, with detachment. That was no longer possible.

At the flint mines, a quarter of a mile away in the opposite direction, under the midday sun, he could see soldiers and overseers standing about. One lifted a water bottle to his lips and drank. Other figures, slaves, were busily carrying timbers to and fro, or hauling baskets and leather buckets of spoil away from the shaft heads. Down below, in the claustrophobic darkness under the hill, many more would be at work, digging, prizing from the native rock the flint that had made Valdoe wealthy, that had paid for Paoul to be trained and put the clothing on his back.

Paoul could not make the mistake of envying the slaves the simplicity of their lives, but at least the duties of a miner were well defined. He worked his shift, returned to his quarters, ate, slept, worked again. Nothing was required of him but to dig flint. His thoughts and beliefs were his own affair; his prison was made of tangible things—wooden bars, the clubs and spears of his overseers. The Gehans deprived him only of his physical liberty. He wore no tattoo; if ever he escaped he had a real chance of remaining free.

Turning his eyes from the flint workings, Paoul looked more to the west, where a finger of forest yet remained between Valdoe and Apuldram. Starting there, it would be possible, traveling almost entirely under the trees, to find a way beyond the Weald, to the ancient uncut forest farther north. There were no tribes of hunters left, no one who knew, as Tagart's people had known, how to thrive in the wild, but an existence of sorts might be found there. In his childhood, in the group, Paoul had learned the names and edibility of the animals and birds. He had learned how to make a trap and light a fire. The rest he could teach himself.

No. He would never be able to survive alone. Tagart had taught him that. It was the first and most important law of the forest. And if Tagart or Fodich—men who had been born and bred to the life—had been powerless to circumvent that law, what sort of chance would Paoul have?

The sun was very pleasant here. So was the feckless feeling of having nothing to do. But already Paoul knew he ought to be getting back to the residence, in case Phede Keldis or General Teshe discovered Hothen was on his own; and he knew he ought to let as little time as possible elapse before finding Hothen again. It would only make his job harder if he allowed Hothen's resentment to simmer for too long.

But it was with an effort that Paoul started across the temple precincts, toward the narrow gateway in the hedge and the fortress at the top of the hill.

5 Besides the four great Valdoe fairs there were smaller, monthly markets, set up outside the southwest gates and consisting of fifteen or twenty stalls under broad awnings of colored fabric or skin. Their proprietors were mostly peddlers, itinerant traders; a few were more ordinary folk, farmers from nearby villages with seed or produce for sale.

This month's market was officially due to open the following day, but already several stallholders had arrived and were unpacking their wares.

Paoul, returning from the temple engrossed in thought, felt his throat constrict. The subject of his thoughts was there, walking by the stalls with Chreo, her companion; and she had seen him. She waved.

Her wave was perplexing. He had been expecting her to ignore him, to pretend, as usual, that she had not seen him, to avert her eyes. He could do little but wave back. His line to the southwest gatehouse would take him to her; he could not very well proceed without stopping to acknowledge Lord Hothen's wife.

"You're the very person I wanted to see," she said. "Look. That vase over there. The little blue one. What do you think of it?"

The vase, of classical proportions and patterned with great artistry in two shades of sea-blue, looked out of place among its neighbors, the clumsy pots, pitchers, and bowls that were the usual denizens of such stalls.

She did not wait for Paoul's reply. "The man wants thirty scrapers, but Chreo says it's too much."

"Then Chreo is wrong, my lady."

"Exactly, Chreo. What did I tell you?"

Paoul felt again the ache that was inseparable from her presence and the sound of her voice. Today she was wearing the fine gray robe edged with maroon in which she looked, he thought, at her most beautiful. Her hair had been brushed until it shone. It had been tied loosely at the nape of her neck, in just the way he loved it best. In this moment, while her head was turned and she was teasing her staid, middle-aged companion, Paoul was able to study her freely. Then she turned back.

"Does my lady want the vase?" he said.

"Why, certainly."

Her eyes, her brown eyes which until now had always entreated him to keep away, looked directly into his and it was as though a soft barrier inside him—inside her, inside them both—had just been breached. Something had happened. Something had changed. Something reckless was taking hold of him that he did not want to resist. It had to do with the long chain of events beginning with Dagda and Bocher, leading, through his years of training, to the Lady Atane, to the tour, to Kar Houle and the feeble grasp of his hand. It had to do with Tagart and the forest and the miners under the hill. But most of all it had to do with Yseld.

"I'll see what can be done," he said.

The dealer was a swarthy fellow who looked none too honest. At Paoul's approach, however, it seemed as if he suddenly repented of his past triumphs. After a little haggling, Paoul acquired the vase for twenty-five scrapers, which he took from the wallet at his belt.

"Please accept it as a gift, my lady."

"I couldn't. Thank you, but I really couldn't."

"Then you will have offended me and made a mortal enemy."

She laughed. "That wouldn't do, would it, Chreo? We need Forzan Paoul on our side." She took the vase. "Thank you. It's lovely."

He could not understand the change in her. He was seeing a different Yseld.

She said, "Shall we walk together? I'd like to talk privately with you about my husband's schooling."

At this, Chreo dutifully dropped several paces behind, and she in turn was followed by two bodyguards in red and gray, men of the group detailed to accompany Yseld or Ika whenever they left the safety of the inner enclosure.

"My husband gave me his version of what happened at the temple, Forzan Paoul, and now he's sulking. He's such a fool, I don't know how you put up with him. At least his guards had the grace to look embarrassed."

"What did he tell you?"

"Enough. It sounds rather funny as well as stupid. He's not

amused, of course, but then he never is. I only wish I could have been there to see it."

"He is sick, my lady."

"What, in the head? That's one excuse, I suppose."

They walked a few yards in silence. Paoul had the feeling that she wanted to take his arm: he would gladly have offered it. He would have renounced everything for a chance to touch her, to remain in contact with her, to feel her body come closer to his. As it was, this experience of walking beside her would feed a thousand dreams. He did not want to spoil it by calculating how many yards were left to him, but the gatehouse was already drawing near. Once across the outer enclosure, once through the inner gate and along the path to the main door, they would have to part.

"You wished to talk about his schooling, my lady."

"Yes. His schooling. Forzan Paoul, do you think he will accede? Will Hothen be the next Flint Lord?"

"That is not for me to say."

"But you must have some idea."

"The Vansard and General Teshe will decide. I am not party to their decisions. If I knew, my lady, I promise I would tell you."

"It is very important to me."

Now Paoul understood her change in mood. The incident at the temple had made her realize that there was a possibility Hothen might not accede. If he did not accede, then her marriage might be declared void, contracted as it was on the understanding that her husband was to be the future Lord Brennis.

"Do you see why it is so important to me?"

"Yes."

"The law of Hohe is complicated and difficult. But you know it. You have been trained in it. You are the only one I can trust."

"If there are precedents, they will be in our library. I can find out."

"When?"

"Immediately. Once I have placated my lord."

Paoul did not know how all this had happened: his resolutions had been set aside. In the space of a few yards they had become conspirators. She knew his secret. She had known it from the start.

They passed under the gatehouse and ahead he saw the single gate of the inner enclosure. Their time together would soon be up.

"Could you meet me?" she said. "Once you've been to the library."

"In the rest hour after the noon meal. It is quiet then. Would that suit my lady?"

"Yes. But where?"

"In the downstairs day room."

"No. Not in the residence. Outside."

"In the garden, perhaps."

"Yes, in the arbor. Will you meet me there?"

"At the second hour."

"I'll be waiting."

"And in that case too?" she said.

"Yes. Nullified. The husband was made to yield to the cousin's claim. His wife and issue were entailed on the cousin."

"What does that mean?"

"His wife and children were given to the cousin as part of the title."

"When was this?"

"Over a hundred years ago. But it makes no difference. Once the Prime has ruled, his precedent must always be followed. That is the basis of the law. Only the Prime himself can change it."

She looked down at her lap.

Paoul gazed at her, listening to her breathing. He could smell her perfume, the same that she wore sometimes at the night meal, only now it was much stronger, as if its fragrance were an integral part of her, brought to life by the heat of her body. She had not changed her clothes, but as a concession to the warmth of the afternoon she had loosened one of the minute fastenings at her neck, revealing the side of her throat.

At this time of day no birds were singing; the only sound from the garden was the drone of the bees, visiting bloom after bloom on the branches overhead. The shrubs of the arbor were so thick that only a sprinkling of sunlight penetrated the interior to the flagged floor and the quaintly formed stone bench. The bench was not long: she was seated close beside him, on his right. He had never sat this close to her before. He had never sat this close to any girl. In all his imaginings he had never dreamed of anything as vivid or stultifying as this. He wanted to break out of his dream, to touch her, but did not know how to begin.

"Was there ever a case of a wife going free?"

"Not that I know. In law, a wife is regarded as property to be disposed of as the owner wishes. But if a man does not want a wife he has inherited as part of a title, he is bound to offer her in the first instance to her former husband. The same goes for children. Their father may buy them back, provided he has the funds. The price is set by the High Council, and a third is paid into their office.

"That's barbarous."

At one time Paoul would have been shocked to hear such a term applied to the methods of the Prime. But now he made no comment.

"So," she said, "if Hothen does not accede, I will be given to the next Lord Brennis as part of the Valdoe domain. If he does not want me, I will be offered back to Hothen. And if Hothen can't or won't pay the price, I'll be sold to the highest bidder. Is that right?"

"That's my understanding of the law."

"But what if my father pays the price? Can he do that?"

"There is no reason why not."

"So he could buy me back from Hothen."

"Provided Hothen fails to accede. Otherwise, the marriage contract is binding and cannot be revoked."

"But there is a faint chance, isn't there?"

Paoul nodded.

The rest hour was nearly over. In a few minutes he would have to return to the residence for the afternoon's lessons. He did not want to go but, by shifting slightly on the bench, he must have reminded her of the passing time, for she stood up. He too rose.

"Forzan Paoul," she said. "I am so grateful. I did not mean to burden you with my troubles. Especially when you yourself always look so sad."

"Surely not." He was genuinely surprised: an ability to contain the emotions was a stated object of the taug.

"The others might not notice. In fact I'm sure they don't."

"But you do."

"Yes. I do."

There was a light breeze blowing, the lightest imaginable, barely enough to stir the leaves. It was coming in off the calmness of the sea, a stream of pure, sweet air like the first breath of summer. In the pause that followed before she spoke again, Paoul became aware of its subtle sound in the foliage.

"Are you very unhappy, Forzan Paoul?"

He gave assent with his eyes. In a low voice he heard himself saying, "Do you know the reason?"

"I think so."

Her whispered reply was like the breeze, the secret sound of acquiescence. The final restraint of his yearning had been removed. His equilibrium, hers, had gone: the space between them was melting away. He felt her arms around him, her fingers on his neck, and under his own hands was the weave and texture of her robe and beneath it the incredible reality of her body. Endlessly rehearsed in his imagination, this was like nothing he had ever known before. His face was against her cheek, buried in the fragrant softness of her hair. "Paoul," she said, "Paoul," repeating his name until it became a sigh, a command to hold her with all his strength, just as she was holding him. "Forgive me. Forgive me."

Her words had no meaning. What was happening was beyond meaning. Too close to focus, he saw her eyes wet with tears; as the first strength of their embrace gave way, her face turned further to accommodate his, and the pressure of her arms on his neck brought their mouths almost into contact.

"No," she said. "No. We mustn't."

For a hopeless moment he tried to insist; but she was resolute. She gently pushed him away.

"Please, Paoul. It's enough that we know."

"Yseld—"

"Don't say any more. Paoul, we are who we are. And you are a priest. There can be nothing for us. Nothing but pain. They will catch us, and you will be killed."

"My love—"

"No, Paoul. This must never happen again. I should never have asked you here."

He reached out for her hand: she withheld it.

"I must go. I must go, Paoul. Please let me leave."

To let her go now was impossible. She was part of him; he could as well tear himself in two. But there was no choice.

With a last look back at him, she fled.

6 At the end of the afternoon, when Hothen's lessons were finished for the day, Paoul received a note from Kar Vever. Much sooner than Paoul had expected, Enco had arrived, and Paoul was to go to the vansery common room to meet him.

Paoul was glad to have an excuse to leave the residence. The afternoon's lessons, at Hothen's request, had been conducted in the garden, in the pavilion. On warm days the ladies of the retinue often took refreshments there, and Paoul did not trust himself to face Yseld so soon in company. In the event, though, she did not appear. She was keeping to her quarters, just as fearful of betraying him as he was of betraying her. Tonight, at the meal, would be soon enough to begin the pretense that nothing had passed between them today.

But more than this, Paoul was relieved to get away from Hothen's company. Although he had managed to achieve a sort of resolution of their quarrel, and had even elicited a grudging and halfhearted apology, Paoul knew the incident was not likely to be forgotten. For the first time this morning he had seen the depth of Hothen's resentment, which was matched only by Paoul's jealousy and dislike. Eventually there would come a violent confrontation, after which Paoul feared he would be unable to carry on. To be free of Hothen would be a blessed release, but Paoul was dreading the day. His only concern now, mad and dangerous and forlorn as it was, was the prospect of no longer sharing Yseld's roof, of being prevented from seeing her again.

The vansery common room, in the southwestern corner of the main building, was filled with early evening sunshine. Paoul recognized Enco at once, although half a dozen other priests were present and, sitting with his back to a window, Enco's features could scarcely be made out: as he rose to his feet with an exclamation of greeting, he became a silhouette against a dazzling background of gold.

He clasped Paoul's hand. "It's good to see you again."

Kar Thurman, with whom Enco had been talking and who had also risen on Paoul's entry, acknowledged Paoul with a subdued smile. "Shall we continue our discussion later, Kar Enco?" he said. "For now, I must ask you to excuse me. I have many things to do for the ceremony this evening."

"Of course," Enco said, with an easy confidence he had not possessed at school. "I am most grateful to you for your interest, Kar Thurman."

"Ceremony?" Paoul said. "What ceremony is that? Something unscheduled?"

"Have you not yet heard?" Kar Thurman said, and immediately Paoul understood why his smile had been subdued; and why the conversation in the common room, he now noticed, was rather quieter and more restrained than usual. "I'm sorry. I thought you knew. Kar Houle is dead."

Momentarily Paoul's composure deserted him. He had been expecting this blow, but he found himself, after all, unprepared for it. He shut his eyes. "No one told me," he said.

"He died this afternoon, in the fourth hour."

Just at the time Paoul had been with Hothen in the pavilion, toiling through a lesson in arithmetic that should not have taxed a twelve-year-old. "How did he . . . how did he die?"

"Quite peacefully, Kar Vever says. I was not there myself."

"Is he still in his room? May I see him?"

"Of course."

Paoul turned to Enco. "Do you mind?"

"Not at all."

"Perhaps Kar Enco would also like to see him," Kar Thurman said. "Kar Houle was much loved and admired here."

Despite his friendship with Enco, despite his eagerness to talk with him again, Paoul would have preferred to go alone. He wanted to spend a few minutes in private with Kar Houle before the grand obsequies began: the rites this evening were likely to be attended by most of Valdoe. But it was too late. Enco had already accepted Kar Thurman's invitation.

The rush blind at Kar Houle's window had been let down. A second wicker table had been introduced and on either side of the bed burned a small scented lamp. The aroma in the room was of resin, of pine trees or firs, a smell Paoul had not known since leaving Hohe.

Kar Houle was still in his bed, but the bedding had been renewed, he had been dressed in a fresh nightshirt, and already, in preparation for this evening, his head had been shaved of all hair: only his eyelashes remained. Without his beard, and with his hands placed in the classical position, left upon right, above the solar plexus, he looked somehow more serene, but nothing could disguise the awfulness of his appearance. It was a marvel that this skeletal frame could have endured so long, a tribute not only to the human body but also to the doctrine of the taug.

Enco moved to the foot of the bed, and suddenly Paoul was reminded of another room, far away, where they had stood in contemplation of a corpse. The smell then had been of excrement, not the clean air of the pines; of heat and suffering and the barracks, not of laundered robes and the cool detachment of the citadel. Which room, which body, could be explained by the teaching Paoul had received? The answer came to him: neither. There was sense in neither. What had that young soldier died for? And why should the life of this old man have been prolonged to its maximum term? What had he achieved in all those extra years that the soldier, through his premature death, had not?

Enco spoke. "How old was he?"

"Ninety-eight."

The tenuous idea that Paoul had been pursuing slipped away; his train of thought had been broken, leaving him only with a sense of isolation and loss. If they did hold any secret for him, Kar Houle's remains were unlikely to yield it up when another was present.

Paoul turned aside and was followed by Enco to the common room. They sat down in the same seats; the room had almost emptied.

Paoul tried to smile. "I'm sorry, my friend. This has not been an easy day. You must tell me first about your journey. Was the crossing smooth?"

Enco talked; Paoul, only half listening at first, preoccupied as he was with thoughts of Yseld, Kar Houle, his own precarious future, gradually began to perceive in Enco a profound but indefinable change. This was not the same Enco Paoul had known at Hohe. This was a qualified and practicing kar, mature, purposeful, sure of himself and his abilities. In only eight months of life in the mainstream of the Order, he appeared to have lost whatever it was that Paoul had once valued. Or perhaps, Paoul thought, it was he himself who had changed, and Enco who had

remained the same. Whatever had happened, his closest friend
had become a stranger. He saw that there could now be no question of seeking advice.

Paoul asked, "When will you want to see your patient?"

"There's no hurry. Indeed, it's better if he doesn't even know
he's being treated. The powders go straight into his food."

"He has a food taster."

"That makes no difference. The doses are minute, and they're
quite tasteless."

"But won't the food taster be affected?"

Enco grinned. "Not unless he shares his master's symptoms,
in which case he can only benefit. But let's not talk about that.
There'll be plenty of time for Lord Hothen later. I want to hear
what you've been up to since you returned to your native land."

Enco was evidently impressed that Paoul had been chosen as
tutor to the future Lord Brennis. He accepted with equanimity
the obvious but unspoken fact that Paoul had used his position
to effect a reunion with his friend, a procedure that, in the ideal-
ism of their schooldays, would have filled them both with horror.

After giving an account of his own career, Enco brought Paoul
abreast of the latest comings and goings at Hohe. Among these
were the retirement from the school of the Chief Reciter, whose
place had been filled by their mentor on the tour, Ilven Fend.
Since his initiation, Enco had got to know Ilven Fend on a more
informal basis, as an equal, and he repeated to Paoul some of the
stories Ilven Fend had told him about the tour, about matters
which Ilven Fend had thought it best to conceal from his charges.
At Vinzy, for example, he had chosen to disregard a late but
ambiguous correction of Commander Yahl's smoke signal, a correction warning them not to set out for Chaer. They had been
behind schedule, and a detour would have been difficult. "Makes
your hair stand on end to think of it now, doesn't it?" Enco said.
His manner became more serious. "There's another thing I think
you ought to know. It concerns Starrad. He wasn't expelled, as
we were led to believe. He was killed."

Paoul endeavoured to keep his expression as matter-of-fact as
Enco's. "What?"

"Of course, they couldn't tell us at the time. We were only
novices. But it had to be done: it's standard procedure. After all,
Starrad was already in the higher school. He'd been warned there
was no going back. We all had. They couldn't just let him leave."

"How did you find out?"

"It's no secret. Ilven Fend told me. If you remember, he was on dormitory duty the morning Starrad was caught."

"Yes. Of course." Paoul's mind, already numbed by the events of the day, could barely take this revelation in. It made no new impact; it was almost as if he had been expecting something of the sort. But, although numb, his mind was still able to function. "What about his paramour?" he said, adopting the very tone that Enco had used. "The fishmonger's daughter. What happened to her?"

"Killed too, I imagine."

"And her family?"

"The same. The reputation of the Order was at stake. Who knows what he'd been telling them? The Prime had no alternative."

Paoul looked up. The senior ilven had entered and was coming across the room.

"Forzan Paoul," he said, with a gesture of acknowledgment for Enco. "May I have a word? We're finalizing the arrangements for the funeral."

All red priests were trained in ceremonial: the funeral had been organized quickly and efficiently, without need of rehearsal. The torches, firebrands, and banners had been ready for days; the musicians and choristers had known in advance the sequence of dirges and laments. During the late afternoon the bier had been set up and a tomb prepared in the vansery barrow, for it was considered proper to inter a body as soon as possible after death, preferably at the onset of night.

The rites began at sunset. After a service in the vansery, Kar Houle's body, wrapped in a green and vermilion grave robe and suspended on three richly embroidered straps, was carried in procession to the temple. At Kar Houle's request, Paoul was one of the bearers. The column was led by Phede Keldis; at its rear walked General Teshe and Hothen, behind them Lady Teshe and Yseld, and then Ika, guided by a liveried page. Behind them came the General of Valdoe, all the higher Trundlemen, the leader of the Village Council and his wife, and representatives of the barracks and of the freemen's guilds. The passing of the senior kar was an occasion for solemn and spectacular ceremonial: the first stage of the interment, the Celebration of the Earth, was witnessed too by most of the soldiers and freemen in the Trundle, who had gathered at a respectful distance on the hill. Even the returning day shift from the mines, and then the arriving night shift, were allowed by their overseers to pause and watch for a few moments.

The rest of the ceremony was for the priesthood only. The laymen retired; the hill was cleared, and even the sentries on the distant ramparts were instructed to direct their eyes elsewhere. And finally, after the temple had been opened and the Rites of Gauhm enacted, Kar Houle was buried and the tumulus remade. The sacred semicircle of thirteen torches was left blazing in the night breeze; taking their banners and firebrands, the priests followed the flag-marked path back to the summit.

The second part of the interment had lasted for over three hours. When at last Paoul returned to the residence, the household had long since gone to bed. He was admitted by the guard and, still in his ceremonial robes, began to climb the winding staircase to the gallery. The stairs were illuminated merely by two dim cressets; most of the lamps in the gallery above him had been doused, leaving barely enough light to show the way.

As he slowly mounted each tread, he delayed his progress by grasping the rail and using it to draw himself on. He was both reluctant and eager to reach the top; he felt exhausted and yet also infused with a lucid determination he had never known before.

The funeral had been for him the final release. As the ritual had unfurled, so Paoul had been reborn. He had accepted Tagart's inheritance and become a man who was free, capable of discerning the ceremony for what it was: a spectacle to impress the pagans and keep them in their place. This was how the priesthood kept its power, and nothing was too precious to be subordinated to that purpose. Kar Houle had given his life to the Order, and his passing had been made a mockery, an excuse for that nauseating masquerade. But, unlike the soldier at Chaer, at the very end Kar Houle had not been deceived. For his final month, or days, or hours—or even from the time he had clutched Paoul's hand in warning—he too had been free.

Watching his wasted body going into the grave, Paoul had been conscious of Enco standing nearby. Enco had become just what they wanted. He had survived the selection process that Starrad had failed; in eighty years from now Enco, like this other kar, would be lauded and inhumed. He too would have devoted his life to the Earth Goddess, and already Paoul knew what his reward would be.

And so, as the congregation had retreated, leaving the thirteen flames roaring softly in the breeze, Paoul had made his choice. He had chosen freedom. He had abdicated safety, comfort, and the security of the Order. He had renounced his calling.

Whether he lasted another year, or only a week, he would exercise within himself the freedom that was his birthright. They had tattooed him: there could be no physical escape. He would continue the outward life of a priest until such time as they became too clever for him and he was caught.

He reached the top of the stairs. As his eyes came level with the gallery floor he noticed, to the left, a faint strip of lamplight under Yseld's door. The other rooms were all dark. His own room, two doors along from hers, was to the right. That was where he had intended to go.

Paoul found himself stopping, one hand on the carved serpent's head of the newel. He listened: there was no sound save the quiet lapping of the cresset flames.

At the funeral he had seen Yseld again and known that his longing for her was right. The vows he had taken were wrong: wrong in Tagart's terms, because they denied what was natural and true.

The obstacle of his vows had disappeared. All that mattered now was her safety.

He listened again. The household was silent, as silent as his movement away from the newel and toward the left, as silent as his return would be later, to his own door.

The handle yielded to his touch. Before he really understood what he was doing, her door was open and he had slipped inside and locked it.

She was seated at her dressing board, in a pale cream nightshift. She had unraveled and was brushing out the formal and elaborate plaiting of her hair. Startled, she turned and in bewilderment rose to her feet.

No words were spoken; he held a finger to his lips, afraid that she might yet protest or cry out in surprise. In the arbor she had been resolute, but that was then, and this was now, and as he crossed the floor she moved to meet him. He could not believe how beautiful she was, more beautiful even than before; and in her eyes, her dark and lustrous eyes, he saw not only fear but daring, the triumph over danger, acknowledgment, and desire.

They resumed their embrace, but now it was different. Now began the exploration and merging of their senses. The rapture and sweetness of this, his first kiss, dissolved imperceptibly into others. As his arousal grew, the material of her shift became an intolerable hindrance and she, understanding, immediately reached behind her and it fell away. Dazed, he beheld for the first time a living woman's body.

She delayed extinguishing the lamp until he had stepped free of his ceremonial robes, leaving them in a crumpled heap on the floor. And then, in the darkness, she took his hand and drew him toward her bed.

7 "Master Crogh!" Rian called out, as, her heart pounding, she started after him across the lawn. He had just made one of his visits to the residence, bringing samples of specialist honeys for the chief cook to try and, having secured his usual handsome order, he was heading for the gate.

Rian had seen him many times over the years. He liked to call in person, so important did he consider the patronage of General Teshe, in whose name all purchases were made; and indeed, Master Crogh's reputation as sole supplier to the residence had done him no harm. His increasing wealth had brought increasing girth, and his dense brown curls, like his rather elegant, squared-off beard, were here and there beginning to turn gray. His eyes were humorous. On the few occasions when Rian had spoken to him, she had found him, for a freeman, approachable, friendly, and easy-going. He liked to joke with the servants and slaves, and sometimes even brought them little gifts of beeswax or honeycomb.

But she had awaited today's visit with terror. As the date had approached, she had doubted her ability to see her plan through. It went against all her instincts: she would be risking death to address a freeman like that, especially a freeman of Master Crogh's rank. Just now, loitering by the kitchen door, she had actually decided to abandon her intention and take the way of safety. What difference could it make now, after all these years? Who cared about the feelings of an old woman, a slave? No one. But that was the very reason why she knew she must speak. Her life was almost over. They had stolen it; they had done their worst. She had nothing left to lose. Thus, at the last possible moment, she had decided after all to risk everything, to seize this chance to uncover what above all else she yearned to know.

It had begun eight weeks ago, when Ika had acquired, from a dealer in curios and precious objects, a tiny brooch in copper studded with amber, opal, and coral. The brooch was in the form of a serpent: not quite the Gehan serpent, but a variation on its theme in civilian style and coloring. The opals were uniquely and ingeniously cut, the work of a supreme craftsman: there could not be two such pieces in existence. Although she had not seen it for almost twenty years, Rian had recognized the serpent at once. The first sight of it, in Ika's quarters, had almost made her cry out in astonishment. Beyond all doubt, the serpent had once belonged to Altheme. It had been among the pieces that Rian herself, in the final, panic-stricken moments of the siege, had scooped from her mistress's dressing board and crammed into a hidden pocket in her traveling bag. When Rian and she had been parted, when Altheme had gone off to the forest with the savages' leader, then, as far as Rian knew, the traveling bag and its contents had gone with her.

The serpent was the only clue that Rian had ever found to the fate of the one mistress whom, alone among all her owners, she had loved; the one mistress who had treated her kindly and loved her in return.

Cautiously, reluctantly, Rian had enlisted the help of her younger son, the slave of a former Trundleman who had retired to Valdoe Village. Her son was friendly with the house slave of the dealer, Master Iorach. It transpired that Iorach had bought the serpent from Euden, the grown-up son of Master Crogh. Euden had tried to make Iorach promise not to resell in Brennis, but Iorach had refused. Even so, Euden had taken the price. It was rumored that he was in trouble, being pressed to pay a gaming debt. Of more interest to Rian, it was believed by the house slave that Euden had stolen the serpent from his father. In the past, at long and irregular intervals, Crogh had sold Iorach a few items of good but not exceptional quality: a necklace, a pair of earrings, a coral collar clasp. These, the house slave had always assumed, had come to Crogh by way of legitimate trade. But no order for honey could be worth as much as the serpent, a piece so fine that it could have been made only for a noble, a high noble— almost certainly a member of the ruling clan.

Rian had not dared ask her son to inquire further. Necklaces, earrings, a coral collar clasp: all these had been among Altheme's effects. Somehow it looked as if Master Crogh had acquired them. But when? Where? From whom? And what knowledge did he have of Altheme's fate?

The idea of tackling him directly had not come easily. She knew the gossip about Crogh. He was a former harvest inspector who, through what now began to look like suspicious circumstances, had been able to leave the beilinry and set up at the Village, and in some comfort too. He had risen to a position of prominence on the council, and Rian knew that any man who could do that, easy-going or not, was a man to be feared.

But it was too late to change her mind. She had already called out to him and, puzzled, half smiling, he had stopped on the pathway and was looking back. Rian forced herself on, becoming breathless. Out here, in the middle of the lawn, there was no shade, nor shelter from all the overlooking windows of the residence. She was completely on view. What she was doing was insane.

"Master Crogh, I must speak with you."

His half smile vanished; it displeased him to be accosted thus by a slave. "You? With me? What about?"

"It's important, Master Crogh. We ought to speak in private. Over there, in the arbor—"

"Get out of my way."

"It's about your son, Master Crogh. About Master Euden, and the brooch he sold to Master Iorach."

"Brooch? Brooch? What are you talking about?"

"The serpent brooch. Your son sold it to Master Iorach, but he had no right. It was stolen from the ruling clan. If General Teshe finds out, your son could be executed."

This was a lie, but a convincing one, and she prayed he might suspect it to be true. If he didn't, or if he knew nothing about the affair, or if his son had come by the serpent honestly, then she was lost. This conversation would be reported to Ika, to the chamberlain: she would be punished, tortured, put to death. And to begin with, at the very least, Crogh would strike her down, here on the lawn.

She was waiting for the blow. It did not come. Crogh remained still, and she saw that the first part of her plan had worked. And if the first had worked, so would the second. By threat of exposing Euden—the threat disguised as an attempt to save him from discovery—she would be able to find out whatever Crogh knew about the serpent, its history, and the fate of Altheme.

Crogh glanced uneasily toward the residence. "It's Rian, isn't it? That is your name?"

"Yes, master."

"Since you seem to have something to say about my son, I suppose I ought to listen." He made a show of reaching inside his tunic. "Wait a minute," he said. "I appear to have mislaid my purse. I'll have to go back and fetch it."

The purse was hanging around his neck: Rian could clearly see the cord. This was just a ploy, a ploy with a double purpose: to forestall questioning in case they had been observed, and to give him a face-saving way of agreeing to meet her in private. His next words came as no surprise.

"Go over to the arbor, Rian. I'll join you there presently."

There was only one place where it could possibly be: among the confidential parchments in the Vansard's quarters. Paoul had unearthed everything else. He had found the provenance of the serpent, the original bill of sale, and the inventory of the Lady Altheme's other jewels. He had found the inventory of the Trundle taken after the siege and the list of missing valuables, among them the serpent and all the pieces Rian had remembered. He had consulted again Kar Houle's record of his induction and, to his unspeakable relief, and with a prayer of gratitude for the Order's pedantic insistence on thoroughness and precision, had found every one of the essential details faithfully noted in that flowery, old-fashioned hand: the repeated doubts about Paoul's parentage, the exact date of his birth, Tagart's name and physical description and his identity as Paoul's "putative father." He had found everything but the vital scroll relating to the Lady Altheme, the deposition that Rian had given to Torin Hewzane's men. In this she had described the circumstances of her mistress's departure from the Trundle, naming Tagart as the leader of the group of nomads among whom she had last been seen, giving an account of the missing jewels, and, most important of all, substantiating any other reports that the Lady Altheme was with child, Rian distinctly remembered mentioning the time at which the pregnancy had begun.

Paoul was still unable fully to take in the news Rian had broken to him just before the night meal. Perhaps he never would be able to adjust to it, not completely. If her excited suspicions were proved correct, then he was not what, all his life, he had believed. He was not the son of Mirin and of Tagart, leader of the southern tribes. He was instead a member of the ruling clan, son of the Lady Altheme and of Brennis Gehan Fifth, Lord of Valdoe. He was Hothen's half brother, Ika's nephew. During the meal he had seen them with new eyes, comparing their features with his own. The resemblance, now that he was aware of it, was too great to be coincidental. It was a horrible and unwelcome sensation to feel himself suddenly so close to them, severed from the father of whom he had always been so proud. Yseld was rightfully his. But for an accident of birth, he would already have been married to her.

The meal had demanded enormous self-control. Even Yseld, during their customary polite and neutral exchanges, could not have guessed what was going on inside him. He had longed to tell her; but after the meal there had been no safe opportunity to talk, and anyway it was too soon. Before telling her, he had to be sure. He had to visit the library.

The search had taken longer than he had anticipated. By the time he had finished, it was too late to return to the residence. At midnight his free day began and, as far as the household knew, he would be spending the night in the vansery. He had practiced this same deception last week. It was one way of reducing the risk.

Since that first night, he and Yseld had been together eleven times. Her room was much too dangerous to use again. There was nowhere safe inside the residence, and guards were kept posted at the entrance and at the gate of the inner enclosure. But, by using a circuitous route, it was possible to reach the downstairs day room and from there, climbing through the window, they could escape into the garden unseen. And so, almost every night, for the two or three hours before dawn, they had met in the pavilion.

Tonight they had met here again.

After leaving the library, retrieving a length of rope he had left hidden in the vansery grounds, Paoul had skirted the palisade of the inner enclosure until he had reached the darkest and quietest spot. There, nor far from the shrubbery, he had climbed over and made his way to the pavilion. He had waited for several hours before hearing her footfall on the path, and then, on their improvised bed of cushions, she had joined him.

Their passion was so intense that until now she had put all thought of the future in abeyance. She had refused even to let him speak of it, but tonight he insisted.

In the long hours he had spent waiting for her, Paoul had decided, much against his natural inclinations, not to disclose any of what Rian had told him or what he had so far found out.

Without the final evidence there could be no effective claim; to raise and then dash her hopes would be more than he could bear.

So he merely said that this was to be their last secret meeting. He could not yet tell her why, but it involved finding a certain parchment. If he found it, there would forever be an end to these furtive assignations. They could be together openly, as man and wife; they could have it all. But they had to be patient. They could not afford to jeopardize the future. Their happiness was at stake.

"But you are a priest," she said. "A priest can never marry."

He did not tell her why she was wrong. He could not tell her that membership of the ruling clan took precedence over all else, even the priestly vows. It was the one, the single, the sole escape from the Order. And further: if his claim were upheld, he would inherit Yseld automatically as part of the Valdoe domain. Her dowry had purchased her the position, not of wife to Hothen, but of consort to the future Brennis Gehan Sixth, whoever that turned out to be.

Although she tried to question him, he refused to be drawn. "You once said you trusted me," he told her. "You will have to trust me still."

"Of course I trust you. I trust you with my life."

"Then let's have no more questions."

With that he kissed her. Fighting his own as well as her desires, he made himself break away. It was nearly dawn. They had to get dressed.

He helped her find her things, and fastened his tunic and leggings and drew on his boots. While she finished tying back her hair, he picked up the cushions and replaced them on the bench seat that ran along the inner wall.

Together they went to the step. The east was already faintly gray; a robin which had been singing in the darkness was now joined by a wren. Over the hill, in the distance, came the first calls of a carrion crow.

"When will I next see you?"

"Soon," he said. "Very soon."

"Paoul, be careful."

"I will."

"I cannot live without you, Paoul. Do you know what I am saying?"

"Yes. I have thought about that too."

"If you don't find this parchment, how much longer do you think we'll have?"

"Yseld, it is time to go."

They descended to the path. In the deep night under the cherry trees, they kissed again before parting. "Take care," he said, as she vanished into the dark, moving toward the lawn.

Within minutes he was back at the vansery. No one saw him come through the gate or enter the main building at the rear.

His excuse, his reason for being here, was that he wished to spend the morning of his free day in private study in the library, starting before the residence was awake. Rather than disturb the servants and the guards, he had told the chamberlain that he would sleep in the vansery, as before, in one of the small chambers reserved for visiting priests. These chambers lined a short corridor near the common room. The one in which Paoul was meant to have slept was at the end, next to Enco's.

Before leaving to meet Yseld, he had disturbed the bedding on the narrow, hard-based cot. There was a negligible chance that his absence would be discovered: once he had retired for the night, a priest's privacy was strictly respected, for the hours of darkness were an important time for meditation. Disturbing the bedding had been a needless precaution, but one that would give him the basis of an explanation if the unexpected had happened. He had also pulled three short lengths of stalk from the rush matting and left them bent in such a way that, if the door were opened widely, to its normal extent, they would be moved and their relationship with each other destroyed.

They were still in place. The room had not been entered. Paoul silently shut the door and went over to the cot.

He made himself lie down. He needed sleep, but sleep was impossible. Already he could hear the first sounds of the vansery coming awake, and he had yet to devise a means of getting access to the confidential archive. He knew where it was kept, in the inner chamber of Phede Keldis's office. He would need no more than a quarter of an hour to pick out the appropriate scroll, read it, and return it to its compartment. The problem was to find a time when the office would be unattended during daylight.

In the next room he heard Enco rise. A moment later Enco's door opened and closed as he left to perform his ablutions. What were his plans for the day? How would he react if told how his friend had spent the night? Would that shake his confidence, his smugness and self-esteem?

The treatment of Hothen had so far yielded no results. Already Enco had confided that he was beginning to doubt it ever would. He had said that Hothen's defects were congenital, the result of inbreeding. If nothing could be done for him, Enco would soon be going back to Hohe.

Paoul shut his eyes. How weary he was, how sick of it all, of the priesthood and its values. To think that he had once dreamed of nothing more wonderful than a career at the citadel!

The dawn gong sounded and the solution came, and with it a surge of new energy and excitement. Paoul got to his feet, straightened his clothes, and hurriedly made the bed. Phede Keldis almost always conducted the dawn litany himself; his assistant would also be there, leaving the office empty just long enough for Paoul to enter the inner chamber and consult the archive. Then he could join the service at its end, standing near the door at the rear of the hall, and no one would ever have to know.

8 Paoul had found it. He had found the scroll. He had seen Rian's deposition, among a sheaf of private documents relating to the ruling clan, and in it the essential framework for the successful prosecution of his claim. He had had to delay before leaving the vansery, but now, overjoyed, he was hurrying back to the residence.

The dealer Iorach was now the key. He was an honest man, Rian had said; his testimony would prompt General Teshe to interrogate Euden, Crogh's son, and then Crogh himself. There might well be some difficulty here, although Crogh could not deny his son's possession of the serpent and would be hard put to explain how he had acquired it unless he admitted the truth: that the serpent, together with the other pieces he had subsequently sold to Iorach—for which Iorach would also have bills of sale—had indeed come from Bocher's village. There was no evidence that Crogh had come by the jewels illegally; he could easily have bought them, just as he had told Rian, and just as, in Kar Houle's report, he claimed to have bought Paoul. It was not a crime to benefit from the ignorance of the farmers. Far from it: the only crimes recognized by Hohe were crimes against the empire. And even if, as seemed likely, Crogh had accepted both Paoul and the jewels as a bribe, there was no possibility that Bocher, presuming he was still alive, would ever condemn himself by admitting it. All Crogh had to do was stick to his story, the one he had given Kar Houle, and he would be safe. In protecting himself he would substantiate the link between Paoul and the jewels; between Paoul and the Lady Altheme.

The evidence was essentially flimsy. After all this time, how could it be otherwise? In different circumstances, Paoul knew his claim would not get far. Minds like his own would rip it to shreds. But, with Hothen as he was, and his coming of age now only five months away, the claim stood an excellent chance. Paoul fulfilled all the requirements of Lord Heite, and more. Not only was he the son of Brennis Fifth, but he was the legitimate son, the firstborn. The claim would receive support from all quarters of the High Council: the Order, ever anxious to extend its influence, could not wish for a more pliant Lord Brennis than one of its own. Knowing the way the High Council worked, there was little doubt in Paoul's mind what the ruling would be.

He still could not believe there was every chance he would have Yseld for life, with the freedom to be with her just as he chose. He could not believe that he, Paoul, might soon be the Lord of Valdoe, the man who held sway over the whole domain and whose influence could, in time, be brought to bear on the citadel. What slow and subtle changes there would be! Secretly, subversively, he would work for reform. He would seek to free the slaves, to reduce the taxes, to diminish and divert the power of the Prime. But above all he would work for the golden dream: to extend the control of self beyond the priesthood, to pass this priceless gift to all. "Pagans," they were called; but who were the real pagans, the heathen criminals who abused the greatest faculty of man? There could be no going back to the forest. It was too late for that. The marvels of Tagart's age had gone. Man was coming to another age, not of decay, as the Order said, but of potential unfulfilled. But it never would be fulfilled if he were deprived of the single faculty on which the world's welfare hinged, the faculty indivisible from that which Paoul loved and worshiped most in Yseld: the human spirit.

They had talked of all this; it seemed as if they had been talking forever. Lying together in the pavilion, he had told her all his doubts and dreams, and she had told him hers. She had never been under any illusions about the Order or the Gehans. What he had taken years to realize had for Yseld been the hateful background of her life. Since birth she had been exposed to it; her own marriage was an example of her family's greed.

Very soon now, her unhappiness would be at an end. Paoul would tell her first, and then he would find Rian, the kind and faithful Rian, a woman who deserved none of the treatment that Valdoe had meted out. When she had told Paoul of her discovery she had wept with joy, saying again and again what a miracle it was, again and again how much he reminded her of his mother, her former mistress, the Lady Altheme. She had made no mention of it, but he was sure she had guessed the truth about him and Yseld, and he was equally sure she would never give them away.

Yes, he would find Rian and take her to the Vansard, and immediately begin his claim.

The guard at the residence gate was a new man Paoul had never seen before. His unsmiling face was completely at odds with Paoul's euphoric mood; so too was the grayness of the day. Crossing the sheep-cropped lawn, traversing the irregular granite stepping stones to the porch of the side entrance, Paoul noticed a wizened old gardener, a slave, morosely at work near the arbor, picking spent blossoms from the shrubs and tossing them into a wicker bin. To reach the higher blooms he was using a crook, bending down the branches, stripping them, letting them spring back. As one of the stouter branches sprang back a dark cluster of leaves was torn off and fluttered to the ground.

They touched the lawn and Paoul felt the first painless stab of premonition. Something had changed here. Something was wrong.

The side door opened and Rian appeared. She did not come out; she remained anxiously in the porch, her hands clasped. She must have been standing by the window, watching for him, awaiting his arrival.

Then, somehow, Paoul knew that Yseld had been caught returning to her room. He knew. The porch and door, approaching with unreal slowness, Rian's face, her anxiety, the cloudy morning, the swish and slap of the tortured foliage, everything confirmed it.

"Forzan Paoul," Rian said, pulling him inside, into the gloomy dankness of the lobby. "I have something terrible to tell you." The lobby smelled of stale milk. A bucket had been spilled here a week before. There were many garments hanging on the rack: the servants' robes and mantles, the gardeners' leather aprons. She was holding his arm, as a mother holds her son's. "Forzan Paoul, you must promise me you'll stay calm. You must do nothing sudden, nothing foolish."

Still it was unfolding at the same unreal rate; but now he realized that the stab of premonition had gone much deeper and left a widening wound, a wound filling with agony and disbelief.

"Sometimes, Forzan Paoul, my Lady Ika cannot sleep. This morning, very early, she called out to my Lord Hothen. She had heard the Lady Yseld. I think she must have stumbled at the foot of the stairs and hurt herself. The light there is very bad."

His wound was worse, even worse than he had feared; his last hope of life was crushed by the look in Rian's eyes.

"If it hadn't been for my Lady Ika . . . if you'd heard her questions . . . Forzan Paoul, she put ideas in his head. She wanted to know where the Lady Yseld had been. She accused her of seeing the kitchen boy, just because he's handsome and the Lady Yseld was once kind to him. Hothen called his guards. They dragged the kitchen boy out of bed and beat him. They beat him with clubs. Then Hace . . . Hace burned him. He burned him till he screamed. He confessed to everything my Lady Ika said, foul things, disgusting things, and then they killed him. And then . . . then . . . then Hothen . . . Forzan Paoul, I am so sorry. I loved her too. Pity him, Forzan Paoul. Pity him. He has killed the Lady Yseld."

9 Today, two months and more after Yseld's funeral, Paoul felt able at last to visit her grave alone. This morning Hothen had been removed, pronounced unfit and sent to the mainland with his mother: his place would be taken by one of Lord Heite's nephews. By the autumn there would be a new Flint Lord at Valdoe.

Paoul had lost all interest in his claim. Without Yseld, it could serve no purpose. And, although he had not yet summoned the courage to admit it, he had a bigger aim in view.

The temple and its precincts were deserted when he arrived. The sky had cleared after an early evening squall; the rain had softened the turf and wetted the grass on the tumulus. She was buried at the western end. No fragment of her wreaths remained. Only a small stone marker, bearing the single beautiful character of her name, distinguished her grave from the vacant soil.

Standing here, Paoul realized that his craving for death, for peace, had changed. It had become secondary but intrinsic to that chilling design which he was still afraid to contemplate. At first, in his guilt and despair, he had wanted to join her. He had wanted to complete the pact at which she had hinted in their final moments together. He had wanted to kill himself by killing Hothen.

He had almost done it. He had almost rushed upstairs. Without Rian, he would have been unable to contain the first access of his rage, but she, the slave, had been wiser than a priest. In the crucial instant she had checked him and given him back his self-control. He would never lose it again: her words had revealed to him the course of his future purpose, if only he were strong enough to take it.

"He's not worth killing," she had said, and she was right. Hothen, his half brother, was not the cause of Yseld's death. Nor even was Ika, nor the negligent Teshe. The cause was not even here in Brennis. It was at Hohe, at the center of the Gehans' circle, the same circle that had made Rian a slave, Rian and all the others, the same that had made a slave of Paoul.

The empire's goddess, Gauhm, had killed his Yseld. The true Earth Goddess had been murdered by the false. But Yseld had been much more to him than that: it was to her gentle spirit that he should build her monument. He would have to remain alive, submerged in all he loathed. He would have to remain alone, completely alone, until, working from the center, he had done so much damage that the Gehans' empire could not survive.

Death would be easier. Death needed no resolve.

But they had fitted him perfectly for his task. They had taken an innocent child and made him into a future Prime.

Facing across the tumulus, toward the sea, Paoul turned his eyes southeastward, toward the citadel, and knew he had no choice.

Thirty-eight years later, almost to the day, Forzan Paoul, former Principal of the Temple School, Surveyor of the Vanseries, Honor Companion to the Gehan of the Gehans, and now Moderator of the Supreme Board of the High Council, was unanimously declared successor to the ailing Prime.

His accession took place in the winter. In the spring it was noticed, first by the lakeman, and then with increasing alarm by the men in the temple and in the barracks, that fewer pairs of herons had returned to breed. The heronry, for over three centuries the symbol of the continuance and prosperity of the Gehan empire, had in large part been unaccountably abandoned.

The following spring, no pairs at all were seen to build. The islands were deserted: the birds had gone elsewhere.

RICHARD HERLEY was born in Hertfordshire, England, in 1950. A trained biologist, he has devoted himself to writing since his graduation from Sussex University in 1971. For as long as he can remember, he has been interested in natural history and has a firsthand knowledge of the Sussex Coast, the setting for much of *The Earth Goddess*.